'James McBride's first book, *The Color of Water*, a memoir published in 1996, sold more than 1.3 million copies and was a bestseller for two years. Now he has produced a novel, *Miracle at Sant'Anna*. It evokes such power and beauty, pathos and love, that it may very well outstrip its precursor . . . A searingly, soaringly beautiful novel . . . The book's central theme, its essence, is a celebration of the human capacity for love. Even in the course of virtually unbearable warfare and deprivation – with carnage and devastation, hunger and hopelessness blotting out all other realities – people are able to touch each other, to care. That, McBride insists, is the enduring, immortal miracle of the human race, for all its imperfections.' *Baltimore Sun*

'A haunting meditation on faith that's also a cracking military thriller . . . *Miracle at Sant'Anna* flows along with cool, clean prose . . . Profoundly spiritual but rarely preachy, *Miracle* turns out to be less a Good Book than a good book – a miracle in itself.' *Entertainment Weekly*

'McBride has a broad vision, an evocative style and an affection for cause and bizarre-effect plotting that recalls Paul Auster.' *Sunday Herald*

'Excellent first novel . . . McBride is realistic about racial prejudice and explicit about the dreadfulness of all fighting, but still hints at the possibility of justice. He offers hope.' Jessica Mann in the *Sunday Telegraph*

'War, cruelty, passion, heroism and race crammed into one lyrical tale.' *List*, Glasgow

'Exceptional storytelling skills . . . McBride has fictionalised only a small part of the soldiers' war but in doing so he has distilled the essence of what he has learned, not only about the battles in which men died, but about the way men lived. Like the war, this is a story with many fronts, many layers. The author peels them back to reveal what lies beneath. At times, what is exposed is ugly, but that is no reason to look away.' *South China Morning Post*

Also by James McBride

The Color of Water

About the author

James McBride is an award-winning writer and musician. He has been a staff writer for the *Washington Post*, *People* magazine and the *Boston Globe*. His memoir and tribute to his mother, *The Color of Water*, spent more than two years on the *New York Times* bestseller list, was published worldwide, and was the winner of the prestigious Anisfield–Wolf Book Award. As a composer, he won the American Music Theater Festival's Stephen Sondheim Award for his jazz/pop musical *Bobos*, and has composed songs for Anita Baker, Grover Washington Jr., and Gary Burton. A jazz saxophonist, he has performed with Rachelle Farrell and with legendary jazz performer Little Jimmy Scott. He lives in Pennsylvania.

Miracle at Sant'Anna

James McBride

SCEPTRE

Copyright © 2002 by James McBride

First published in Great Britain in 2002 by Hodder and Stoughton
First published in Great Britain in paperback in 2003 by Hodder and Stoughton
A division of Hodder Headline

The right of James McBride to be identified as the Author of the Work has been
asserted by him in accordance with the Copyright, Designs and Patents Act 1988.

A Sceptre Paperback

2 4 6 8 10 9 7 5 3 1

A CIP catalogue record for this title is available from the British Library

ISBN 0 340 82318 6

Typeset in Berkeley Book by Palimpsest Book Production Limited,
Polmont, Stirlingshire
Printed and bound in Great Britain by
Mackays of Chatham plc, Chatham, Kent

Hodder and Stoughton
A division of Hodder Headline
338 Euston Road
London NW1 3BH

Dedicated to the men of the 92nd Infantry Division,
the people of Italy,
and the late Honorable James L. Watson of Harlem, New York,
who epitomizes the best of both.

AUTHOR'S NOTE

This book is a work of fiction inspired by real events and real people. It draws upon the individual and collective experiences of black soldiers who served in the Serchio Valley and Apuane Alps of Italy during World War II. I have taken certain liberties with names, places, and geography, but what follows is real. It happens a thousand times in a thousand places to a thousand people. Yet we still manage to love one another, despite our best efforts to the contrary.

Contents

THE POST OFFICE

All the guy wanted was a twenty-cent stamp. That's all he wanted, but when he slid his dollar bill across the post office counter at Thirty-fourth Street in Manhattan, the diamond in the gold ring on his finger was so huge that postal clerk Hector Negron wanted to see whom the finger was connected to. Hector normally never looked at the faces of customers. In thirty years of working behind the window at the post office, he could think of maybe three customers whose faces he could actually remember, and two of them were relatives. One was his sister, whom he hadn't talked to in fourteen years. The other was his cousin from San Juan, who had been his first-grade teacher. Besides those two, the rest didn't count. They melded into the millions of New York schmucks who staggered to his window with a smile, hoping he would smile back, which he never did. People did not interest him anymore. He had lost his interest in them long ago, even before his wife died. But Hector loved rocks, especially the valuable ones. He'd played the numbers every single day for the past thirty years, and he often fantasized about the kind of diamonds he would buy if he won. So when the man slid his dollar bill across the counter and asked for a stamp, Hector saw the huge rock on his finger and looked up, and when he did, his heart began to pound and he felt faint; he remembered the naked terror of the dark black mountain towns of Tuscany, the old walls, the pitch-black streets as tiny as alleyways, the staircases that appeared out of nowhere, the freezing, rainy nights when every stirring leaf sounded like a bomb dropping and the hooting of an owl made him piss in his pants. He saw beyond the man's face, but he saw the man's face, too. It was a face he would never forget.

Hector always carried a pistol to work, and the next day, when the newspapers ran the story of how Hector pulled the pistol out of his front pocket and blew the man's face off, they talked about how Hector always carried a gun to work because he lived in Harlem and Harlem was dangerous. Hector was old. He lived alone. He'd been robbed before. He was afraid. The New York Times and the Post carried the requisite interviews of fellow postal employees gathered around a taped-up doorway saying he'd seemed about to snap and that he was ready for retirement and how they couldn't understand it all, but only one person, a rookie reporter from the Daily News named Tim Boyle, wrote anything about the statue head. It was Boyle's first day on the job, and he got lost going to the post office, and by the time he got there, the other reporters had left and all of Hector's coworkers had gone. Boyle panicked, thinking he was going to get fired – which if you're a reporter for the Daily News and you can't find the main post office in midtown Manhattan is about right – so he talked the cops into letting him ride with them up to Hector's ramshackle apartment on 145th Street. They went through Hector's things and found the head of a statue, which looked expensive. Boyle rode with the cops to Forensics, who checked it out and found nothing. But one of the cop's wives was an art lover, and the cop said, This thing don't look normal, so they took it to the Museum of Natural History, who sent them to the Museum of Modern Art, who sent for a man out of NYU's art department, who came over and said, Shit, this is the missing head of the Primavera from the Santa Trinità.

The cops laughed and said, Is that the Niña, the Pinta, or the Santa María?

The guy said, Hell, no. It's a bridge in Florence.

And that's how Tim Boyle saved his job and Hector Negron made the front page of the International Herald Tribune, which on that December morning in 1983 was tossed from a tenth-story window of the Aldo Manuzio office building in Rome by a tired janitor named Franco Curzi, who wanted to get home early because it was almost Christmas. It floated down and pirouetted in the air a few times and finally landed on a table at the sidewalk café below, as if God had placed it there, which He, in fact, had.

A tall, well-dressed Italian man with a well-trimmed beard was sitting at a table having his morning coffee when the paper landed on the table next to his. He noticed the headline and grabbed the paper.

He read holding the coffee cup in his hand, and when he was done, he dropped the cup and stood so abruptly his chair skidded out behind him and the table slid forward three feet. He turned and began to walk, then trot, then run down the street. Passersby on the sidewalk gawked as the tall man in the Caraceni suit and Bruno Magli shoes tore past them at full tilt, his jacket flying behind him, his arms pumping, running down the crowded tiny streets as fast as he could go, as if by running he could leave it all behind, which was of course impossible.

INVISIBLE

On December 12, 1944, Sam Train became invisible for the first time. He remembered it exactly.

He was standing on the bank of the Cinquale Canal, just north of Forte dei Marmi, in Italy. It was dawn. The order was to go. One hundred and twenty black soldiers from the 92nd Division bunched behind five tanks and watched them roll toward the water, then clumsily waded in behind them, rifles held high. On the other side, just beyond the river plains and mostly hidden in the heavy mountain forest of the Apuane Alps, five companies of Field-Marshal Albert Kesselring's 148th Brigade Division, seasoned, hardened German troops, watched and waited. They sat silently. Hardened, seasoned, exhausted, they sat burrowed into the sides of the heavily wooded mountain, peering into their scopes, watching every move. They'd been there on the Gothic Line six months, a thick line of defense that stretched across the Italian peninsula, from La Spezia all the way to the Adriatic Sea, planting mines, building concrete bunkers, laying booby traps and tripwires. Exhausted, starving, knowing the war was lost, most wanted to run but could not. There were reports that many were found dead, chained to their machine guns. The orders were straight from the Führer himself. Any man who deserted, any man who gave an inch would be shot without ceremony or trial. Their orders were to stand firm. There was no backing away.

Train watched as the first of the tanks hit a mine on the other side of the bank and the Germans opened up with everything – mortars, eighty-eights, and machine-gun fire. He heard a frightened voice behind him screaming, 'Kill me now! Kill me now!' and he wondered who it was. The smell of cordite and gunpowder drifted into his lungs. He felt his heart seize and stop. Then he heard someone yell, 'Go, soldier!' and felt a shove, and he ran, splashing, to his own death.

He had no choice. He didn't want to run. He didn't trust his commander. The man was from the South. Train had never seen him before that morning. He was a replacement for the old captain, who'd transferred out two days before – whose name Train couldn't remember either. The men were strangers to him, but they were white, so they had to be right, or maybe not, but Train was from North Carolina and he didn't know how to stand up to white people like the coloreds from the North did. Train didn't trust them either. They brought trouble with their high-falutin' ways and long words and college degrees, always making the captain – what was his name? – mad. He remembered the first colored soldier he'd ever seen, back home in High Point, North Carolina, just before he was drafted. It was his first-ever bus ride in the city, and the man had spoiled it. The soldier got on the bus wearing a crisp Army uniform with lieutenant's bars and a shoulder patch with a black buffalo on it. He took a seat down front. The bus driver said, 'Move to the back, boy.'

The Negro opened his mouth, outraged, and said, 'Fuck you.' The driver slammed on the brakes and got up. Before the Yankee could move, there was a chorus of hissing and cursing from the rear of the bus. It was the other blacks next to Train. 'Cut it out,' one blurted. 'You makin' it bad for the rest of us.' 'Whyn't you go home, you mooley bastard,' shouted another. Train, stunned, tried to look away, the slight bit of shame that washed over him replaced by relief as the Yankee soldier glared at the blacks next to him, flung open the rear door of the bus, and stomped out, huffing and muttering at them in furious disgust. The bus roared away, blowing black diesel fumes in his face.

And now Train was following one of those light-skinned, know-it-all Northern Negroes into the drink, a lieutenant from Harlem named Huggs. He called himself 'a Howard University guy, ASTP,' which Train guessed had something to do with reading but wasn't sure since he couldn't read himself. It was something he had a mind to learn one day because he would like to read the Bible and know his verses better. He even tried to think about his Bible verses as he drove his legs into the water and the din around him grew louder, but he couldn't remember a single verse, so he began singing 'Nearer My God to Thee,' and as he sang, the metal shrapnel and bullets began to ping off the tanks around him and he could hear their treads snapping as they hit mines that blew up. He waded slowly up to his hips in the clear canal and suddenly felt quiet and peaceful, and then – just like that – he was invisible. He could see better, hear better, smell better. Everything in the world became clear, every truth clairvoyant, every lie a blasphemy, all of nature became alive to him. At six foot six, 275 pounds, all muscle, with a soft-spoken charm, tender brown eyes, and deep chocolate skin that covered an innocent round face, Sam Train was everything the Army wanted in a Negro. He was big. He was kind. He followed orders. He could shoot a rifle. And most of all, he was dumb. The other men laughed at him and called him 'sniper bait' and 'Diesel' because of his size. They placed bets on whether he could pull a two-ton truck or not, but he never minded them, only smiled. He knew he wasn't smart. He had prayed to become smart, and suddenly here he was: smart *and* invisible. Two for one.

He stopped completely still in the water as the sounds of death and machine-gun fire seemed to die all around him, as if someone had turned down the volume and replaced it with the peaceful crowing of a rooster that he could hear all by itself, as if it were singing solo. Standing in the water as men rushed past him, falling, screaming, weeping, he gazed upward at the mountain before him and marveled at the lovely olive trees that lay in the groves above the German batteries, which he could see as clear as day. He saw the bobbing green of the Germans' helmets as they raced from one smoking artillery cannon to another. The helmets blended perfectly with the shorn leaves and rocks and ridges of the mountains behind them. He marveled at the sun peeking over the ridge as if for the first time. Everything seemed perfect. When Train saw the smarty-dog Huggs from New York spin back toward him with his face shot off, then flop into the water like a rag doll, he felt no fear. He was happy, because he was invisible. Nothing could touch him. Nothing could happen to him. He decided it had to be the statue head.

He'd found it in Florence the first day he'd arrived, next to a river where the Germans had destroyed a bridge. Everybody in the army wanted souvenirs, but for some reason nobody was interested in it. There must have been four companies that marched past that marble head, but no one grabbed it, maybe because of the weight. But Sam Train had carried a forty-six-pound radio in training camp for six months and that had never bothered him. He picked the head up because he wanted it as a gift for his grandmother. He kept it in a net bag laced to his hip, and before the day was over, three guys had offered him ten dollars for it. 'Naw,' he said, 'I'm keeping it.' That night he changed his mind and decided to test the market. He wanted to see if the Italians would buy it, because he'd heard they would pay twenty dollars for a carton of cigarettes. Before digging his foxhole outside Florence, he walked into town to look for an Italian, but he couldn't find a soul. The streets were empty, barren, save for an occasional rat that leaped out of the wreckage and quickly disappeared into the rubble again. Finally, Train found an old woman wandering down a deserted street. She was the first Italian he had ever met. She was ragged and filthy, with her head wrapped in a scarf and her feet swathed in rubber tires worn like sandals, even though it was winter. He held out the statue head as he approached. He offered it to her for fifty dollars. She smiled a toothless grin and said, 'Me half American, too.' Train didn't understand. He dropped the offer to twenty-five. She turned around and staggered away as if drunk. He stood, blinking in misunderstanding. Halfway up the block she straddled the curb, spread her legs, held her dress out, squatted, and pissed, steam coming from the piss as it hit the ground. He was glad he didn't sell it to her. It would have been a waste.

He was thinking about the woman squatting over the curb, pissing, as the murky parts of Huggs's face floated past him in the water. Then he heard a soft plop and felt a sucking inside his chest and a pain in his head. Suddenly, he no longer felt peaceful. He could feel his invisibility slipping off like a cloak, so he ran like hell, past two burning tanks, past a bobbing arm connected to a bobbing body, straight across to the other side of the canal, where a group of soldiers cowered behind a rock in a grove of trees, a man named Bishop among them.

He flopped on the canal bank and heard Bishop say, 'Oh, shit. You been hit in the head.'

Train wiped the moisture from his face, glanced at it, realized it was blood, and lay on his back and died. He felt his spirit leave his body. It was as if his spirit had drained out of the bottom of his shoes and floated away. He was truly invisible now.

'Thank you, Lord,' Train said. 'I'm prepared for Thee.' He waited to feel the sweet nothingness of death. He opened his mouth to taste the sweet smell of heaven and felt instead stinking, hot chicken breath blowing down into his lungs. It tasted like dog shit and hog maws mixed together. He opened his eyes and saw the big, black, shiny, eel-like face of Bishop stuck to his – Bishop stuck to his mouth. He sat up straight.

'Goddamn, you crazy?' Suddenly, the booms and din around Train seemed to screech to an unbelievable roaring pitch. He heard moans and screams of death. He heard fire crackling as nearby tree limbs and branches snapped under the thunderous slams of eighty-eight shells that whirred past, blowing branches and bark down on them like rainwater. It was as if some giant, inhuman beast had broken loose and was out to destroy the world. He looked across the canal and saw the unit retreating, the dozens of bodies in the canal, a white captain waving them back in, and then his view was blocked by Bishop's huge, black, shiny face and several glistening gold teeth, which adorned the front of Bishop's mouth like a radiator grille. Bishop grabbed him by the lapel and roared at him over the din, *You owe me fourteen hundred dollars!'*

It was true. He did owe Bishop fourteen hundred dollars from poker and craps, but that was before today. Before he'd learned to become invisible.

Just as suddenly, it got quiet. The screaming meanies quit, the German machine guns quit, the American ack-ack guns quit, and the only sound Train could make out was the crackling of a burning tank in the canal just short of shore and the soft murmuring of someone who was obviously burning to death inside it. He suddenly remembered where he was and what had happened to him.

'Wasn't I hit?' he asked Bishop.

Bishop was a minister from Kansas City. They called him Walking Thunder. He was a short, trim man with smooth skin that covered a handsomely sharp, coal-black face, with dimples and devilish laughing eyes that seemed to wink all the time. His uniform always appeared starched and neat, even in battle. His voice was like silk, his hands slender and delicate, as if they had never held dirt, and his gold-toothed smile was like reason itself. He had a church of two hundred parishioners back home who sent him care packages every week, full of chicken and cookies, which he used to barter at poker. Train had heard him preach once at training camp and it was like watching a steam pump sucking coal on a hot July day. He could make the hair on the back of your neck stand straight up on end.

'You was hit and you was dead and I brung you back,' said Bishop. 'Don't nobody know about it but me, and that's fine. But you owes me some money, and until you pays it, you ain't goin' nowhere.'

'You puttin a mojo on me?'

'I ain't doing no mojo. I wants my money. Now you go git that white boy out that haystack over there yonder. He's yours to deal with. I sure ain't goin'.'

'What white boy?'

'That one.' Bishop pointed to a stone barn about two hundred yards off and fled, splashing back across the canal as the bombs and artillery splashed around him and didn't touch him.

Train turned on his side and watched as a haystack the size of a small bush crept along the barn wall, then stopped. Underneath it were two tiny feet clad in wooden shoes.

2

CHOCOLATE GIANT

Beneath the haystack, the boy tried to imagine himself, but he could not. There was no front, no back, no middle, only where he was. At dawn, he'd awakened to the sound of thunder overhead and ignored it, crawling to the doorway of the tiny barn where he slept to see if the usual bowl of soup was there. It was not. Neither was the old man who normally brought it. He had not seen him in two days. The boy didn't even know the old man's name. The old coot in vest and dirty shirt simply appeared one day and began talking to him, and from that day forward he'd been the Old Man. The boy could not remember how he'd come to the Old Man. The Old Man had given him a job pulling a few olives from his trees and crushing grapes, then placed him in the barn each night to sleep, leaving a bowl of watery soup there each morning. The boy could not remember how long he'd been living in the Old Man's barn, or why he was living there. His memories were like tiny single slivers of glass blowing through a wind tunnel with a giant fan at one end and him at the other, the slivers jarring and jumbling about, slicing through the air past him, dangerous and deadly when they hit, even more dangerous when they missed, for more often than not they were lost in the roar and din and shrill yelling of fleeing villagers and German eighty-eight shells that landed closer and closer to the Old Man's farm each day. People moved in and out of his clouded vision like ghosts.

One by one, the neighbors came by to warn the Old Man, and through the shreds of what was left of his mind, the boy watched blankly as they nodded at him and talked to the Old Man with grave voices saying, Leave now, for the sake of the boy. The war is almost over. The Germans will lose. The Americans are coming. For the sake of the boy, leave. But the Old Man shrugged and said, Germans or Americans, it's all the same. They will take my farm and use my olive twigs to make fire. I can't have it. The boy can leave when he wants. He is of no relation. He is slow in his mind. I keep him here because his feet are always clean and he crushes grapes well.

Two days before, the boy had watched the neighbors withdraw one by one, their meager belongings piled onto the backs of mules and in wagons, a trail of entire families of women, grandfathers, and shoeless children, heading south toward the Americans, nervously glancing at the boy as he went about his duties in the Old Man's olive field, until a solitary figure remained, a woman, who tried to pick him up but dropped him when he screamed and bit her and tore her dress. 'You are a devil,' she proclaimed, and left. He watched her go, perching on a high rock on all fours like a dog, his head pointed to the sky. The cool wind blew the leaves across the dirt road she departed on. Later, a man and his young daughter approached, and the man offered the boy an egg, but the sight of it frightened him. The man laughed as he cowered in fear from the egg, but the man's laughter soothed the boy, so he took the egg and observed silently as the man and his daughter ran down the road. When they were out of sight, he cracked the egg and sucked it dry.

The shelling that drew closer and closer to the barn each day never bothered the boy. He found the noise to be a comfort. The thunderous roar, the shaking of the barn, the whistling and angry chatter of machine-gun and automatic-rifle fire dulled his senses and drew him away from that most painful place where he had once lived, a place where strawberries were red, and candy had real names like peppermint and orange, and trees grew apples, and water flowed from a beautiful fountain in the piazza of a village someplace. He had seen all that once, but he could not remember where. He had no name, no face, no key, no clean shirt, no toothbrush, no mother, no father, no someone who loved him, he was not himself and he was not anywhere. He, too, was invisible.

He watched as the bobbing helmets of the Germans grew nearer. Through the shreds of what was left of his mind, he suddenly remembered what the Old Man had said before he'd disappeared two days earlier. The Old Man had been very clear. He had said it several times. He had pointed his finger at the boy and said, *If you are in the barn and see the Germans coming, run to the top of the hill and whistle toward the house, then hide in the haystack behind the barn.* The boy had delayed when he'd awakened because he was starving. He'd spent fifteen minutes looking for the bowl of soup the Old Man normally left just inside the barn door, having eaten chestnuts and flowers for two days straight. By the time he finished looking for the soup, the Germans were too close and he'd run up the hill and hidden underneath the haystack, because he could see them coming. A lot of them. And it was too late to whistle.

His mouth hung open as he stared, fascinated, at the helmets of the German soldiers, which bobbed closer and closer to him from the mountains above. He knew he should be afraid of them, but he was not. His fear of them was merely an instruction given, like 'Don't touch the knife,' or 'Stay away from fire.' Peering through the hay as they approached, small dots on the mountainside, dipping and dodging, dropping into trenches and crevices, then rising and running forward a few feet more before falling to the ground again, the boy remembered suddenly that he actually had a friend among them, but he was not sure which one it was. Perhaps if he asked, one of them would help him find him. He decided to stay where he was.

Hearing a voice behind him, the boy shifted in the haystack. He turned and saw his friend Arturo. Arturo was his imaginary friend who sometimes appeared to discuss matters – food, toys, how to make a soccer ball from rolled hay – but he usually disappeared when the shelling started. He was a tall boy with white hair, suspenders, and long pants, and unlike him, Arturo was already seven. The boy was surprised to see him. Arturo stood before him holding a soccer ball made of hay tied with string.

'Look,' he said. 'Watch me throw this over my shoulder.'

The boy shifted the entire haystack around to watch, his back to the charging Germans, as Arturo tossed the ball over his shoulder. It rolled toward the barn. 'Get it and kick it back to me,' Arturo shouted. The boy complied, running toward the barn door with the haystack still over his head. But Arturo arrived first and kicked the ball into the barn. The boy flung the haystack off his head and followed the ball inside.

Inside, it was dark. The ball bounded into a corner, and the two tumbled after it. The boy reached it first and kicked it high against the wall. It struck the wall at the same moment that a shell landed nearby, and the thunderous boom lifted them both off their feet and they toppled to the ground, laughing.

'That was a big one,' the boy cried. He looked about, but Arturo was gone.

The boy frowned. Arturo always did this. Always disappeared at any moment.

He yelled, 'Arturo, how come you're not coming out?' Then he saw him on the other side of the barn, against the opposite wall.

'Over here,' Arturo said. 'Come this way.' The boy moved toward him, and as he did, there was a tremendous crash, as if a hurricane had suddenly entered the room. Great clouds of dust kicked up, and the walls shook. The boy felt himself being lifted off the ground and flying high in the air. He flew past the stone wall he'd been standing next to, a wall with stones wedged so tightly and carefully by a Tuscan farmer years ago that it had withstood hundreds of machine-gun bullets and artillery fire from previous weeks of fighting. The wall cracked and burst apart, rocks flying everywhere. The boy felt himself spinning in circles and cried out, but his terrified howls were lost in the mad whirlwind of roaring, booming wind. He landed on the floor, and large chunks of the roof fell about him like raindrops, covering him with rubble, leaving a small gap through which he could see the sun shining brightly. He lay on his back in shocked silence and watched, transfixed, as an eight-by-eight beam that spanned the eaves of the roof slowly pulled itself out of place on one side as if being lifted by a giant hand and landed atop the rubble covering him with a distinct pop, making everything dark.

Then he felt nothing. He was clear. All was well. It was quiet.

He lay there for seconds, minutes, hours – he could not tell, because it was dark and he did not know what time was and had only seen a watch once somewhere long ago. He had heard someone speak of time before, but that memory lay deep in the jagged-glass wind tunnels of his mind and he could not find it. He wondered how old he was. He decided he was six. Then he wondered how he had wondered it, since he lived with no front, back, or middle. He suddenly realized that since he'd lost track of time maybe he'd lost being six, too. He felt hungry. His chest hurt. He opened his mouth and cried, 'Help! I'm six! Help!'

He heard a rumbling sound from above him. A voice. A piece of the rubble was being pulled away. Then another. A sudden sliver of light cut through the rocks and the plaster dust as it billowed about. A slab was lifted from across his head. The sun struck his face like a punch. He shut his eyes. Then a figure blocked out the sun, and he opened his eyes again.

At first he thought it was the Old Man, but it wasn't. This man was a giant, a huge chocolate giant, staring down at him from underneath a battered American helmet, its chin strap dangling lazily in the sun, bandoleers crisscrossing his massive chest, rifle slung horizontally across his back. The giant was straddling the rubble with massive boots, one knee touching the ground, the other leg stretched over the beam covering the boy's chest. His skin was as black as coal. His teeth were white as diamonds. The boy had never seen anything like him.

'Good God,' Train said.

The boy had heard of men like this, somewhere in the corners of his jagged-glass wind memory, but he could not recall. 'Where is your tail?' he said in Italian.

The man ignored him and looked around, his huge head swiveling, his large brown eyes rolling from left to right in their sockets.

'I don't have any oil to drink,' the boy said. His chest ached.

The giant looked at the beam pressing against the boy's chest. He placed his large hands around it, grunted heavily, and tried to lift it. It would not budge. He tried again, and the beam shifted slowly and the boy cried out. The sound of his voice seemed to scare the giant, and with one mighty heave he pulled at the huge beam again. Sweat ran down his face in rivulets and into the corners of his wide mouth. He gritted his teeth, and from within his black face the white teeth shone like tiny lightbulbs. He thrust his mighty head toward the ceiling and said, 'Lordy . . .' and lifted, his huge hands trembling as the beam slowly rose up, higher and higher.

Only then did the pain hit the boy, it hit him so hard he felt like he'd been jerked into a fire and flung into the jangled glass of his own memories. It washed over him with such force that he couldn't contain it. He felt himself being lifted, high, toward the sun, and he heard the soldier cry out, 'Hey, Bishop! Bishop!' and then the Negro colossus stuck his ear to the boy's mouth to see if he was breathing.

The boy could not resist. Chocolate. A giant chocolate face. He reached out to touch the man's face. Then he licked it. It tasted terrible. But then sweet unconsciousness came, and it was as sweet as anything he could imagine.

3

THE CHOICE

The Germans came down to the Cinquale Canal from the mountains in a pincer movement, going around the barn on both sides as they rushed forward to meet the American attack. Lying behind the wooden beam with the boy, Train could see them through the jagged ruins of the barn, which was completely open on one side. The beam and stones of the wreckage covered them somewhat, though any of the Germans who ran by could have looked in and seen them if they had wanted to. They didn't seem to have a mind to.

In his invisibility – Sam Train felt it coming and hoped he was right – Train marveled at how tiny the Germans were. He expected them to look like the ones he'd seen in the newsreels back in training camp at Fort Huachuca, Arizona: straight-backed, strong, fit, neat, with starched uniforms and shiny helmets, high-stepping by the thousands as they marched past in formation, arms outstretched in that funny salute as they greeted the biggest white man of them all, Hitler. Instead, he saw soldiers that looked like skeletons, some without hats or helmets, boys and old men, with torn and ragged uniforms, emaciated, exhausted, panicked, stumbling past and yelling at each other as if their hair were on fire. One lurched by laughing madly in a high-pitched voice; another ran past sobbing like a child. Some were dressed like Italians he'd seen everywhere – in fact, he could've sworn he saw two Italian mule skinners from Fifth Battalion that were in camp the day before – and right as he was thinking how unfair it was that they could switch sides anytime they wanted, being white and all, a few more Italians appeared from another direction and shot the two Italian mule skinners he had just seen. 'Lord,' he murmured to the boy. 'I don't know who's who.'

The boy paid no attention to this, largely because he seemed to be dead. Train squeezed himself farther behind the beam, moving the child's body a little closer to it to keep him out of sight of the open end of the barn, and examined him closely. He laid his own head flat on the ground behind the beam, facing the kid, their noses almost touching, his face just inches away. He nudged the boy gently to see if he was breathing.

Train had never touched a white person's face before, even though, he thought glumly, this one looked dead. He had met a white child in his hometown of Mt. Gilead once – Old Man Parson's little grandson. The boy had come out to the field to watch him pull his mule one afternoon and had even held Sam Train's hand, but his ma had seen him out there and shooed him back into the house.

Train took his hand off the boy's face and regarded him as the shouts and machine-gun fire began to head down the mountain away from him. The boy, even catatonic, was beautiful. He was dark, olive-complexioned, with smooth skin and soft black hair that glistened. His head was shaped like an onion, giving him an almost dowdy look, set off by eyes that were

wide apart and a rounded chin that was shaped like an O. He was skin
and bones, his pants cut off at the ankles, sliced off with a knife, no hems,
and his bruised feet were blistered and swollen from malnutrition. His
swollen feet looked as if they belonged on a man, and if he hadn't been
so terrified, Train might have thought to laugh.

The sound of machine-gun and artillery fire seemed to descend farther
down the valley, but Train could still hear moaning nearby from those
who'd been shot. Suddenly the enormity of his situation began to collapse
on him – he realized he was cut off from everyone and trapped on the
wrong side of the canal – and he turned his head away from the boy and
started to vomit uncontrollably. The image of Huggs's face floating in the
water seized his mind and wouldn't let go. Some of Huggs's brain had
splattered on Train's ear when he was hit – it had looked like oatmeal
– and Train rubbed his ear furiously as he vomited, unable to stop.

After a while, the sun came up full in the sky, and it began to get
warmer, and the firing died down. The vomit next to his face began to
stink, so Train turned his head the other way and saw the boy lying on
his back, eyes still closed, breathing in quick short breaths like something
was caught in his throat. Train was afraid the boy would start moaning,
but he did not.

Instead, he tried to sit up.

Train pulled him down firmly.

'Don't move no more,' he snapped.

The boy's dark eyes widened, and he slid back out of arm's reach.
Train realized his mistake and made a series of shaking motions with
his hand to calm the boy. It had no effect. The kid began to whimper
softly, and Train could feel panic rippling through his spine.

He considered shooting the boy. No one would know. He wanted to reach out and cover the boy's mouth, but he had slid too far away and Train was scared to move. He rubbed the magic statue head at his side quickly to no avail, then desperately searched through his pockets for something to make the kid shut up. His fingers came upon a hand grenade. He shoved that thought from his mind and settled on a wet, mushy chocolate D bar in his front pocket. It was sticky and nearly melted from the canal water and his body heat. He placed it on the ground and, with trembling hands, slid it across to the kid, who stared at it a moment, then grabbed it, sniffed it, and greedily stuffed the whole thing in his mouth, paper, chocolate, mud, everything.

'More,' the boy said in Italian, his mouth full, licking his fingers.

Train covered his own lips with a finger to 'shhh,' but the kid ignored it.

'More!' he cried.

Train rose on his elbows to inch toward him and as he did, out of the corner of his eye, he saw the German soldier trotting nearby. The German wasn't staggering forward in mad desperation like his fellow soldiers. He was jogging downhill slowly far behind them, as if they all were running to an event at the state fair and he was the last of the pack to get there and didn't mind it a bit, a sort of not-too-fast, no-need-to-hurry, the-fat-bearded-lady-isn't-going-anywhere kind of trot. He was ten feet off, his rifle held low, and he was almost past when he suddenly turned in Train's direction.

Train and the German saw each other at the same time, and even as Train clumsily swung his M-1 up with his left hand, his head dizzy, hastily propping the gun barrel on the wooden beam, hoping that the safety was off and nearly wetting his pants at the same time, he realized he wasn't invisible anymore, and he cursed the boy and Bishop, too, for putting the mojo on him. He had found a way to survive the war, and they had ruined it.

'I'm invisible,' he cried, and he shut his eyes and fired, shooting with his left hand and propping himself up with his right. The gun barrel danced wildly, bullets pinging through the wreckage and zinging everywhere.

The German soldier hesitated for a moment, then dropped like a sack of potatoes. His boots flopped awkwardly in the air and plopped back down to earth again.

Train sprang to his feet and ran.

He was ten feet off before he realized the webbing at his side was empty. The statue head was gone.

He turned around just as two more Germans appeared from a clump of bushes about a quarter of a mile away up the ridge and began to run at him. He stood, frozen for a moment, looking back at the statue head, which had fallen out of the netting and had rolled back to the barn near the kid, who was now writhing around. Train was still out of range. He had time to go back and get it. But with the rifle in his left hand, his free hand could grab only one.

Which?

The boy.

Or the statue head.

The boy.

Or the head.

He stepped back and grabbed the statue head and ran toward the canal. He saw what appeared to be the back of a German soldier wading out of the canal and disappearing into the woods on the opposite side, so he turned around and ran the other way, past the barn, toward an olive grove that was downstream and behind it.

The boy was still lying near the beam in the destroyed barn when Train sprinted by crazily the second time. Train ignored the boy, hearing rounds kicking up on all sides of him.

The black Americans from F Company had made a fight of it farther up, where the canal was shallower, and had driven the Germans back across to Train's side. They lay out of range, on their stomachs on the bank across the creek, and could see Train leaping and running through the high mountain grass, holding the head of the statue like a football as machine-gun fire, bullets, and artillery shells chewed up the earth all around him. From across the creek, some of them laughed.

Train was all the way to the safety of the olive grove when he looked back and saw the kid, scrambling in wounded, terrified confusion, desperately trying to drag himself over the wooden beam and deeper into the safety of the barn rubble. The kid had somehow managed to maneuver the upper part of his body across the beam but could go no farther. Chocolate was smeared on his face. His tiny arms frantically clung to the beam, and his legs kicked to no avail. Machine-gun and artillery fire began to kick around the barn, and the Germans began to walk artillery shelling toward it.

This action prompted a round of cursing and vicious fire from F Company on the American side, who could see the boy but could not reach him. The German gunners in their artillery positions high up on the opposite slope could not see the boy at all, and the desperate urgency of the American firing propelled them to direct their cannon blasts at the boy with an even greater fury.

In that moment, Train realized he had to go back.

He strapped his rifle to his back and, still holding the statue head, leaped out from the grove. As he sprinted across the field again, the

Americans across the creek gave covering fire. But their attempt at protection didn't matter. It came on him again. True and real. Invisibility. He could've walked over there with an ice cream cone like it was Sunday morning after church. Nothing would touch him. He could see better, hear better, smell better. There was no noise, no pain, no fear. He felt the rush of fresh Tuscan morning air on his face, heard every bush, every tree, every rock, which seemed to speak to him, shake his hand, saying, Hello, Sam Train. Good morning, Sam Train. We love you, Sam Train. What can we do to help you out today, Mr Sam Train?

This, he thought as he leaped over rocks and gullies, is what it must feel like to be white.

He snatched the kid in one long arm and ran for the cover of the olive grove again. Every single tree, branch, bush, and rock was smoking with lead and cordite as he ran. Bullets and shells smacked against the plants and trees, which fell en masse, as if a giant lawn mower were sweeping the plains, and as he ran he heard them cry out. Since they had spoken kindly to him and he knew they could not speak to anyone but him, he howled for them, for he knew they depended on him to tell the world of their pain, since his invisibility made him privy to their feelings whereas the rest of the world was not. He was responsible to them, he knew. When he reached the edge of the grove and made it into the safety of the olive trees, he was unhurt and feeling wiser and deeper inside than he'd ever felt in his life.

Then, instead of turning to run across the canal back to the Americans, he ran in the opposite direction, deeper into the grove and toward the mountain behind it.

Across the canal, heaving with sweat, having been driven farther downstream by the fire of the Germans, who had overtaken their position

JAMES McBRIDE

in numbers, the three remaining members of Train's squad, Bishop
Cummings, Hector Negron, and Second Lieutenant Aubrey Stamps,
ceased their covering fire and watched him in disbelief.

Stamps turned to Bishop. 'What the hell you do to him?'

'Nothing.' Bishop didn't want to talk about it. His little hustles with
the ignorant Negroes from the South were none of Stamps's business.

'You know that nigger's dumber than a dime. You sent him over
the hill?'

'I didn't tell him to risk his neck for nobody,' Bishop said. He and
Stamps could see Sam Train's back as he dipped in and out of the
trees, climbing higher and higher into the ridge, the little boy slung
over his shoulder, his face a white speck in the dark green of the
mountain.

The fire was dying down. The Germans were heading up the canal
toward Poveromo. Some were setting up camp on the other side of
the canal, within full view but out of range. The fighting had gone out
of everybody. Stamps heard a German yell in thickly accented English,
'Hey! You niggers cut our phone wire.' He heard laughter from the
American side.

Stamps watched Train's back as he continued to climb.

'Well, we gonna get him or not?' Stamps asked.

Bishop snorted. 'You the big lieutenant, not me.'

Stamps was undecided. He had no idea what to do. This was his first
time leading a squad. Huggs, the squad leader, had been dead ten minutes.
They'd slugged it out to get across the canal, and when he'd radioed the
base to deliver artillery fire so they could maintain their position and
move the Germans back up the mountain, the captain had told him, 'It's
impossible for you to be over there. Get back here.' Stamps had radioed

28

three times, and each time, the captain, Nokes, had cut him off, called him a liar, and told him to get back. If Nokes had shelled Stamps's coordinates on the other side of the canal, the Germans would have been cut off on one side and the Americans would have it right now, he thought bitterly. His company, Company G, had crossed with Company H on their right. All they had needed was artillery support to the right of Company H to help them hold off the flanking Germans while they pierced the bank, established a foothold, and moved their tanks across. Instead, Nokes had shelled to their left, on Company F's side – which already had their own artillery support – leaving companies H and G exposed. Stamps would bet a hundred bucks that he knew why. H and G companies both were commanded by Negro first lieutenants. F Company was commanded by a white captain. Nokes, from his safe position a mile back at the fire-control center, couldn't see either. He had fired on F Company's side because their white captain had radioed that they'd made it across, too, and when a white man said something happened, by God it was gospel. As a result, H and G companies were just about destroyed. Stamps didn't know Captain Nokes at all. The man was brand-new. As far as he knew, the guy had no knowledge of how to fire artillery. He was a transfer from an engineering company. Huggs was the one who had told him how to do everything. Now Huggs was dead in the fuckin' canal, and this scared sissy was running the show till he got his transfer out, which he most certainly was trying to do like most of the white captains did, trying to get away from the niggers.

'Hector, your radio working?'

Hector Negron was twenty-one, a Puerto Rican from Spanish Harlem. He sat in a crouch, smoking a cigarette, staring sleepily at Stamps. He was in shock from all he had just witnessed, and at times of extreme nervousness, he shut down and became sleepy. He'd been meaning to see a doctor about it.

'Sí. But it's a diaphragm job. Just your voice powers it.'

'Get on it and see where everybody is.'

'Everybody is everyplace.'

'What the fuck you mean by that?'

'Look around you. You see anyone talkin' on a radio? Our lines are cut. The battalion got out of Pietrasanta two hours ago. They was fighting with spoons and typewriters and pots and pans over there. I think they fell back to the other side of Valdicastello, or south toward Monteggiori. Who knows? The batteries in the wireless radio got wet and it's out. Last I heard, the Germans were on it, anyway.'

The Germans had taken up positions on the other side of the canal. Stamps heard the German shout again, 'Hey! You niggers come back and fix our wire.' He heard an American yell, 'Tell your momma I'll be right over.' He heard laughter from the American side, silenced by a single burst from a German eighty-eight, the shell swishing low, skimming across the canal and landing on the American side with a thunk as the Negroes scrambled. The shell was a dud. Now the Germans were laughing.

Stamps lay in the mud and watched Train as he moved higher and higher up the cliffs behind the Germans, a small dot on the side of the mountain. He thought he was dreaming. He'd known Train six months. Train was too dumb to do anything so stupid. 'Goddamn,' he muttered. 'That nigger's lost his buttons.'

Bishop lay next to Stamps, watching too, and after a moment, he rose and began to walk downstream, looking for a place out of German range to cross.

'Where you going?' Stamps asked.

'Y'all go back if you want. The only person who's got any luck around here is him. Plus, he owes me fourteen hundred dollars. That kind of money can set me up for the rest of my life. Even if the rest of my life is today.'

Stamps and Hector watched Bishop's broad back as he crossed the creek, through the chest-high waters swirling around him. When he reached the German side, he trotted into the olive grove and began to climb the hill behind it that led to the Apuane Alps and, beyond them, the Serchio Valley.

After a moment, Hector and Stamps followed.

4

THE MOUNTAIN OF THE SLEEPING MAN

The American ground campaign in central Italy in December 1944 was unlike any other war fought in Europe during World War II. France had its rolling hills, its beautiful villages, its sweeping countryside where the enemy was easy to spot, its romantic Resistance fighters organized by General Marshall's Americans. Germany had its snow and its black forests, its long, vacant tundras, where General Patton led his tanks and troops with cheering press correspondents A. J. Liebling and Ernie Pyle at his side. But in central Italy, the war was fought out of the public eye, at night, in winter, in cold, chaotic blackness, by Gurkhas, Italians, Brazilians, British, Africans, even Russian defectors, and most of all, by American Negroes, who were convinced that the white man was trying to kill them, in mountainous terrain where icy winter rains and high winds lashed the trees and bushes with hurricane force, pushing aside sanity and loosing all the ghosts and goblins of Italy's past. The lovely mountains of Tuscany, mountains that would years later inspire dozens of gushing travel books from breathless American writers, were not friendly to the coloreds. They were rude and discourteous, dangerous and deadly. A single well-aimed artillery shot from a hidden German eighty-eight would land in the center of an advancing American company and leave several troops dead, scattering the rest. The fleeing soldiers would retreat in terror up the sides of mountains, where the muddy, choppy terrain seemed to reach out and grab their knees – to stretch the legs full length over the black slopes was impossible. With each stride, the ground rose up unevenly to meet their feet, and as they stumbled forward under ruthless German fire, the craggy slopes would suddenly pitch them into ditches that dropped ten feet or more, or the earth beneath their feet would end completely and the terrified soldier would find himself sprinting at top speed with nothing but air under his feet. Then, if he were wingless and faithful to God, he would drop three feet to crumple into a ravine; or if he were unlucky, he might plunge three hundred feet into solid stone or muddy, rocky earth that would collapse around him and bury him. The Negroes were terrified of the Tuscan mountains at night, even those who had been raised in America's farm country, and with good reason, for even the Italians were afraid of them. Thirty years after the war, Italians in the Serchio Valley, near the towns of Barga, Gallicano, and Vergemoli, were still pulling skeletons of colored soldiers – some of them still locked in a death embrace with their German counterparts – from the ravines of the Tuscan mountains, and even then, three decades after the war, the Italians, tough mountain men and women themselves, didn't want to touch the bodies, for those mountains held their secrets like the secrets of a young maiden's heart, jealously and with great zeal, and to disturb that curious mixture of belief and denial was to invite trouble indeed. The Negro skeletons only added to the haunted legacy of mountains already full of five centuries of lore about wolves, witches, half-men and half-goats, child-gobbling goblins, woman-snatching moon monsters, angry cave fairies, toads that bit you and drained your life blood, sleep-walking witches that entered rooms with rats crawling out of their mouths, and other creatures whose victims were found in the mountain's muddy ridges: children who simply disappeared forever; farmers whose hair fell out and grew back like cotton days after they encountered an angry cave fairy; a village violinist expired after an argument with a half-man half-goat, the violinist found hanging from a tree by a violin string, his whistling violin still heard seventy years after he disappeared. The Italians of Tuscany were respectful of their beautiful, haunted peaks. They did not see them as mountains but as pieces of life, and as with all things familiar, they gave each a nickname: the Horse Mountain, the Table of the Thirsty Wizards, the Kingdom of Echo, the Laughing Witch Who Came Back, the Hill That Swallowed a City, and the most frightening of all, the Mountain of the Sleeping Man.

He is easy to see from any point in Barga and the surrounding Tuscan villages of the Serchio Valley. Even during the day, he is a frightening sight. He is huge. He lies on his back, his jaw extending with fury, his forehead huge and dense, with a crop of hair cut in Marine style jutting fiercely skyward. His angry, thick skull is topped by a colossal eyebrow furrowed in rage, his monstrous chest protrudes with mutinous strength, his steel-like legs bent at the knees knife skyward. Once you see him, you cannot escape him. He follows you everywhere you walk, morning, noon or night, his gargantuan face just over your shoulder – an enraged, snoozing ogre, about to awaken. Italian children were afraid to look at him. Shepherds crossed themselves when their herds wandered near his ridges. His shadow blocks the sunlight in the morning, and in afternoon the sun tiptoes across his gigantic brow so slowly that workers at the nearby Aracia iron mine often laughed that evenings never come to the Serchio Valley because the sun hasn't the guts to slip any farther past the sleeping man's brow lest it awaken him and be smacked clean into space.

The myth goes that he was a young shepherd who had fallen in love with a shepherdess long ago, but she was in love with a young sailor who was at sea. Despite his constant pleas and beautiful gifts, the maiden refused the shepherd's entreaties and offer of marriage, so he vowed to wait until she changed her mind. He waited for years and years, but the young maiden never relented. She sat high in the mountains staring at the sea – so he lay on his back and stared at the sky, vowing to block her view of the sea until she changed her mind, angry that she would not acknowledge the love he so freely demonstrated. And there he lies to this day, sleeping, waiting, his huge chest blocking out the sun, his massive forehead nearly touching the moon, his thick hair crusted with snow, and most of all, those furious eyes which, from a distance, appear to be two eyes, but up close are only one eye and a true geological miracle: a huge oval encirclement of rock that rises up to the height of a five-story building. If he has the courage, a man can stand inside the sleeping giant's eye, at the dead center of the circle, and gaze at the roofs of every village in the Serchio Valley below. And if he has the courage and listens closely, he can also hear the thunderous pounding of the giant's angry broken heart.

It was within the sleeping giant's eye that the German forces of Albert Kesselring's 168th Panzer SS Division, among the most dreaded and fearsome warriors that ever walked the face of Europe, placed four regiments – fourteen thousand men in total – to plan a surprise attack on the exhausted and thinning ranks of American Negroes of the 92nd Buffalo Division, so named by the Native Americans who saw the first black cavalry as having hair akin to that of their beloved buffalo. And it was Kesselring's forces that Colonel Jack Driscoll of the 92nd Division saw in a fuzzy aerial photograph in his intelligence report nine hours after the failed Cinquale Canal attack that separated Sam Train from reality and diced four companies of the 92nd into bits.

Driscoll sat outside his pup tent glaring at the photo and reading the intelligence report as roaring jeeps, growling tanks, and harried colored soldiers rushed all around him. Tall, slender, thirty, Boston-born, with a lean face and blue eyes that always held steady, Driscoll, his thin frame folded onto a crate, reached into his pocket and pulled out a cigarette, ignoring the bustle around him. What's the point in hurrying now? he thought bitterly as he glanced at the soldiers and tanks hurrying past. All the fun's over.

The Cinquale was a disaster, as he knew it would be. It was par for the course with the 92nd Division, where nothing ever went right. Someone had the bright idea that an end run could be made around the Ligurian Sea to avoid mines the Germans had placed from the coastal plains all the way up through the Apuane Alps and into the Serchio Valley. To try to take the canal without securing the high ground on the other side seemed such a stupid idea that Driscoll was surprised anyone would want to take credit for it, but he was there when General Parks, his superior by two ranks, had outlined the plan. Driscoll had no respect for Parks. The man had run a successful undertaker's business before the war, and as far as Driscoll could tell, he was just ringing up future business. Now here they were, nine hours into the Cinquale Canal, and the jig was up. Fourteen tanks from the 597th and 598th field artillery units were all shot up. The beachhead was extended all of a thousand yards inland, thirty-three men were dead, 187 wounded, and the fuzzy aerial photograph in his lap showed at least a division-sized group of regiments sitting in place four miles away. It wasn't possible. He didn't believe the photo.

He lit the cigarette and carelessly tossed the match, which landed next to several barrels marked 'fuel.' Ten pairs of Negro eyes watched him. He ignored them as he sucked in the smoke. Let it burn, he thought bitterly. The 92nd is going down in flames, and me with it, he thought. He watched as a Negro soldier walked over and stubbed out the burning match with his boot, then returned to a group that was standing at a tent across from Driscoll, staring. There was a time when ten Negroes staring at him would have made him nervous, but that was long ago. Driscoll smoked, ignoring them. He didn't hate them like a lot of white commanders did. He didn't even dislike them. He hated their trust in him. He turned his head back to the report, smoking silently and looking at the photo one more time. The inscription on the back said '11,000 feet.' That was all.

He stood up. He had to pass this on to the old man, General Allman, commander of the 92nd Division. Allman had been under a lot of pressure lately, and even though he was a tough old geezer, Driscoll was worried about him. A graduate of Virginia Military Institute, five feet two inches of steel-blue eyes and grit, Allman didn't think coloreds were qualified to command, and he said it. He didn't think many of the whites assigned to the division were up to the task either, and he said that, too. The coloreds hated him, and the second-rate white officers weren't crazy about him either. His only son was missing in action in France; racial unrest, fights, shootings, and stabbings were tearing the division apart; and the big boys up in England and France had underestimated the Germans' strength in Italy, which was why they were getting their asses kicked right now. Allman already knew the score on the canal, but he always wanted the gory details anyway, plus he needed to see this photograph. The photograph was muddy, a fake, Driscoll decided. Of unknown origin, possibly altered to appear British. No way would the Germans waste that amount of men and resources on this stretch of Italy. If they made a stand, it would be at La Spezia or at the Brenner Pass, near the Austrian border. But he'd let the general decide. That was his job.

As he rose, Driscoll noticed a lieutenant standing among those watching him. He had gone to a museum in Pisa on leave two weeks before and was surprised to find a group of Negroes from the division there admiring some of the paintings, this lieutenant among them. There was something in the man's face Driscoll did not like. He called him over.

'What's on your mind, Birdsong?'

'Um . . . Captain Nokes is interrogating a prisoner in regimental headquarters two, sir. Perhaps . . . perhaps you'd like to hear what he has to say.'

Driscoll frowned. The Negro division lived on rumors. The last one, about two colored soldiers hanged from trees outside Lucca for sleeping with an Italian prostitute, nearly caused a mutiny in one of the companies. He decided to nip this potential for rumor in the bud. 'Let's go,' he said.

He followed Birdsong to a large regimental tent. Standing inside was Captain Nokes, the white captain who had just transferred in, and a small Italian priest. Captain Nokes's eyes widened when he saw Driscoll. He snapped to attention and saluted.

'What's wrong?' Driscoll said.

'Nothing, sir. Just questioning this priest here.'

'You know Italian?'

'I can speak a few words, yes.'

Driscoll watched Birdsong shift uncomfortably.

'What's he talking about?'

'Nothing,' Nokes said. 'Well, a few things about where we can find some German prisoners is all. But nothing out of the ordinary.'

The priest was very young, with a large, brimmed hat and the flushed face of a drinker. He had no shoes. His collar was filthy, soot-black, and his face sweaty. He had the largest pair of ears that Driscoll had ever seen on any human being. He said something frantically. Driscoll had been raised in the Roman Catholic church and knew Latin fairly well, but his Italian, he had to admit, was terrible.

He looked at Captain Nokes. 'What does he want, food?'

'No. He said something about a church and a fight between the Germans and the Italian partisans. We'll check it out, sir.'

Out of the corner of his eye, Driscoll saw Second Lieutenant Birdsong purse his lips, looking troubled. Driscoll turned to Birdsong.

'Didn't I see you in Pisa at the museum two weeks ago, speaking Italian?'

'Yes, sir. I grew up in South Jersey with plenty of Italians. I also studied German in college.'

'What did this man say?'

Birdsong replied, 'He said something about a large number of German paratroopers planning to come through the Serchio Valley in ten days or so. Around Christmas. Through the Lama di Sotto ridge.'

Driscoll straightened in alarm. The Lama di Sotto ridge was in the aerial photograph he had just seen. 'How many Germans?' he asked.

'Two or three regiments.'

'Companies or regiments?'

'Regiments.'

'Ask him that again. Two or three *companies* or *regiments*?' A company was two hundred men. A regiment was four thousand.

Birdsong asked the question.

'Regiments, sir,' he said.

'Where'd he hear that?'

'From some Italians in his village and a German he saw here.'

'A German he saw *here*?'

Lieutenant Birdsong directed Driscoll's question to the Italian, who responded.

'A German at the POW camp back at division headquarters,' Birdsong translated.

'There's two hundred German prisoners there,' Driscoll said dryly.

'That's what he said, sir.'

Captain Nokes shrugged. 'It's a lot of story there, sir.'

Driscoll ignored Nokes. He had worked intelligence before. He had to consider the source. In his hand was a fuzzy photo taken from eleven thousand feet, of unknown origin. The man before him was a living source, a priest. Through Birdsong, he grilled the priest: Name. Birthplace. Parents' names. Dates, when and where he'd served. Birdsong translated flawlessly.

After half an hour, Driscoll had heard enough. He turned to Captain Nokes. 'Who's your first lieutenant?'

'Huggs. He was killed this morning in the canal.'

Driscoll pointed to Birdsong. 'This man speaks excellent Italian. How come he's not a first lieutenant?' Nokes's face took on the pallor of a man at a funeral. He was a short man with a downturned mouth, small, darting eyes, and lips the color of veal – a leather-skinned roughneck from Mississippi. The kind of officer, Driscoll noted wryly, that the division seemed constantly to attract, a reject and a transfer – somebody else's problem.

Nokes barked, 'In fact, I've been keeping my eye on this man, Colonel, and was about to promote him.' Driscoll was willing to wager a month's pay that Nokes didn't even know Birdsong's name.

'Promote him now and have him take this priest down to the POW camp. Let him pick out the German he's talking about. Then let him write up the S-2 intelligence report and have it to me by fifteen hundred hours.'

It seemed like too much information for Nokes to process, and as his face twisted and contorted with the effort, Driscoll silently cursed the Army policy that dictated that only Southerners were qualified to lead colored men. Nokes's 'Yes, sir' bounced off Driscoll's back like a rubber ball, as Driscoll had already turned and left the tent.

He went to his tent and lay on his cot, troubled by what the priest had said. The information the priest offered was days old and probably useless. It was not corroborated other than by the photo, the veracity of which he still doubted. Still, the whole business bothered him. It had to be checked out right away, even though nothing could be done about it. The colored division was spread too thin as it was, fifteen thousand men over a thirty-mile front five miles wide, with the Germans fighting from concrete bunkers that were impervious to small-arms fire, and a huge railroad gun in La Spezia that was kicking the shit out of them. The Germans, ingenious fighters that they were, had placed a ship's 406-millimeter cannon on a flatbed car, secured it, and wheeled it into a railroad tunnel. Anytime they wanted to, they rolled the cannon out, fired it, then wheeled it back in.

The giant beast wreaked havoc, hurling shells weighing 560 pounds for thirty-eight miles. American bombers could not reach it. They needed a ship to float into the harbor and knock that goddamn thing out. But naval support cost money. Money meant politics. And politics, for a colored division? In Italy, which was poor and not strategically important? With the Negro press kicking their ass about the segregated Army's treatment of coloreds, and good white boys dying in Normandy under Patton and Marshall? With General Allman, who had the guts to tell his superiors what he really thought, who was about as politically correct as General MacArthur? Forget it. The gun stayed, and it kicked the shit out of them. One single goddamn gun, he thought bitterly.

Driscoll sat up and told his orderly to summon Captain Rudden. Rudden was from Maine. He was one of the few captains in the division whom Driscoll trusted.

Rangy and tall, with a slow, careful manner and dark eyes that sucked in everything around him like bilge pumps, Rudden entered, followed by his first lieutenant, a man named Wells, a stocky colored man with a huge head and bug eyes that stared blankly. Several white captains had tried to make Rudden get rid of Wells – they were scared of him – but Rudden refused. 'He's the best first lieutenant in the division,' he boasted, which is why Driscoll liked Rudden. Rudden knew a good soldier when he saw one.

'Sir?'

'I got a report that Germans are planning a push down the Serchio Valley, through Lama di Sotto ridge. Two or three regiments.'

Rudden's eyes widened. 'Regiments?'

'You been running patrols back and forth over there. You hear anything about that?'

'No, sir. But G Company has a squad that's probably sitting right on that area, sir.'

'What's the state of G Company?'

'Shot to hell, sir. Twenty-four dead, forty-three wounded, plus they have a squad missing up in the Serchio Valley.'

'How many in it?'

'They went out as twelve, crossed the Cinquale Canal, and two came back, two wounded, four dead, and four missing, still on the other side of the canal. One of 'em's a lieutenant.'

'Who's the lieutenant?'

'Stamps is his name.'

Driscoll knew him. A good soldier. Cool and smart. Stamps had come out of the Army's Advanced Special Training Program, which sent the smartest coloreds to Howard University for special training. It was a program the Army had started to raise the intelligence tests of the division, which were low, since only forty per cent of the colored draftees were literate. Driscoll had seen Stamps back at training camp in Arizona. The kid knew his business.

'Radio contact?'

'Yeah. Captain Nokes got them on the SCI-536 when we pushed across the Cinquale. They were on the other side and got just beyond Hill Maine near Strettoia, at the enemy weak point. They called for artillery fire, which might've pushed the Krauts back and collapsed their hold on the canal, but Nokes didn't fire. Instead, he called them back.'

'Why the hell did he do that?'

'He couldn't see them and didn't believe they'd crossed, so they got hung up. I had F Company upstream about five hundred yards. It was pretty hot over there. There was a kid caught in crossfire. One of 'em grabbed the kid and ran up the mountain. Stamps and two others followed him. They're gone now.'

'You got their names? Maybe one of 'em speaks German. We need some German prisoners to confirm this report. We need them badly.'

Rudden produced a sheaf of papers from his pocket and circled four names. He handed the list to Driscoll.

Driscoll took the list and said, 'Get Nokes over here, and tell him to bring a squad with him. He sent 'em. He'll get 'em.' He was furious at Nokes. The screwball had stayed back at the fire-control center to direct artillery while he sent his men into the canal. It was his choice, but a good captain like Rudden went with his men. Driscoll wished he'd been at the canal that morning instead of having to direct the attack from division headquarters. He would've pushed Nokes into the canal himself.

Rudden turned to leave just as General Allman entered. Driscoll flipped the report on his lap to the floor, rose, and saluted.

'Don't bother,' Allman said. He wore an air of resignation on his face. 'Don't say a word. Don't mention Parks to me one time. He's a stupid bastard. He's going to run for senator once this war is over, that's all he thinks about. I told him we need more howitzers. I told him we need fire support. Trying to take a beach without securing the high ground above it! He did the same thing at the Rapido River and got the Thirty-sixth Infantry Division all shot up, and now he's killing my colored boys, too. Goddamn bastard.'

Driscoll was silent. He waited a moment before asking, 'Any word on your son?'

Allman's face softened a moment, and Driscoll thought he saw a glint of despair shoot across the old man's brow. The kid had been missing nine days. Just as quickly, Allman's face straightened and he said, 'None. Give me what you got on the canal.'

'Forget the canal for a minute. I just got a report from an Italian priest who says the Germans have two or three regiments on the other side of the Serchio Valley and are planning a push in ten days, at Christmas.'

Driscoll watched Allman's eyes widen, then harden. The old man, Driscoll had to admit, was a tough old bastard. 'Where is the priest now?' Allman asked.

'Sent him down to S-2 intelligence.'

'We got any corroboration?'

'Nothing. An aerial photo that looks pretty inconclusive. But a squad from G Company Three-seventy-one was over there and hasn't come back. We had radio contact and lost it.' Driscoll said nothing about Captain Nokes's not sending artillery fire behind the squad at the Cinquale. If Allman booted Nokes, he might get replaced by someone worse. If he had to continue protecting lizards like Nokes, Driscoll thought bitterly, the 92nd would never take central Italy, no matter how worn-out the Germans were.

Allman waved his hand. 'If we listened to every report from the Italians, we'd still be back at Anzio. You sent a squad for 'em?'

'Done.'

'Try to raise 'em on the radio and tell 'em to get a German prisoner. Meanwhile we'll gather tomorrow morning at oh-seven-thirty and lick our wounds. Let's get some replacement officers so we can stay in position. We got boys up there melting away like butter. You see Miller's report yesterday? They had ten guys heading back to the aid station helping one wounded who'd been shot in the foot. The next soldier doing that is court-martialed, understand?'

Driscoll nodded.

Allman turned on his heel. 'I'm sick of it,' he muttered. 'Sick of this melting-away crap. Bunch of sissies.' He walked out of Driscoll's tent, so mad he forgot to take the report with him.

Driscoll decided not to press it on him. It could wait. Instead, he sat down and lit another cigarette, thinking of the aerial photo and the priest's information. He wasn't going to worry about another crisis, he decided. Intelligence wasn't his job. Yet the photo bothered him, like an itch that can't be scratched. The steady supply of German prisoners who were turning themselves in had suddenly diminished – gone down to zero – and that was a bad sign. If Driscoll were planning a big push, he'd do the same thing, make sure nobody got through to spread word to the enemy. They needed a German prisoner, badly. He looked over the list of names of the squad in the Serchio Valley: *Negron, Cummings, Stamps, Train.* His finger stopped at the last name. He did not know every draftee in the division, but he damn sure knew this one. This was the biggest Negro he'd ever seen in his life. He couldn't forget him. He'd met him his first day at training camp, back at Fort Huachuca, Arizona.

It seemed like a million years ago. It was July, hot as hell, desert hot. Driscoll was standing in front of division headquarters and ordered the huge colored soldier standing nearby to take the supply truck parked out front over to the post quartermaster to draw rations for the newly arriving troops.

The giant Negro got into the two-and-a-half-ton truck, started it, and drove it directly into the building where Driscoll was standing. He damn near knocked it off its moorings.

Driscoll stormed out of the building, cussing the man up and down, ending with, 'Where the hell did you learn to drive?'

The man looked apologetic. 'I'm no driver,' he said. 'I never drove nothing but a mule.'

Driscoll told the guy to move over, got in the truck, and drove it to the quartermaster's himself. En route, he asked, 'What's your name, soldier?'

'Train.'

'First name or last?'

'My ma calls me Orange 'cause I likes oranges, but most calls me Train.'

Driscoll marveled at the man's size. He was so big he had to crouch to fit into the cab of the truck. His hands looked like meat cleavers. They were clasped nervously in front of him. 'You ready to say hello to Italy, Private Train?'

The huge man's face crinkled. 'Who's Italy?'

Driscoll thought Train was joking, until he looked over and saw the man's face was dead serious.

'I ain't fussy 'bout meetin' folks,' Train said nervously. 'I never met no woman, though. Not for dating and jook joints and the like. Never had no girlfriend. If Italy's a woman, maybe you could tell me what to say to her.'

Driscoll was astounded.

'Haven't you seen a map of the world, soldier?' he asked.

The giant looked out the window as the barracks spun past him, building after building, and beyond it hot, white desert. 'The world is a big place,' Train said softly. 'It seem too big to fit on one piece of paper.'

Sitting in his tent near the Cinquale Canal, Driscoll set down the list with the four names on it. No doubt about it. That was him, the giant he'd met that first day in camp. The guy who said the world was too big to fit on one piece of paper.

Too bad, he thought bitterly. The big galoot was sitting in the path of twelve thousand Germans and couldn't even read a map. He hoped the information he had was wrong. If it wasn't, he felt sorry for the poor bastard.

5

THE STATUE HEAD

The statue head that Sam Train found on the bank of the Arno River in Florence and carried into battle began its life as a chunk of rock in a marble mountain in 1590 in the town of Carrara, forty miles north-west of Florence. A marble worker named Filippo Guanio, dangling precariously from a rope strung from the top of the mountain, chiseled a long, straight line down a ten-foot outcropping and attached fourteen metal loops to the rocks. He was pulled up to the top of the mountain by his fellow workers, walked twenty feet over, then descended again, chiseling another line ten feet long and attaching fourteen more metal loops. He then worked his way twenty feet across the bottom, attaching twenty-two metal loops, forming a ten-by-twenty-foot box. He then strung a long, thick rope through each loop so they all were connected and formed a kind of cradle. With five other men, he carefully chipped away at chiseled lines near the loops until the big piece of rock broke loose and dangled freely from the mountain, held by only a single thick rope, and bounced precariously against the ledges while six men and two mules at the top of the mountain hung on for dear life to keep it from falling to earth. The men at the top were successful in defying gravity; the piece did not fall, but it bounced along the side of the ridge like a pendulum, tapping lightly with deep *booms* as it swung back and forth. Unfortunately for the workers who had freed the piece in the first place by hammering at the chiseled lines, there was no one available to pull them to the top since everyone up there was straining to the last muscle and was dreadfully occupied, to say the least. They were on their own, still suspended by ropes and clinging to the sides of the mountain, and as the piece bounded wildly out of control, they desperately scrambled to get out of the way. Filippo saw the chunk coming and frantically tried to move, but the huge piece hit another outcropping of rock and skittered crazily, losing its rhythm and bounding high. It swung wide of the mountain, then blocked out the sunlight as it came down and caught his arm, crushing it and ripping it away. The arm, still clothed in Filippo's sweater from shoulder to hand, dangled from the giant rock as it bounded away – it was as if the giant hunk of marble had deliberately grabbed the arm for itself – before it dropped to the side of the mountain below, where it landed in a pile of marble rubble, never to be found. Only then was Filippo, the nerve endings of his arm dangling jagged and bleeding from its socket, hastily hauled up to the top. He received an extra three hundred *scudi* and four bottles of wine from the mine's owner for his troubles that day, and went back to work two months later as a mule skinner.

The huge marble stone was lowered to the ground and placed on the back of a wagon, then carted eighty miles north to the port city of Genoa by twelve mules and a team of drivers. There, it was placed aboard a ship bound for France, where it was unloaded in La Rochelle and taken by another mule train to the studio of a starving French sculptor named Pierre Tranqueville, who had been commissioned by a duchess de' Medici, wife of the Duke of Florence, to carve one of four statues that would sit atop each corner of the Ponte Santa Trinità, the most beautiful bridge in Florence, whose looping curved arches conform to no line or figure in geometry and are believed to have been drawn freehand by a linear genius, rumored to be Michelangelo. The duchess wanted each statue to represent a season. She assigned the 'summer,' 'winter,' and 'fall' statues to Italian sculptors. Tranqueville, who was commissioned to do spring – *primavera* in Italian – was the only Frenchman. The duchess chose him because he was recommended – indirectly – by one of her chambermaids whom Tranqueville happened to have had the good fortune to pork on his one visit to Italy, when he'd scraped up enough money to visit the great marble statues created by Michelangelo, of whom everyone had heard. The chambermaid had recommended him to the duke of nearby Barga, whom *she* happened to have had the good fortune to pork on several occasions, and who in turn recommended him to the duchess, in order to show the lovely chambermaid how much sway he had with Her Highness.

The commission was the biggest of Tranqueville's young life, and he worked on the statue like a slave for four years, during which time his wife died, his mistress left him, and his only daughter ran off with a painter at the age of fourteen. Tranqueville cursed the statue every day, because despite the size of the commission, he became convinced that the statue that was to bring him fame and fortune had instead brought him only bad luck. Still, he slaved on. His money ran out, his creditors were breathing down his neck, his landlord waited in the wings to evict him, but Tranqueville worked without pause. When the gorgeous piece was finally completed, Tranqueville sent it back to Italy via the same route of mules and men, along with a gracious note to the duchess, thanking her for her generosity and hoping that his piece was the best of the four she had commissioned. Not receiving a swift reply and being flat broke, having taxed all his resources, soul, and savings, he became disconsolate and heartbroken, feelings which later gave way to rage. Two months after shipping the *Primavera* to Florence, Tranqueville stabbed his former mistress to death, flung his daughter's husband off a cliff, beat his daughter so senseless that for months afterward she had to eat food chewed for her by a nursemaid, then took his own life by swallowing a towel.

The statue, in the meantime, was the toast of Florence. It was mounted on the bridge with the three waiting others and drew flocks of admirers, even peasants, who commented that the *Primavera*'s tragic beauty – her long neck, the graceful curves of her shoulders, the swoop of her luscious arms, and her beautiful, shy head tilted forever downward – connoted the deep secrets of a woman's heart as well as the purity of spring for which the statue was named, and the lovely countenance of a young maiden's ever expectant soul awaiting love in the fresh bloom of youth. The duchess, who had secretly harbored some reluctance about hiring a foreign artist, was now so delighted she took several weeks to decide what kind of remuneration to offer the unknown but gifted French sculptor. She finally decided on a commission of four statues for the nearby Ponte Vecchio, which paralleled the Santa Trinità on the Arno River, along with a generous commission to create any five statues of herself in marble that the artist pleased.

The letter bearing this good news from the duchess was sent to Tranqueville wrapped in Chinese silk and scrolled paper edged in gold, with forty-eight gold pieces tucked inside. It arrived nine days after Tranqueville had stuffed the towel down his throat, just as his creditors and landlord were arriving at his studio to clear out his belongings and decide what to do with his daughter, who was homeless, husbandless, and currently living in the back of his studio with an old peasant woman who fed her chewed bread and watery soup twice a day. The creditors and the landlord split fourteen gold pieces among themselves and awarded the rest to Tranqueville's daughter, who though unable to make much sense of the proceedings and the flush of activity that suddenly blossomed around her, was quite happy to receive chestnut soup and chewed wild boar for her twice-daily meals as opposed to crusty, day-old bread covered with the crusty hag's spit. The remaining gold pieces were enough to take care of her for the rest of her days, which, unfortunately, would number very few.

When word of Tranqueville's death reached Italy, the duchess was distraught. She had had no idea of the dire poverty the artist had been living in, and insisted that had she known she would have sent for him immediately and given him a place at her side as a royal artist in her court. She sent enough gold bullion to Tranqueville's daughter in La Rochelle to feed an entire village for a year, then took to her bed in grief for several days, disheartened that her one great artistic discovery had taken his own life before she could introduce his genius to the world at large – and thus immortalize herself in the process, since her future plans for him included several busts of herself.

Meanwhile, the tempest around the statue began. The other three artists, Florentines who had been commissioned to sculpt the works *Fall*, *Winter*, and *Summer*, were furious about the attention the Frenchman received. This is Florence, they argued. We see no difference between his piece and ours. Cultural imperialism, they cried. French snobs! Several city councilmen from the newly formed city government, seeking favor with the populace and a rival duke, took up the cause, and a good old Italian brouhaha started. There is a saying in Florence that Florentines don't agree on anything. They simply say no to everything and continue saying no again and again, deciding only many months or years later whether to agree, disagree, or stay out of it completely – and this only after several commissions have been formed, everything has been discussed, nothing has been decided, and the whole matter has been completely forgotten. Fourteen centuries of continually getting their asses kicked by successive rulers, dukes, counts, conquerors, Lucchesians, Pisans and Romans have, if nothing else, taught Florentines the value of silent virtue and cautious negativity. That virtue remains in Florence to this day.

In the meantime, the tempest around the statues grew, with the populace taking sides, this side sponsoring tours with rival dukes and duchesses, the other side passing pronouncements declaring that a holiday be named for their favorite of the four statues, and so forth. During this time, the duchess took to her deathbed, and in the wake of sentimental fashion that accompanies the dead and dying, not to mention the duchess's declared dying wishes that the statue be honored for the great art that it was, the value of the *Primavera* skyrocketed. The French ambassador to Florence, hearing of the controversy, took one look at the *Primavera*, hopped a ship to France to see King Louis IV of Mont St Michel, and returned to Italy with an offer of two hundred thousand French florins for the *Primavera*, arguing coyly that if the Florentines could not agree as to the greatness of a French genius, why the French certainly could. This offer prompted a torrent of outcries from all Italian factions, who sent word to the French ambassador through the newly formed Florentine city council that while the duchess might be ill and dying, the statue was bought and paid for with Florentine money, labor, and blood, and with all due respect to the King of Mont St Michel and the great nation of France, he could take his two hundred thousand French florins and stick them up his ass. The French ambassador took umbrage, and lawyers were summoned. Tempers mounted. Politicians drew up resolutions. More committees were formed. The French called in a lawyer from the nearby province of Liguria, who argued that there was no contract between France and Florence and that copies of Tranqueville's commission must be produced in order for the Florentines to prove ownership. There was no copy to be found, as the duchess's chambermaid, the lover of Tranqueville and the Duke of Barga, had taken note of the controversy and swiped the document in hope of cashing in on the whole bit later on. Now she was too frightened to reveal her deed and took to her bed, feigning illness. The Florentine city council, unable to produce the document, and by now thoroughly enraged, sent for Filippo Guanio, the marble worker who had lost an arm pulling the giant rock from the marble quarry at Carrara.

When four soldiers on horseback in full knight's regalia from the duchess's court appeared at his door, Filippo the marble worker thought he was either dreaming or going to prison for stealing dozens of limestone slabs off the mountains at Carrara and using his toes and his remaining hand to carve them up into figurines, which he sold for a good price. He jumped through a back window and tried to run. The soldiers caught him, threw him on a horse, and took him to Florence, where city officials stuffed him full of olives and wine, gave him a set of new clothes and a mule, and placed him before the marble *Primavera* on the Santa Trinità bridge, whereupon the poor man declared to all present, This is indeed the piece of marble that cost me my arm, and I would know it since it is my arm that lay crushed against it and fell down the mountain. Then, to the astonishment of all present, the drunken man cursed the *Primavera* from head to foot, calling the piece 'a low, filthy whore of a statue and not worthy of the time of a great duke-in-waiting like myself, and certainly not worth my arm.'

He was quickly hustled away – but the point, the Florentines argued, had been made. The *Primavera* was Florentine. It had been etched in Florentine blood. No Frenchman, be he a lowly ambassador or Louis IV, would touch it. The French ambassador backed down, withdrew the offer, and the squabbling among the Italians about the four statues began anew. It quieted down some after the duchess's death, in 1602, died after the Romans conquered Florence in 1639, was revived again when Italy was united in 1861, then ceased again in 1914, after the First World War began. After the war, the bickering started up anew, as each of the four statues began to show its age and needed repair, and no one could agree as to how – and by whom – they would be repaired. That ended when Hitler's army invaded Italy in 1943 and in 1944 blasted to pieces nearly every bridge in Florence, including the Santa Trinità, destroying every statue on it except the *Primavera*, which miraculously survived. She stood alone now on her corner post, a testament, her proponents murmured smugly beneath their breath, to God's decision as to which was the greatest work after all, though by accident of default or irony, one of her arms was blown off and presumed to have fallen into the Arno River, and like Filippo the marble worker's, that arm was never found. So the score of fate, it appeared, was even.

The *Primavera* nearly survived the war, until November 1944, when a tired German artillery gunner named Max Faushavent received a message via his radio that Americans were marching dangerously close to Florence, and his regiment needed two artillery fires in Fiesole, four kilometers above the city. Faushavent was sleeping next to his battery when the order squawked over his radio, and he awoke in a panic, not hearing the exact coordinates. Faushavent had never seen a Negro before in his life, and when he scrambled to his feet and peered over the edge of the ridge where his battery was hidden and saw colored American soldiers marching beneath him along the Arno River near the destroyed Santa Trinità bridge, he thought he had died and gone to hell. Without thinking, he loaded up and fired two shots at them before his screaming compatriots told him he was firing backward – Fiesole was the other way – but too late. His shots fired wide and missed, scattering the Negroes. One shell landed in the Arno River and the other landed at the base of the *Primavera*, the lone statue remaining on the Santa Trinità bridge, which had cost Filippo Guanio his arm, the artist Tranqueville his sanity, the duchess her stature, and the French their pride. The shot blew the statue off its base and sent the *Primavera*, now worth millions, hard to the concrete, where she landed with a thunk, severing her other arm, which flew into the Arno River, and also severing her lovely head, which rolled several feet away and landed in the gutter, where it was found by a Negro soldier from Mt Gilead, North Carolina, named Sam Train, who could not unload it for fifty dollars and who was now rubbing it inside a deserted barn in Tuscany, three kilometers beneath the eye of the Mountain of the Sleeping Man, with a dying boy in his lap, trying to make himself invisible again.

6

THE POWER

The three soldiers caught Train about a mile up the ridge, sitting in the loft of a deserted barn with its doors blown off. He sat with his back against the wall, rubbing the statue head, his pants caked with mud. The boy, in shock, was cradled between his legs, swaddled in Train's field jacket. Outside, the sun was disappearing behind the clouds, and it had started to rain. Train's gun lay near the open doorway, which faced the mountains. His pack lay on the floor next to him.

Stamps was the first inside the barn and climbed up to the loft, furious, as the others waited below. His nerves were shot. They were at least two miles from American lines. He thought he saw the backs of at least two German patrols to the west as they'd climbed the ridge. He was in a state of near panic. 'What's the fuck's wrong with you?' he said.

Train shrugged and turned to the side, his body in a crouch. The boy in his lap did not move. He held the boy up to Stamps as an offering. The kid's arms draped back, lifeless.

'Y'all can take him now.'

Stamps didn't want to touch the boy. 'Hector, come here and take a look.' Hector, the radioman, was the only one trained as a medic.

Hector dropped his radio, scrambled up the ladder, took one look at the kid, waved a hand across the kid's face, and said, 'He needs a hospital.'

'I ain't say put a spell on 'im. Look 'im over,' Stamps said.

Hector didn't want to touch the boy. He climbed down the ladder. 'Wasn't my idea to come here,' he said. He felt like he wanted to throw up, he was so scared. He was a draftee, a Puerto Rican. He had no part in this war. He was stuck between colored and white in the division. His cousin Felix had been drafted the same day as he had and had been sent with the all-white 65th Division to France. Felix had written him and told him he was frigging all the French girls he could find. And here he was stuck with these guys, following Diesel the dope, because he looked more colored than Felix. It had been bad luck from the first day. They tried to make him into an Italian translator at training camp because of his proficiency in Spanish. After completing the four-month course, he purposely flunked the final when he was told he would become an officer afterward. He hadn't wanted to become an officer for this very reason, because he might find himself in shit like this, with somebody asking him what to do. He didn't know what the fuck to do. The kid was hurt. They needed to get the fuck outta here. He felt like he was losing his grip.

Stamps looked through the blasted barn's doorway. He could hear renewed firing in the distance below them. He couldn't tell whether the firing was moving away or coming closer because the sound reverberated in the mountains all around them, but somebody had gotten a second wind. He turned to Train. 'We gotta book outta here now. Train, button him up and let's go.'

Train remained curled in a ball on the floor and didn't move.

Stamps stepped around to the front of Train and knelt, his rifle slung across his back and his ammo bandoleer packed so full it hung nearly to the floor. Tall, thin, with long arms, a lean, handsome face, and skin the color of chestnuts, he and a small squad had been sent into battle his first week in Italy without ammo and had barely survived an attack by a German patrol. Since that day, he carried enough ammo for two men.

'You goin' over the hill, Train?'

'What hill?'

'What's gotten into you?'

'Lemme be.'

'We spent three hours looking for you.'

'Well, you can see I'm found. Now g'wan.'

Stamps eyed the kid, who lay across Train's shoulder now, his eyelids fluttering slightly, looking feverish and pale yellow.

'We got to get this kid to a hospital.'

'I don't know nuthin' 'bout no kid,' Train said. He held the boy up high again, the field jacket draped around him like a sacrificial blanket.

Stamps turned and climbed down from the loft, to where Bishop waited below. 'You talk to him while me and Hector take a look around,' he said disgustedly.

'Why me?'

'You the one made him lose his grip, man!' Stamps walked away, furious, stepping to the doorway of the barn to reconnoiter the outside, but seeing the forbidding hills and ridges around him, walked no farther than five feet before deciding to reconnoiter from the safety of the blasted-out doorway.

Bishop dragged his heavy frame up the steps. He approached Train, who sat hunched in a ball in the corner, and stood in front of him, his hands on his hips. Train could see the far wall between Bishop's legs. He noticed that Bishop's brand-new boots, which he'd won off Trueheart Fogg in a poker game, were muddy and ruined.

'Where you going, Sam Train?' Bishop said softly. Train rubbed his hands along his face, his big shoulders heaving slowly as he breathed. He turned to look up at Bishop, whose eyes stared at him like headlights. Even when he was angry, Bishop's eyes seemed mirthful and sly, like there was a secret between them that only he knew.

'I know you, Bish. You kin talk the horns off the devil's head. I ain't fixin' to go back.'

'I ain't ask you that. Did I ask you that? I asked you where you was going.'

Train sighed heavily. 'Dunno where I'm going, Bish. I'm ain't going here no more.'

Bishop figured he could move this mountain. There was always a way to move a mountain. If he had the time, he could've made Sam Train stand up, throw the boy out the window, and carry him, Bishop, all the way down the mountain on his back, clear to division headquarters, all by talking. Talking was his magic. Talking was his balm. But they were in the middle of who knows where, and with Germans around. There wasn't any time for any fuckin' magic. Bishop just wanted his money. He took a more direct approach. 'Well, we do got to go back,' he said softly.

'I never felt so lonesome in my whole life, Bishop. I been dreaming a lot,' Train said.

Bishop shot a look over his shoulder to make sure that the loft was empty, then leaned down to talk in a low voice, so the others wouldn't hear. 'Nigger, I ain't interested in your dreams,' he hissed. 'You got my money.'

'I'll pay you. I ain't never gone bad on no debt. I knows how to turn invisible now. Want me to show you?'

Bishop stood up. 'Stop talking crazy! We got to go back so's you can pay me.'

'I can pay you right now. I got something worth more'n fourteen hundred dollars.'

'What's that?'

Train held up the head of the statue, the priceless *Primavera* of Florence, the seventeenth-century prize created by the great Frenchman Pierre Tranqueville, which he'd found in the gutter next to the Arno and couldn't unload for fifty dollars. In the dim light of the barn loft, the dirty piece of marble looked like a piece of whitened shit.

Bishop stared at it. 'Naw. That's just a hunk of rock. I wants my cheddar in cash.'

Train's brown face wrinkled in confusion. 'I don't understand why I'm heah, Bishop. It's a mistake. They got the wrong man. I'm staying right in this heah spot till it's all over.'

'You can't do that, Train.'

'Why not? Nothing the white man say counts out heah. You said that yourself many times.'

'This little boy is white. You nearly died gettin' him.'

'No, I was getting my statue head back. You can have him. Heah.

Please take him.' He held up the child, who now was stirred awake by all the jostling and tried to cling to him. Bishop reached for the child, who shrank back against Train.

'He don't wanna go,' Train said miserably. 'Carry 'im, he's little, Bishop.'

'They gonna put you in jail, Train.'

'I hope so. If I could pay 'em to do it, I would.'

'You'll pay me first, though.'

'G'wan. I told you I would . . .'

Bishop shrugged and climbed down from the loft. Stamps approached the ladder. 'Well?' Stamps said.

'I can't do nuthin' with him.'

Stamps mounted the ladder again, his footsteps thundering as he climbed, shaking the loft. He stood in front of Train, hands on his hips. 'Get up, Train, let's go,' he said.

'I got this child heah who won't go.'

'You're using that child,' Stamps said.

'The same way the white man is using me.'

'Don't start that mess. The boy ain't got nothing to do with that.'

'Everybody got something to do with everything.'

'Goddammit, don't double talk me, soldier!'

'He don't wanna go back! G'wan. Take him! I don't want him.'

Stamps could feel his heart pounding so hard it felt like it was going to burst through his mouth. He had a tremendous headache. His hemorrhoids were killing him. There were better ways to desert. Shoot yourself in the foot. Help a wounded soldier to the aid station and take off. Get trench foot, a condition in which the mud and rain made your feet swell and develop such painful, debilitating sores that you couldn't walk. Train could've deserted ten times before. In Pietrasanta, when they were hung up in a paper factory for four days by German fire, soldiers fleeing with their eyeballs rolled back in terror, Train could've shot himself in the foot ten times or punctured his leg with a knife and called it a shrapnel wound and no one would've said a word. Why now? He had no idea. The Negro draftees from the South like Train were a puzzle to Stamps. He could not understand their lack of pride, their standing low, accepting the punishment that whites doled out, never trying to take the extra step. Yet in battle they were often tenacious fighters, smart, fierce soldiers who reacted to stress with calm and deliberateness. Why didn't they save a little of that fight for the white man back home? Instead, they walked around like idiots, superstitious of every damn thing, carrying cats' bones and Bibles and wearing little black bags filled with potions around their necks, with names like Jeepers and Pig and Bobo, kow-towing to the white man at every step. He didn't understand it and he didn't want to. To him, they were everything he did not want to be: dumb niggers, spooks, moolies. He'd been a champion swimmer at his segregated high school back home in Arlington, Virginia, the only Negro good enough to make the all-white regional team that won the state championship. To celebrate their victory, the coach took the team out for ice cream. He bought vanilla ice cream for the other swimmers. For Stamps, he bought chocolate. Stamps refused to eat it. The coach was indignant and demanded an explanation, but Stamps refused to explain. Even as a kid, he had wanted to be treated equally, and he couldn't understand how anyone could feel or think otherwise. He was exhausted by these country Negroes. He'd seen them all his life, at the bus stop, in his neighborhood, the women swabbing floors, shelling peas, sitting on porches, laughing and joking like they didn't have a care in the world, the men drinking themselves to death, hollering to heaven every Sunday, calling each other Deacon this and Brother that while robbing each other blind over nickels and dimes, fighting over women, making babies they would later beat up and abuse, while Mr Charlie was kicking their ass. Passive-aggressive Negroes. That's what Huggs used to call them. He'd known Huggs for four years. They'd gone to officer candidate school together. He felt a bit of shame creep over him as he realized he was glad it was Huggs that got hit and not him. Train had been standing right next to Huggs in the canal, and Stamps suddenly thought that maybe that's what had made Train snap. Watching Huggs get blown to spaghetti. That could send any man over the top.

'Okay.' He sighed. 'I'll get Captain Nokes to let you escort the child back to division headquarters. You can take him all the way there, then go to ordnance and work in supplies. I'll get Lieutenant Birdsong to write it up. He's colored, he'll do it. You'll be twenty miles from the front, all the way back to Viareggio if you want. Get all the tail you want down there for two dollars.'

Train shook his head. 'I ain't going back. I'm done fighting for white folks. Up here, it don't count what they say. It ain't like back home. They got no say here. White folks got no say here,' he repeated. The thought panicked him as he said it. The white commanders liked him. They always said he did good. They knew everything. He trusted them. Now they were dying, too. He'd seen that. His world was upside down. He watched Stamps glare at him.

'You're acting like a goddamn fool,' Stamps said.

'I'm setting here till I figure out what's next,' Train said.

'What's next is the Krauts come down that hill in the morning, that's what's next.'

'They won't find me here.'

'Where you going?'

Train rubbed his statue head silently. He decided not to tell anyone anything else about his invisibility. He pointed out the doorway of the barn to a ridge to the southwest, Mt. Cavallo, right at the eye of the Mountain of the Sleeping Man. 'Ain't no firing that way,' he said.

'You don't know what's there,' Stamps said. 'The boogie man's that way.'

'Well, he got to move over, 'cause Sam Train's coming to shake his hand.'

Already, Stamps could see the flares starting to light up the sky. 'It'll be dark in a couple hours. We'll rest till oh-four-hundred tomorrow. Then I'm sending Bishop and Hector up here, and if you're not ready to go, we're arresting you and taking you back. You're lucky Captain Nokes isn't here. He'd shoot you on the spot.'

Stamps ground his foot into the floor of the loft, pushing some hay back and forth. This was a truly fucked-up situation. He hated Nokes. It was Nokes's fault that Train had snapped. If Nokes had fired the artillery right, they'd be back at camp getting ready for Christmas dinner in a few days. He had a sudden vision of himself pointing his rifle at Nokes's face and spraying bullets at it. He quelled the thought as the kid stirred, then sat up. He leaned over to look at him.

'Get some sulfa powder from Hector and try to give it to the kid,' Stamps said. 'It'll bring his fever down. He got a fever, don't he?'

'I don't know what he got.'

Stamps tried to place his hand on the kid's forehead, but the shaking boy watched him through fluttering eyelids and drew away, pushing his body into Train's chest.

'What you gonna feed him?' Stamps asked.

'I gived him some food I got, some chocolate and D rations. He likes the hash.'

'Okay. Take some of Hector's if you run out. And feed him good. He's got a long walk tomorrow.'

Stamps reached for the loft's ladder.

'I ain't got no disserpation with you, Lieutenant,' Train said.

'Disserpation?'

'Fuss. I ain't got no fuss with you.'

Standing on the ladder, Stamps felt his heart sagging. He had marched with Train for six months, trained with him, fought with him, shared latrines and foxholes with him, and realized he had never gotten to know him. He didn't want to get to know him. It was better that way. It was better that he thought of him as a dumb nigger, because if he didn't, Train reminded him of somebody else he knew, somebody he loved very much . . . his own father.

'All right, Train. Get some sleep and be ready tomorrow.'

Train watched as the sun began its descent behind the forbidding mountains. Over the scattered firing in the canal below, he heard a woman's voice on a loudspeaker, saying warmly in English with a German accent, *'Welcome to the war, Ninety-second Division. What are you Negroes fighting for? America doesn't want you. We want you. Come to us. I got something nice and warm for you. You can have all you want,'* followed by the blaring sound of relaxing jazz. Still crouching, Train turned away from Stamps, the flares outside silhouetting his huge brown face against the mountains. 'Tomorrow may never come,' he said softly.

*　　*　　*

70

The boy dreamed of a woman standing on a hill. And in his dream she waved at him. Her hand was frozen in the air. He did not recognize her, but he saw her clearly, at the edge of a grassy field near a tree, hand held high. She seemed tired. He stood and watched as she waved, then she faded away. When he awoke, he was lying on the floor, the chocolate giant crouched over him, watching. Underneath the giant's arm was the head of the woman from his dream. The giant had only her head. The boy regarded the *Primavera*'s head, his eyes wide in fright.

'Ain't nuthin' but a good-luck charm, boy. Got magic in it. You wanna touch it?'

The sound of the giant's throaty voice was soothing, but when he held the statue head out and picked up the boy's hand so that he could touch it, the boy drew his hand back.

Train placed the head on the ground. 'I guess you hungry, ain't ya.'

The boy ignored him. His chest hurt and he felt cold. Something inside him, deep inside, was not right. He looked up at the giant and felt as if a great haze were covering his eyes, as if he were looking at the chocolate giant through sheer white curtains. He watched as the giant shifted, slowly pulled out a tin of K-ration hash, speared some with a field fork, and offered it to him.

'You like this, don'tcha?'

The boy ignored the fork and stared mutely as the giant's lips moved. He had slipped again to that quiet place where there were no voices and no sounds. He decided to check with his friend Arturo to see if he was home. He closed his eyes. Arturo appeared right next to the giant's shoulder, both of them hovering above him. Even standing up, Arturo wasn't as tall as the crouching giant. The boy noticed that Arturo was wearing suspenders and no shoes.

Arturo scratched his head absently. 'I have lice,' he said.

'Where am I?' the boy asked.

'You are in the world.'

'What's the world?'

'The world is a giant's head, and we're living on his head, and when he turns his head, it's your birthday.'

The boy watched Train take off his helmet and sigh, then scratch his nappy head of hair.

'Who is he?' the boy asked.

Arturo was indignant. 'He's a chocolate maker who gives it out for free. And did you save some chocolate for your friend? You did not!'

'I did,' the boy said. 'I saved you some.' From his pocket, he produced a piece of D-ration chocolate that Train had given him.

Hovering over the child, Train watched incredulously as the boy pulled the piece of chocolate from his pocket, held it in the air, and chatted with it amiably before devouring it.

'That was good,' Arturo said. 'I have had that only twice before in my life. Tell me about the chocolate maker. Does he drink motor oil and eat babies?'

'No,' the boy said.

'Touch him and see.'

Lying on the floor, the boy reached up and motioned for Train to come closer. Train complied, thinking the boy wanted to whisper something to him. Instead, the boy raised himself on his elbows and gently ran a hand across Train's face, then through the rough texture of Train's wooly hair. 'If I turn your head,' the boy said softly, 'it will be my birthday.'

Train didn't understand. He felt the little hands pulling at his head, the innocent young eyes searching his face, and shame washed over him like water. A white person had never touched his face before. Never reached out and stroked him with love, and the force of it, the force of the child's innocence, trust, and purity drew tears to his eyes. He expected to feel nothing when the boy touched him, but instead he felt mercy, he felt humanity, he felt love, harmony, longing, thirst for kindness, yearnings for peace – qualities he'd never known existed in the white man. The boy ran his hand over Train's face and held the big man's nose. His innocent eyes searched Train's, and as their eyes locked, Train could see inside him and saw not derision, or fear, or loathing, but hurt and searching and pain from a thousand indignities. He saw light, darkness, flickering hope, but most of all he saw in the child's face a reflection of himself. He had never seen that in the face of any person before, white or colored, not even a child. He stared at the boy, transfixed.

'Good God, boy, you got power in yo' hands,' he said.

The boy dropped his hands from Train's face and lay back. He was exhausted. He saw Arturo watching.

'Can I ask you something?' the boy asked Arturo.

'Sure.'

'Who am I?'

Arturo seemed troubled. 'If you have to ask, I don't know.'

The sound of thundering footsteps mounting the ladder caused the boy to turn his head, and in that moment Arturo disappeared. Stamps hurriedly climbed into the loft and with two steps was standing over Train and the boy.

'Get up, Train! We got to roll,' he said.

Train, still staring at the boy, spoke from his crouch. 'He got the power, Lieutenant,' Train said. 'He got the power!'

'What?'

'The boy. He sat up and touched my head. He got the power of God in his hands. He blessed me. I could feel it. This is my lucky day. Yes, Lord, thank you, Jesus – praise God! He got the power. Wanna feel it? Touch his hands, Lieutenant.' Train grabbed Stamps's hand and tried to force it on the boy. 'You'll feel it, too. Touch him.'

Stamps yanked his hand away. 'Get a grip on yourself, man! Hector saw something out there. We gotta look – now. You comin' or not?'

Train rose to go, excitedly gathering his things as Stamps stared incredulously. 'I think your cheese slid off your biscuit,' he said. 'You need a fucking doctor, I think.'

'Don't need no doctor.'

'Then why did you run this way in the first place? Whyn't you just run back to our side instead of getting us all fucked up way out here?'

Train shrugged. He didn't have a side. One way had seemed as good as the other. No white man could protect him out here. 'I ain't ask you to come,' he said. He didn't need Stamps and the others now. He had protection – two protections now, the statue head neatly tucked into his waistband and an angel, a real one. He picked up the boy and cradled him. He began to hum 'Take Me to the Water,' a soft, deep, throaty hum from within his chest, as he approached the ladder, turned, and climbed down. Stamps followed him, still furious.

The boy settled in the giant's warm arms as the deep singing voice covered him like a blanket. He felt like he was swaddled in cotton. He buried his head in Train's chest. He wished Arturo would come back so he could tell him the feeling of it, the feeling of being buried in chocolate and hearing the sweet music, but Arturo would not come, so he slept again and dreamed of the woman waving at him. He wanted to ask Arturo why the woman kept waving at him. He wanted to know why she was waving at him to go away.

7

THE CHURCH

The four soldiers had got about a hundred yards down the ridge toward the American side when a German patrol spotted them and chased them back up the ridge and down the other side of the mountain, toward the Serchio Valley, and now they were lost. They walked for four hours in the freezing rain, over jagged ridges, through valleys, past caves, along perilous cliffs. They had no map, a dead radio, no idea where they were going other than that they were traveling away from the last patrol they'd seen and that they had to find shelter and food before night. Whenever they saw a fire or a cluster of houses, they walked into the hills to get around it, and in doing so walked within four hundred yards of half a dozen American forward artillery observers and Italian partisans who could have saved the boy's life: Lieutenant Horace Madison in Seravezza, Lieutenant Jimmy Suttlers in Cerreto, Bruno Valdori of the Valenga partisans in Ruosina, all sitting quietly in warm houses next to warm fires eating hot food, awaiting orders to deliver coordinates that would rain artillery fire down on the mountain towns where the Germans were hidden. But once the soldiers got past Ruosina, there were no forward artillery observers around for them to blunder into. They'd ventured far beyond the American outposts, and they were on their own. The freezing rain fell heavier as they trudged farther and farther into the mountain forest, transforming the already slippery slopes into thick, red mud.

With each slip in the mud, Stamps, who was in the lead, cursed aloud, 'Dumb bastard, sending that fool over the hill.' He couldn't get over it. He didn't blame Sam Train. He was convinced now that Train had snapped, and everybody knew Train wasn't the sharpest knife in the drawer in the first place. But Bishop, he had power over men. Even Stamps owed him money from cards. They'd never gotten along. Bishop represented the kind of Negro that Stamps despised; his type set the race back a hundred years with his silly grinning and shining in front of whites and hustling his Negroes with God talk and playing cards.

As Bishop huffed and puffed up the ridge behind the other men, Bishop heard Stamps and ignored him. Bishop's liking or caring about a person was in strict proportion to how much he could use them, so he wasn't worried about Stamps. He was worried about himself. He was furious with himself for following Train across the canal. He couldn't understand why he'd done it. The thing about Train owing him money was an excuse. Everyone owed him money. And as for sending Train to get the boy, he had no idea what he was thinking. He had seen the two feet under the haystack, it didn't seem right, there was a lot going on, he couldn't hear anything, Huggs was hit and his face was splattered everywhere, the white cracker Nokes didn't believe they'd made it across the canal and didn't fire artillery support, he thought he was going to die anyway, what the fuck. He had panicked and sent Train to do what he himself had no intention of doing. If he believed in God, he would've prayed then, but he didn't believe in God. The preaching thing he did back in Kansas City was just a ruse to get some money out of some dumb niggers. Giving Train artificial respiration and bringing him back to life on the beach at the canal – that was some bullshit, too. He'd read about that in a magazine someplace, how a guy fell off a roof and a doctor shocked him back to life by pushing air down into his lungs. He didn't know why he'd tried it. He thought that big mumbo-jumbo nigger was dead, and he was thinking about all that money, that's what it was. Shit, fourteen hundred dollars was a lot of flow.

As Bishop climbed behind the others, watching the steam rise from Sam Train's back in the eerie, foggy rain, Bishop tried to decide which made more sense: fighting and keeping your pride like the Negro papers said, or bailing out and keeping your life intact. Nothing ever worked right in the division anyway. The good white commanders had transferred out before the company even left the States. The black first and second lieutenants ran everything, and they never knew more than five minutes of what the next mission was. Take this hill, take that hill. For what? The enemy came right back and took it the next day anyway. When Bishop first saw the mountain slopes they had to attack, he thought maybe jail was better. The Germans had blasted and burned away all the trees and houses and foliage so there was no place to hide. The Germans shot down. The Americans ran up. It was a turkey shoot. Their first mission outside Lucca, they had a good white captain named Walker, a man from Mississippi. Walker was a courageous bastard, Bishop had to admit it. Walker refused to stay back at headquarters and give radio orders like the other white captains. He told them, 'When we climb that ridge tomorrow morning, I'll be right there next to you,' and he was. When the order came to jump, Walker stood and said, 'Let's go,' and the Germans sliced, diced, sissy-fried, cut up, spanked, and chopped up every single foot of earth in front of Walker, and every soldier behind him who was stupid enough to stand up when he made the order got his ass shot off. Walker made it ten feet before he leaped into a foxhole. A shell came right after him and blew him to pieces. Incredibly, what was left of him got up and staggered another five feet before the other bits of him collapsed, and not all of them at the same time, either. Lieutenant Huggs, he got his face shot off at the Cinquale Canal. All his friends – Jimmy Cook, Skiz Parham, Spencer Floor, Hep Trueheart, all of 'em deader than Calpurnia's flapjacks. Now the whole thing was so fucked up he couldn't stand it. He was still out here, Captain Nokes was back at base sipping tea, probably, and Stamps was running things, all because he'd panicked and followed the dumbest nigger in the world.

'It's working,' he growled, as Hector climbed in front of him.

'What's working?' Hector asked, the rain dripping off his helmet.

'This stupid idea I had. To see how dumb you niggers were, following me across the canal. This kid's gonna die, anyway. And us with him.'

'Cut it out, Bishop,' Stamps snapped, as he climbed ahead. 'We don't need ministerin'. We got to find shelter to get outta this weather.'

'I ain't ministerin',' Bishop said. 'I shouldn't be here with you dog-faces nohow. The only reason I came over here is 'cause my tailor lives here.'

Hector laughed, but Sam Train saw nothing funny. 'Kid here needs a doctor,' he said. 'What y'all gonna do about it?' He stopped underneath an outcropping of rock that partially shielded him from the downpour to check on the boy, and the others huddled in close. Racks of rain slopped down from the slab of rock like a waterfall. Train slowly peeled open his field jacket, which covered the kid. The boy's face was the color of white plaster, his tight little hands balled into fists. Occasionally, his eyes flickered open, then fluttered shut again. For the first time, Train noticed that his breathing seemed labored, and even over the pouring rain he could hear the child's breath wheezing in and out, as if something were rattling in his throat, making the ripping sound a playing card makes when it's stuck in the spokes of a bicycle rim.

'He don't need no doctor. He needs a hospital,' Stamps said. 'Hector, take a look while I check the top of the ridge.' Stamps trotted ahead.

Hector didn't even bother to glance at the kid this time. He waved his hand at Train, who looked at him hopefully. 'I told you before, he needs a hospital.' He felt sorry for Train's kid, but not that sorry. He'd seen a thousand of them in Naples, begging at street corners, tugging at the soldiers saying, 'Meet my sister. Big titties. Tight pussy.' They reminded him of himself growing up back in San Juan, begging for food at sidewalk cafés, snatching leftovers as the owners chased him down the street, his silent mother praying at mass, his drunken father screaming and punching her out at home. Hector couldn't stand the thoughts. He turned away and crouched on his haunches, watching Stamps slip up the muddy ridges.

'Whyn't you look at him?' Train insisted.

'I seen him,' Hector said, watching Stamps struggling up the rocky crevices.

'Whyn't you put some o' that powder on him that you got. I seen you use it before.'

'What powder?'

'The magic powder.'

Hector looked at Train sideways. 'Sulfa powder. Is that what you talkin' 'bout, Train? That's for fevers. I'mma give him that in this rain? He don't got no fever. He got a chest injury or something inside, I don't know.'

'Well, do something.'

Hector yawned. He suddenly felt sleepy. His nerves were giving way. He watched as Train stared at him, his large eyes bulging with hope like a dog's eyes. Hector imagined Train as a dog. He'd be a big, black puppy. 'Let's get outta this shit first,' he said.

Train turned to Bishop. 'Bishop, can't you make 'im look at 'im?'

Bishop peered at the ridges around them. The rain made a fizzing sound as it hit the leaves and trees. 'Don't talk to me 'bout no little white boy,' he grunted. 'You would never see me grabbing no li'l' white boy like you done.'

'But you tol' me!'

'Told you, hell. It was your idea. Wasted your time, too, trying to save him. What for?'

'I done what you tol' me to!'

'I ain't tell you to get us kilt. This is a white man's war, boy. Niggers ain't got nothing to do with it. This boy ain't got no life nohow.'

'Why not?'

''Cause a life of goodness is not what white folks has chosen for they children. The Bible says it, Proverbs Twenty-two sixteen: "Raise up a child the way you want him to go, and he will not depart from it." He's trained to hate, boy. His life ain't worth a dollar of Chinese money.'

Train blinked in confusion, the rain shrouding his giant features. 'He ain't done nothing to you.'

'Two hours ago you didn't want 'im.'

Train said nothing. That was before he knew the boy was an angel. The boy was his now. The boy was an angel of God. He had the power. Train couldn't give him away now.

Stamps returned from above, slipping and sloshing down to a stop underneath the rock outcropping, sliding as if into home plate. The rain was falling in sheets now, and he had to shout over the splattering of the downpour. 'It's gonna be dark in ten minutes,' he said. He pointed. 'There's a church bell tower behind that ridge. We'll hold there. Maybe we can make a fire inside the church.'

Hector took the lead and Train went last, carrying the kid, who lay limp against him, tiny as a chicken in his arms.

The church lay beyond a village composed of several houses dug into a dark mountain beside a road that curved along a beautiful sloping ridge. They crawled along the underside of the ridge, sticking close to the dirt road, cut through the woods to bypass the village, and came upon another dirt trail that led to the church. They followed the tiny trail past a small graveyard. Farther up, the road widened and curved again, and they could see, at the very top of the ridge, the church bell tower and a few pastel-colored houses dotting the distant hills behind it. It was a good place to build a church, Bishop thought. If he were really holy and wanted to build a church, he'd build a church here, too. He had just been about to build a new church back in Kansas City when he got drafted. It was the story of his life, that just before he made a big score, his luck ran out. He'd served six months at Parchman Penitentiary in Louisiana under the name of Mason June for fraud and theft, breaking rocks on a chain gang and sleeping with his teeth on edge after winning cigarettes at poker from the other inmates, big, stupid men like Train – tough, grizzled cotton pickers with long arms and short brains who liked his smooth talk and easy-handed way of dealing cards, finding his funny stories about the white man an ease from the burden of their own tortured, boring existences, which promised no future other than long nights of pining after whores and country women, who promised only a dull life and more plowing. He got into preaching afterward. It was a lot easier than fleecing card players in jook joints, where sharecroppers in overalls often found courage at the bottom of a bottle of suds once they figured he'd duped them. Besides, the big-city pimps were moving in and crowding his business, and when they pulled out their pistols, they touched the trigger and told the hammer to hurry. The Bible was an easy study, with lots of extra poontang and chicken dinners thrown in. He had actually grown up in church back in Louisiana, but watching his deacon father punch his mother out every Saturday night, then pray to high holy heaven on Sunday mornings, robbed him of any illusions about God's work. If God's around, he's a loser, Bishop thought, and I'm gonna play him. He spent his last fourteen dollars on a bus ticket to Kansas City and set up shop in front of an abandoned plumbing supply store downtown, serving free lemonade on hot July afternoons and preaching like a madman to tired housekeepers and old gardeners who wandered past on their way home from work: Put down them heavy pots and pans and come to God, he said. Put down that heavy sack and come over here, 'cause Somebody Special wants you. And He don't have no anger. He don't know no pain. He don't give no orders. He's a pain-getting-rid-of-er. That's His job. To get rid of your pain faster than this lemonade can go down your little red lane. Why? Ain't no why! He ain't got to explain Hisself! He'll hurl your enemies down to low stones like he hurled Satan outta heaven, 'cause He's mighty. He's the baddest kitty kat in the firmament! He got the mojo and the sayso. He knows truth. He knows justice. He knows your pain. And He will heal your pain right now, for free, if you just trust in Him. Ain't no cost to it! Ain't no buy-now-pay-later to this. You ain't rentin' no couches here! God-don't-want-your-money-tainted-by-the-filth-of-man's-sinful-touch and you can *take* your money home and put it under your mattress where it belongs, 'cause I don't want it, *I want your soul!* You got an appointment to keep, and I'm the *secretary!* I'm here to tell you that Jesus is coming! The train's *leaving* the station, and I'm collecting tickets! Don't be left out. Don't wait! Leave your money home, but bring your soul! All aboard! Get what you need! Get God! I got what I need! How 'bout you?

The money poured in like magic, and more people came. Bishop rented the plumbing supply store, and the congregation grew. They called him Walking Thunder, and when he preached he was so good at making the lightning come that at times he actually believed in God. During those moments, fright would cover him like a blanket and he would disappear from his congregation for a few days and drink joy juice till the feeling passed. He was in the flow, he had it good, he had found his niche. But the Army wanted him, and he made the mistake of showing up at the induction center thinking they wouldn't sign up a Negro preacher – they made preachers into chaplains with the rank of captain, he was told, and even a fool knew that no white man wanted a nigger being a captain and telling him what to do. By the time he figured the game was played by the white man's rules, that captains, even Negro chaplains, had college and divinity school degrees, he was doing push-ups at training camp. Now his new church back home was just a dream, and here he was trying to collect his fourteen hundred dollars, staring at a white man's church in a white man's land in the pouring rain with a nigger who was carrying a white man's son who was gonna die, and they'd be blamed for that, too – if the Germans didn't smoke them first. He needed a drink.

Hector, in the lead, slowed as the others gathered around him at the side of the road and stared at the church. 'That's where the Germans would be if they were near here. Camped inside,' he said.

'Don't see no Germans,' Stamps grunted. 'Just keep goin'.'

'This is close enough,' Hector said. 'We don't need to walk in the front door and get our asses shot off. There'll be Germans around here soon enough if they're not here now.'

Stamps was exhausted. 'We stay in there or out here. One or the other. You and I'll go take a look. You take point.'

'Shit no,' Hector said. 'Point or not, it don't matter who's got the point if there's a whole regiment in there having dinner and there's only four of us. If you and me get hung up there, who's gonna back us up? Them two?' He pointed to Bishop and Train. 'I say we go together.'

Stamps felt his command slipping from him, but there was nothing he could do. He was so tired he wanted to lie down right in the rain and rest forever. 'Shit, it don't matter. Let's all go.'

Hector moved forward slowly, crouching, advancing to the edge of the road. He lay on his stomach and peeked around the curve. He lay there for what seemed like an hour, then finally got up and motioned for the others to follow as he dashed across the road and took cover in some bushes on the other side.

Train felt himself going invisible again, and he fought the impulse. Invisibility, he felt, always brought problems. He had not wanted to get the boy and he would not have done so had he been visible and in his right mind, angel or not. He would not have waded into the Cinquale had he been visible. He would not have done any of those things. But they were done now. The boy was his responsibility now. He still owed Bishop money. He still did not know where he was. Everything needed clearing up. If the boy stopped breathing, he thought, that would be a disaster. The notion began to terrify him, that the boy would die. Train had seen dozens of kids dying before, in Lucca, in Naples, starving, begging, their wounds wrapped in gauze, big pus-filled sores on their feet and legs, but they were not connected to him, them being Italians and him being colored. But this one was different. He had felt it. How to explain to them that the boy was an angel? How to explain to God that he'd let an angel die?

He rose and followed the others, dashing across the road. His feet splattered the mud, telling him he was not yet invisible, which meant problems, too. Invisibility meant life but problems. Visibility meant being seen and shot. There was no way he could win. Bishop trotted over, and he and Train huddled together in the bushes and peered at the church, which lay beyond Stamps and Hector, who squatted behind boulders on either side of the road ahead of them.

The church lay in the middle of a tiny piazza. From their vantage point, the men couldn't see any object stirring about it. Debris was piled up in front of the church, the pews had been burned, obviously there had been some sort of firefight. The four men were approaching slowly, in a crouch, spread out by ten feet or so, on either side of the road, when Sam Train spotted Sant'Anna.

Her likeness was set just above the church doorway, which overlooked the tiny piazza, her face jutting out about three feet. The eaves shielded her from the weather. She was just a bust, not an entire statue. Train stared at her, mesmerized. He had never seen a white person so expressive in all his life. He glanced at the head of the *Primavera* statue in its webbing at his side, then back to Sant'Anna. They looked so different, yet both were so beautiful. They stirred something inside him, the two of them, easing him into solace, opening the padlocked door of his heart. Train suddenly felt happy, and warm, the two of them together bewitching him with sudden comfort. This second statue was a sign. It had to be.

Without thinking, Train stood up, unaware that he was exposing himself to enemy fire, and slowly staggered forward in the rain as if in a trance, holding the shivering, pale boy in one arm. As Train walked forward, an odd and sudden chill hit him and the smell of fresh death crashed against his nostrils so hard he could barely stand. He suddenly felt like weeping. He tried to turn around and run but could not. His rifle slipped off his shoulders to his waist, and the statue head at his side bobbed and suddenly felt heavy. He covered his face with one hand, still holding the boy, and staggered through the muddy piazza toward the bust of Sant'Anna. He walked with a weaving motion, as if drunk. He ignored Hector, Bishop, and Stamps, yelling at him to come back. He couldn't stop himself.

Train stood before the bust in the pouring rain, hypnotized, staring up, then felt himself rise, floating, until he was face to face with Sant'Anna. He gazed at her quizzically. Her expression was a mixture of sadness, knowledge, wisdom, and joy all at once. Her sedate marble eyes gazed back at him, and it was as if she could see through him. Suddenly, he felt invisibility again. All of the millions of pieces of knowledge and the truths he'd known, and some he could never know, flowed behind his eyeballs: the secrets of plants, why rivers flow north to south, the arithmetic of dams, why dinosaurs walked the earth. He saw cities under water, seas that parted, where wizards live. He understood why steel ships float, the magic of pyramids, the shaping of the mountains, each and every one of God's miracles. And as each revelation flowed by, it paused for a moment, allowing him to examine it mentally in the tiniest of detail. Train shuddered and gazed at Sant'Anna again in awe, and as he did, the saint's head tilted slowly to one side. He watched in disbelief as a large tear formed in one of her eyes and slowly made its way down her face. He reached out to wipe away the tear and found himself standing on the ground, touching Bishop's face.

To Train's horror, he could not remove his hand. It remained, frozen, stuck to Bishop's face. Bishop, all 210 pounds of him, also seemed frozen to the spot, transfixed, staring at Train with a look of shock and compassion, fear, and even understanding in his eyes. They stood, the two soldiers, in the open piazza at dusk, the rain pouring down in goblets, the giant Negro with the child clutched to his chest gently touching the smaller man's face. Train suddenly recoiled in horror as Bishop, as if under a spell, snapped back to himself and flung Train's hand down. 'Get your wrinkly raisin paws off me, you wobbly nigger! Get the fuck off me! What's that smell? Christ!'

Train tried to stammer an apology, but Hector cut him off. 'Look over there, man! There's somebody over there!'

All four soldiers dropped to a crouch and followed Hector's pointing finger. Atop a hill on their right, several yards beyond the burned pews in the piazza, a lone figure stood with its back to them, staring out over a ridge, the wind blowing its pants against its legs. The figure appeared to be a man, and from a distance, appeared to be unarmed. The soldiers fanned out and approached him.

They were ten feet off when Hector shouted at the man, 'Hey!'

The man turned and they flattened, rifles at the ready, save Train, who ducked behind a tree, clasping the youngster.

The man squinted at them through the dark, driving rain, then turned his back to them and looked out over the ridge again, his hands in his pockets. He began pacing back and forth, talking and gesticulating, his feet splattering the mud as he paced. He appeared to be arguing with someone who was beyond the ridge and beneath him, moving his hands as if trying desperately to prove a point. Whoever he was talking to in the approaching darkness was out of their sightline.

'Let's cut outta here,' Bishop said. 'This place gives me the creeps.'

'Watch my back,' Hector said.

Train, Bishop, and Stamps watched the surrounding trees and hills as Hector approached the man cautiously. Five feet from him, Hector called out again, 'Hey!' The man stopped talking and turned to face Hector, who crouched, ready to fire. The man waved a hand absentmindedly and said something to Hector that was lost in the wind and rain, then turned away and began arguing again with the person beneath him, below the ridge.

Hector addressed the man in Italian. The man ignored him, laughing and pacing as he talked, gesturing openly with his hands as if to say, 'You see what I mean?'

Hector slowly crept forward, until he was standing parallel to the man on the ridge, about five feet away. He pointed his rifle at whoever was beneath the ridge, then motioned with his head to the others that it was safe to come forward. They trotted forward and looked down.

There was no one there.

The soldiers turned their attention to the man, who had stopped pacing and was staring at them. Up close, the man looked ragged and spent. His jacket was split and torn. He had only one shoe on. He was filthy and completely drenched. His face was unshaven, with two front teeth missing and several others blackened by cavities. The black teeth together with his rail-thin limbs and the jawbones that jutted from his flattened cheeks gave him the appearance of being a walking skeleton. He glared at them for a long moment, then began pacing again, jabbering in high-speed Italian as he walked back and forth, arguing with the ridge below.

'What's he saying, Hector?' Bishop asked.

Hector's face creased into a puzzled frown. 'I don't know. He's a little cracked, I think.'

Stamps said, 'Ask him can we sleep in the church.'

Before Hector could speak, the man stopped pacing. His face suddenly contorted into a mask of outrage, and he poured forth a barrage of words at Hector, pointing over the ridge. Hector blinked nervously at the fury of it.

Stamps could make out 'tedeschi' – the Italian word for 'German.' That was all.

'Well?' Bishop asked.

Hector shrugged, his face troubled and bewildered. 'Something's wrong with him.'

'What's the gist of it?'

'Dunno.'

'I thought you spoke Italian.'

'I do but . . . He said something about divine truth and the miracle of a female chicken.'

The man pointed over the ridge again, and once again the four soldiers looked down at the sloping landscape. The hill ended at a patch of pasture about a hundred feet long and fifty feet wide. They could see now, in the last glimmers of dusk's light, that the pasture was not a pasture at all. It was freshly dug earth. Several crosses and flowers lay atop it.

'Let's take the tall timber outta here,' Bishop said. 'The Germans done come and gone.'

Train silently agreed.

Hector gave it one last try.

'Tedeschi? Tedeschi?' he said, pointing at the pasture below.

Suddenly, the church bell behind them began to toll in loud, deafening gongs, and the man, who had turned away from them, wheeled and faced them with such rage in his face that the four of them, armed, backed away, blinking. He opened his mouth and roared, and what with the church bell booming behind him and his screaming fury, his voice had the power of a ship's blasting bullhorn.

They turned and ran, through the stinking church square, past the statue of Sant'Anna, past the church, past the graveyard, across the curving road, over the precipice, and down the muddy path that led to the town below, the man's voice ringing in their ears like a ghost's battle cry.

8

A SIGN

In a tiny house just beneath the church of Sant'Anna, in the town of Bornacchi – a town that had sat there for nineteen hundred years before a Negro ever set foot in it – a poor old man named Ludovico Salducchi heard the ringing of the bell at Sant'Anna's and ignored it. It was just one of the sisters at the convent behind the church giving the all-clear, the signal that there were no Germans around. Ludovico didn't care about any Germans, anyway. He had a bigger problem. He had been cursed by a witch, and tonight he was going to get rid of that curse once and for all. He had made up his mind.

He sat on a tiny wooden chair at a table in his living room with several villagers standing around him. They were watching Ettora the witch, the woman who had cursed him, who was also seated at the table. Across from Ettora was Ludovico's daughter, Renata, dressed in the clothing of a man. She wore trousers and a wool jacket, her long black hair stuffed beneath a man's cap. Renata's husband had been missing from the Italian army for five months, and she'd taken to wearing his clothing as a sign of grief. The priest at Bornacchi said it was sacrilegious for a woman to walk around in a man's clothing, but Renata ignored him. Like everything else here, Ludovico thought bitterly, everything, even the respect of the young has been ruined by the war.

He watched Renata clasp her hands nervously as Ettora set a plate of water on the table. Then, from a small bottle, Ettora carefully poured a large drop of olive oil onto the water. Renata's eyes followed the drop closely as it floated across the surface. Ettora said the oil would tell them if Renata's husband was coming back. If the drop moved one way, he was coming back. If it moved the other, he wasn't.

The room stared in silence as the oil slid to one side of the water. There was a gasp. Then it slid back to the other side. The room gasped again.

'Ludovico, don't tip the table,' Ettora snapped.

Ludovico removed his foot from underneath the table, ignoring his daughter's glare.

Ettora never took her eyes from the shimmering drop on the plate. 'Hmm,' she said. She shifted in her chair and squinted. 'My eyes are not what they once were,' she said. She was a tiny woman in a frayed red dress with bracelets that rattled like old bones on her arms, and delicate features on a pretty, slender face. Her sharp, cutting eyes were marvelous in their beauty. Ludovico couldn't stand her. He'd known her all his sixty-seven years – known her parents, her grandparents even, and she his.

The fact is, he had loved Ettora at one time. When she was a girl, those daring eyes that were now going blind had seemed to hold a deeper knowledge. She had been a leader among the girls, her beauty having made her the pride of the village, and as a young boy, he had watched her frolic about in bright dresses and lead the other girls past the village walls to gather the purple and white-tipped lilies that abounded in the fields outside Bornacchi. Her beauty had attracted young suitors from other villages, and, like them, Ludovico had been drawn to the secrets behind those dancing, sly eyes, whose quick slanting glances seemed to undress to the world. He had been young and handsome then, restless. His legs had been full of vigor, his chest full and strong, his hair thick and black, his laugh hearty, and his mind full of dreams that he shared with everyone. At sixteen he had wooed her; he'd led her to the woods behind the village's olive oil pressing plant, where they'd lain in the grass by the river, she telling him all her dreams, he touching her and making her stir from the secret places inside herself. But she was too free in her mind for him. She had thoughts and ideas that were unbecoming to a woman. She wanted to learn to read. What did books have to do with them? She wanted to study the forest, different kinds of trees and flowers. For what? She wanted to know why fire produced heat and steam, why cold water froze to become ice, why chestnut trees bore fruit that could be made into flour while orange trees did not. Useless thoughts, he believed. He wanted a woman who would wash his clothes as his mother did, who went to mass every morning, who looked the other way when he exercised his little indiscretions. But Ettora's beauty was so great he held his tongue, for he was afraid he would never find another as beautiful as she. Only after several weeks of lying in the grass by the river behind the olive oil pressing plant, after she let him poke his finger into her sly hole, did he broach the idea with Ettora that women should not think, that they should wash clothing and cook wild boar for their husbands, and not waste time dreaming about books and silly plants.

Ettora had found his opinion distasteful. Everyone should think, she scoffed. There is so much to learn. Her response had made him fearful –

that and the secrets behind her eyes – and he'd backed away, even though her willingness to allow him to touch her had been a tacit admission of her desire to marry him – and his tacit agreement to ask – which he never did. They drifted apart, and as the years passed, the group of young maidens who followed Ettora outside Bornacchi to pick the beautiful white-tipped lilies and other plants had gradually been winnowed down to a few, then none, as they were married off to men in the village – he marrying one of them, Anna, who, though dry and witless, had been a dutiful wife who had washed his clothes, mended his socks, ignored his indiscretions – of which, unhappily, there had been few – and, before she died of fever, had borne him the one true gift he'd ever gotten from this cursed and difficult life, his daughter, Renata, who was now suffering in this obscene war like everyone else and who, like everyone else, had turned to Ettora for advice.

Ettora, for her part, had taken his rejection in her stride. Her beauty had attracted several young men from nearby villages, but none had found her suitable. Her fire, her intellect, her thirst for knowledge, and the secrets behind her eyes scared them, and they backed off. By age twenty, her marriage prospects were dim. By thirty-five, they were hopeless. She seemed nonplussed, however, and as the years passed and she continued to wander deeper into the woods to learn the secrets of plants and flowers, the young maidens who had followed her into the fields to gather the white-tipped lilies fattened and slowed under the weight of children and demanding husbands, their skin wrinkling in the sun after years of olive harvests, their hands thickening from splitting the tough skin of chestnuts. They began to send their children to follow her into the fields, and also to consult her about matters: Which plant will make my ears stop hurting? Which one will make my little boy's fever disappear? Which will make my husband more virile? for by then it was clear to everyone, including Ettora, that she was destined to become the village witch.

No one ridiculed her for becoming a witch. No one thought badly of her. It was, they decided collectively, a good fate for everyone. There were, after all, good witches and bad witches, and Ettora was a good one, a healer, though it was quickly understood that to rile her or bring about her wrath was to invite trouble indeed. A young man named Umberto, knowing that Ettora lived alone, had made the terrible mistake of stealing some of her gardening tools and a short time later was so badly stricken with shingles that he could not rise from his bed for two months. He'd returned the items with the deepest apologies, offering some of his own tools as a token of goodwill, but Ettora had declined them with a tight smile, saying, You can keep them now because you have paid for them and will pay for them in full three times over. The effect of this smile – and the further bad fortune that had befallen the young thief, whose face was later disfigured in a hunting accident – had a chilling effect on everyone in the village, and it only made Ettora's power seem greater.

Ludovico had watched Ettora evolve with no small amount of regret as the years passed, because while the other women had fattened and slowed under the weight of children and demanding husbands, her beauty remained intact. He did not believe in Ettora's power. He had known her when they were young. He had touched her in all the secret places. He had felt her wet down there, moaning with pleasure, so passionate that she had kissed his eyelids with those thin, beautiful lips. Her beautiful black eyes had pierced him, drowned him in the truest of affections, promising him with their needle-like intensity that she would marry him if only he would ask. And although it had been forty years since that time and he sometimes regretted not taking her hand in marriage, Ludovico had lived with the smug knowledge that he had known her intimates and thus she had no power over him. But now he knew he was wrong. She had not forgotten any of those things he had done to her, touching her in her secret places and making her empty promises. She had cursed him. He was sure of it. That could be the only explanation for why his rabbits had mysteriously multiplied.

He could not account for it in any other way. He'd had twenty-four rabbits before the war began, but when the Germans came, they marched into Bornacchi and quickly demanded them. He had explained that he was a Fascist and that Mussolini would not approve, but the Germans didn't listen. They kicked their way into his rabbit pen, blasting away with their rifles, and in ten minutes the twenty-four rabbits that he'd taken six years to breed were gone. He'd walked through the rabbit pen weeks after the soldiers left, kicking at the shattered wood in disgust, when lo and behold, a lone rabbit popped out. Ludovico had never seen her before. She was spotted white and brown, with eyes the color of birch wood. He named her Isabella and stowed her in the cool earth underneath the floorboards of his bedroom. He grew to love her. She was a smart rabbit, more like a dog actually, and he told no one about her, not even his daughter, Renata, because as the weeks passed the war escalated and food, already scarce before the fighting, began to dwindle. The Germans marched in and out of the village with impunity and stole Aldo Penna's last pig. They took Adriano Franchi's mules, raided his wife's garden, then raped his daughter. Donini Folliati was nearly beaten to death when he protested against a soldier who'd taken chestnut bread from his house. Food was at a premium. Life was cheap. There was no law. The *carabinieri*, the military police, came from nearby Barga when they felt like it and disappeared when the shelling started. So Ludovico kept quiet and crossed himself each morning, thanking the Virgin Mary for blessing him with his single, solitary rabbit that would one day be his meal – if the rabbit was lucky enough to live that long before disease wiped her out or someone stole her.

Several weeks passed, the war continued to escalate, and Isabella the rabbit was still living in a hole beneath Ludovico's bedroom floor without sun and eating hay, which was, mercifully, still plentiful. Her eyes bulged, her fur had fallen out, but otherwise she was fine.

And then one day Ludovico kicked the boards aside in his bedroom floor and found two rabbits.

It was a miracle, he was sure, and normally he would have summoned Ettora so that she could explain it to him, because she knew about these things. But a rabbit was like gold. Its fur alone could be traded for two canaries, a pound of chestnuts, some olive oil, or perhaps even a cup of salt, which was worth more than money. So he kept quiet, thanking God for his little miracle.

When he peeked beneath the boards of his bedroom floor a month later and found four rabbits, he began to pray each day. When the number of rabbits reached six, he began to go to mass every morning. At eleven, he officially rejoined the Church after having wandered away twenty-two years before. At twelve, he became the church sexton. Three times a day, every day, while tending his parched olive fields, he laid down his tools and trudged up the long hill with his broom to sweep the barren aisles of Sant'Anna's church, light prayer candles, and pray to God on his knees. His brother thought he was nuts, his daughter, Renata, thought he was senile. But Ludovico had witnessed his very own miracle. God had given him back everything the Germans had taken.

When he found thirteen rabbits, Ludovico began to worry. His situation was getting dangerous. Starvation was becoming a problem. He had too much. The Germans had camped up at Mt Cavallo, and they came through periodically, hungry and desperate. He began hearing story after story of atrocities and crimes. The partisan movement was growing fiercer. The Germans were striking back with ferocious determination. He blacked them out of his mind. If the Germans found out about his rabbits, he was cooked. He began to pray to God to stop the rabbits, but a fourteenth, then a fifteenth appeared, so in desperation, he had summoned Ettora to his house, ostensibly because of an earache. He was sure she'd cursed him, and he wanted to feel her out, perhaps even confess that he was sorry for what had happened between them years ago. He had held his tongue as she heated olive oil and tossed it down his ear. When she was done and was preparing to leave, she said, 'You have something to tell me?'

'Not a thing,' he answered.

She shrugged and smiled. 'I am working on a spell that will keep the Germans out forever,' she said.

'Work in a bit of bread for me, too, while you're at it,' Ludovico said. Bread was like owls, heard about but never seen.

Ettora smiled. 'Why are you so pessimistic?'

She was looking at him with her piercing eyes. Even after forty years, she knew him. She was looking clear through him. It made Ludovico mad. He decided not to tell her anything. He shrugged.

Ettora gazed at him for a long moment and her smile faded. 'Enrico's son hasn't had milk in four weeks,' she said. 'His family has nothing to eat. Nor do the Salvos, or the Romitis. Everyone in this village has to share more.'

'I share what I have.'

Ettora's stare tightened and her smile vanished completely now. She was sitting at his kitchen table, not ten feet from where his rabbits were buried in his bedroom. She was going blind, everyone knew it, but Ludovico's heart skipped several beats when she took a long look at his bedroom floor. Then she shrugged and got up to leave. 'A sign is going to come to you,' she said. 'I can feel it.'

'I don't need a sign. I need the war to end.'

'That will happen, too,' she said.

He couldn't stand it when she got so cool. He remembered when she was just a young helpless thing, moaning in the grass, his hand over her privates. Now she was an old fox. Well, so am I, he thought bitterly. He watched as she gathered up her things.

Ettora was almost out the door when she stopped and took a long look around. She said, 'And there will be more rabbits.'

'Everyone knows I don't have any rabbits left,' Ludovico said quickly. He was standing ten feet away from at least seventeen. That was how many he'd managed to count that morning. There were two brand-new ones.

Ettora had turned and closed the door of the house behind her, saying nothing, and now Ludovico was caught in a lie. What's more, his rabbits had continued to multiply. He had twenty-five at last count, and was running out of space to hide them and hay to feed them. The hole beneath his bedroom floor had grown to the size of a small cavern, held up by boards. It looked like the entrance to the Mt Aracia mine. It stretched almost to the living room, and the hollow space made his floor sound like the bells of Bologna when shoes struck it. The whole house smelled. To make matters worse, he began to catch everything he fished or hunted. Trout, eels, deer, even wild boar. And his garden was growing. While everyone else's trees and vegetable gardens, destroyed by bombs and looted by the Germans, had remained barren, his olive trees bore harvest. His chestnut trees grew like wildflowers. His vegetables sprouted like weeds. It was horrible for him. In a village compelled by war to divide its resources or starve, Ludovico was forced to share and share alike. The entire village would wait for him to hunt, and when he returned after a day of hiking through the dark woods, miraculously avoiding mines and Germans and wolves and bandits, there would be ten people waiting at his door. He ended up feeding nearly the entire village almost every week. He was exhausted from hunting. His feet hurt. And now, just last week, the final straw had fallen. His electricity had mysteriously returned. Before the war, he'd been the only one in town who had it. It had disappeared after the war began, and now it was back inexplicably, for every bandit and German to see. Someone would surely tell, and the Germans would come to ask questions and search his house, and what would they find? Twenty-five big, fat, tasty rabbits that he was supposed to turn over to them for the war effort. The Germans had grown desperate now, some were starving. The partisans were hurting them badly, and the Germans' response was ruthless and terrifying. He was a marked man. He couldn't stand it anymore. It was all her fault.

He sat in his living room bursting with frustration, with Ettora at the table carefully moving the plate of water and olive oil from side to side. She was ignoring him. She knew about the rabbits. And she knew he knew she knew. All because he'd stuck his finger in her hole many years before. The war was letting every fool with a grudge exact his revenge, Ludovico thought furiously. Well, not here!

Ettora's gaze followed the plate as the drop of olive oil went left, then right. Finally, it broke apart into several smaller drops, and the room moaned. Ettora stood up.

'This outcome,' she said to Renata, who looked aghast, 'means only that you are still apart. It does not mean you will not come back together. Don't be afraid. It's a sign.'

'What kind of sign?' Renata asked.

'A sign that something good is coming.'

'Like what?'

'A good sign is coming,' Ettora repeated.

The rain outside banged heavily against the roof, jangling Ludovico's frayed nerves. He wished it would stop so they would all leave. He couldn't take it anymore. The old witch was trying to kill him. He could feel the anger surge up in his throat, trying to roar out of him. The hell with her signs! He would end the spell now. He would confront her this very moment, and tell her – tell them all – about the rabbits, and to hell with it, let them tear up the bedroom floor and eat the rabbits, every single one of them. The devil was going to show up next if he didn't do something immediately.

Ludovico raised his hand to get the attention of the room, one gnarled finger pointed skyward, and just as he was about to speak, he heard the bump of heavy boots hitting the front steps, followed by a loud knock at the front door.

Silence.

The Germans at the top of Mt. Cavallo couldn't have gotten down the mountain that fast, he thought in alarm. Not without anyone noticing. There were lookouts everywhere. Besides, one of the sisters at the convent had tolled the church bell three times ten minutes ago, signaling that all was clear. The villagers, packed inside the room, stared at each other in alarm.

Then came the sound of another pair of boots hitting the wooden steps, followed by another heavy knock.

The villagers scurried about the room, putting away the plates and olive oil and chestnuts. Ludovico, seated next to the door, waited a moment until all was hidden, then stood and opened the door and realized he had waited too long.

The devil himself had arrived.

Standing in the black, pouring rain was a giant black man holding the white statue head of what appeared to be the Virgin Mary under his one arm. In his other arm was a bundle wrapped in a jacket. The black man was dressed as a soldier, heavily armed, with a long rifle strapped to his back and bullet-filled bandoleers crisscrossing his mighty chest. His nose, widened in exhaustion, breathed air in and out like a pig's snout. Standing directly beneath the giant, Ludovico could feel the hot air whooshing out of his nostrils.

'*Mother of Jesus,*' the old man said, backing away and crossing himself.

The giant stepped inside, followed by three more heavily armed dark men. All four were huge, even the smallest of them was bigger than every Italian in the room, and dripping wet. Stamps was the last to enter. He quickly looked around the room at the gawking Italians, then barked at Bishop, 'Keep watch outside while we find out the deal here.'

Bishop said, 'Man, I ain't staying out there by myself.'

Stamps ignored him and looked at the room of staring Italians again. He closed the door behind him and spoke to Hector. 'Tell them we're Americans.'

'*Americanos,*' Hector said.

The room looked to Renata. She'd studied English in Florence and spoke it better than anyone else in town. Renata sat gaping at the giant Negro with the odd statue's head beneath his arm. He was so tall he'd had to crouch down when he entered the house, and he stayed crouched, his gigantic head swiveling slowly back and forth, moving like the head of a dinosaur as he gazed around. She could not stop herself from staring. She could not shut her mouth. She could not remember a word of English.

Stamps saw the room looking at Renata and settled his eyes on her. Sitting at the table dressed in men's clothes, her small hands open, palm up on the table, her long black hair tucked underneath her cap giving her the look of a souped-up car, her mouth wide open in shock, she was the most beautiful thing he had ever seen in his life. Her huge black eyes looked like globes between olive-shaped, slitted lids as her stunned gaze zipped from one of them to the other. Stamps had never seen anything like that, a woman dressed like a man, and so beautiful underneath it. He noted with appreciation the hips and thighs that lay casually against the cloth of the baggy pants she wore, and he tried not to stare. He was exhausted and thought perhaps he was dreaming.

He spoke to Hector. 'Ask her where the Germans are.'

Hector complied.

Renata blinked and caught her breath. She stared at Train, whose weight made the floor under his feet sag. She was worried that the giant Negro would step into the bedroom and fall through the floor into her father's rabbits, which everybody knew about. The floor groaned under Train's giant feet. Finally, Renata spoke to Hector. 'Are you staying long?'

The three Americans looked for translation to Hector, who paused. Hector was fluent in Italian. In addition to speaking the classic Italian of the Army's translations school, he'd spent plenty of time with Italians back in Spanish Harlem, where his family had moved from San Juan. From the age of ten until he joined the army, he'd spent half his weekends getting the shit kicked out of him by Italian kids and the other half beating their brains out, but he'd never seen any as pretty as this one who sat at the table dressed in men's clothing. Instead of translating, he said, 'No. We just dropped by 'cause his tailor lives nearby.' He nodded at Bishop. Several Italians in the room, including Ettora, two twin cockeyed teenage girls named Ultima and Ultimissima, and a rail-thin woman named Fat Margherita laughed.

Stamps snapped, 'What's so goddamn funny, Hector? Ask the woman where's the Germans.' He looked at Renata. 'Where's the Germans? *Dove tedeschi?*' He said it loud, as if talking louder would make her understand. The room silenced in fear.

Renata sized him up. Long, thin, angular, he was taller than the two who stood behind him, and she guessed he must be the lieutenant, *il tenente*. Hector, with his pointed nose, smooth hair, cleft chin, and smaller stature seemed more Latin. The other dark Negro behind him, with gold teeth, dimples, and sparkling eyes, reaching for his cigarettes, had a coolness, a slickness about him that was exciting, but she instinctively didn't trust him. He reminded her of the jazz music she had once heard in Florence – it was gorgeous, but it could lead to too many bad places. No, the one who knocked her down was the lean *tenente* still glaring at her, all business. He was, she decided, very beautiful. Long arms, wide shoulders, deep hazel-brown eyes, skin the color of chestnuts, his face illuminated by the glow of the warm fire. Even frowning, she thought, he was the most exotic thing she'd ever seen. She suddenly wished she was wearing a dress. She pointed at the window. 'Everywhere,' she said.

Stamps nodded toward Train. 'The boy needs help.'

'What boy?' she said.

He motioned and Train undid his field jacket, revealing the shivering child underneath. He was pale and drenched, breath wheezing out of him, his eyes fluttering, rolling back and forth up into his skull.

The sight of him prompted a flurry of motion from Ettora, Fat

Margherita, and the cockeyed twins, who gathered in close, standing on tiptoe. One of the twins tried to take the boy from Train's arms.

Train drew back. 'Naw,' he said. The women surrounding him began to chatter at Renata in high-speed Italian.

'Where did you find him?' Renata asked Hector. She was having a hard time making her brain function.

'Down the mountain a ways. Who is he?'

'I don't know. He can stay here till he gets better.'

Hector translated for Stamps, who waited impatiently. Stamps shook his head.

'He ain't gonna get no better. He needs to get to a hospital. We're taking him. You all can come. You gotta evacuate the area anyway 'cause of the Germans. Fightin's gonna get hot 'round here once the division arrives. We'll escort you down the mountains.'

This translation sparked another wave of chatter. Finally, Hector said, 'She says she's not leaving, and neither are they. If you want to know more, talk to il parroco at the church up the hill.'

'We just been there,' Stamps said. 'Nothing there but a wacko.'

Hector translated. The villagers looked at each other for a moment. Renata fired off a burst of Italian.

'She says there's no man up there. That's the Sant'Anna church and the convent behind it. Just four nuns live there. She says there hasn't been a man inside that convent for three hundred years.'

'Well he musta snuck in there and filled up on three hundred years' worth of nooky then, 'cause who was that we seen up there, Butterbeans and Suzy?' Stamps said.

The four men laughed. Ettora the witch turned and approached Stamps. Being almost blind, she nearly fell over a chair, so she pivoted, wheeled, and headed straight again, nearly falling on him. She was so tiny that her head only reached his ribs. She pointed a finger at his ribs, her bracelets shaking as she spoke in broken English. 'That's Eugenio. Crazy man. No see Father?'

From across the room, Ludovico watched silently, his heart pounding. He had to hand it to Ettora. She was brave. He wouldn't touch that big man with a flagpole.

Stamps said, 'Don't know nuthing about no father, *signora*. Now I can make y'all go, but I ain't gonna. The boy needs a hospital, though.'

Ettora poked him in the ribs again with a finger that felt like a sharp stick. 'Boy is here.'

'What's up? This kid might die.'

Renata stepped forward and said, 'Where you take him?'

'Hospital.'

The young woman shook her head and spoke for a few moments in Italian, pointing out the window, and Hector's face clouded. 'She says there's Germans on all sides of us as far as she knows: Vergemoli, Callomini, Mt. Caula, all the way up to Barga and down to the Cinquale. She don't know how we got past Ruosina, but she says the only way to Barga, where the Americans might be, is through that mountain pass.' He pointed out the window to Mt. Cavallo, the Mountain of the Sleeping Man.

The four looked out the window at the dark, pouring rain. Stamps imagined the mountain was like Mt. Everest.

'All right. Then we stay here till the weather breaks. Then we move out.'

Bishop's face furrowed into a grimace. 'Move out where? You heard what she said.'

'Bishop, you think too much.'

'Okay, when they come for you, I'll write your folks. I ain't gettin on any goddamn mountain and getting killed. We should stay here till help comes.'

'How do we know help's coming?' Stamps snapped. 'Nokes probably told 'em we're dead. I'm not gonna sit here pootin' chalk and waiting for the Germans to roll up and do the boogie-jump on me. Maybe these people are with them. Maybe the Germans were following us. They might be watching us right now, for all we know. The canal wasn't no fuckin' surprise to them, that's for sure.'

Hector spoke out. 'This ain't the Cinquale Canal, Lieutenant. Shit, this is a new world up here.'

Stamps hated this but knew Hector was right. He fought his own panic. Division would look for them, or maybe not. Till they heard otherwise, they were on their own.

'All right, then. We lay low till tomorrow and try to charge up the radio. The batteries are dead. Ask if they got electricity. Maybe we can charge it up someway.'

Hector complied, and Renata chirped out a response. Stamps watched as Ludovico glared at his daughter, then rose sleepily from his chair, yawned, and grinned, showing one shining front tooth in an otherwise toothless mouth.

'She says her old man here knows how to get some.'

Bishop stared at Ludovico, his tattered vest, his shock of white hair, his toothless grin, his one gleaming front tooth.

'Wow,' he said to the others. 'This one here could get a job snapping holes in doughnuts.' He smiled at Ludovico. 'With chompers like that, ain't no hambone in the world 'fraid of you, is it, old-timer?'

The soldiers laughed. Ludovico, not understanding, grinned harder and nodded back, trying to show he was friendly. He had never seen Americans before. Whether they were really Americans or devils, he wasn't sure. Either way, he knew he was in deep trouble if that big one took two steps back into his bedroom and fell through the floor.

'Cut out the foolin',' Stamps barked. 'We gotta think of a plan to call back to division and get the fuck outta here.' He turned to Hector. 'Ask the *signorina* where we can stay. Then tomorrow the old-timer will show us how to use the electric.'

'No stay here,' Renata said.

'*Sì*, stay here!' Stamps hissed. '*Americano. Bosso.* American government pay for your whole house.'

Hector translated, and the women in the room snickered. Stupid American, Renata thought bitterly, staring at Stamps. He didn't understand Italians at all. Mr Big Shot. Ten minutes ago she would have flung him down and made love to him right on the floor, she was so happy to see him. Now she couldn't stand him. If the Germans caught any of them helping the Americans, they all would be punished and his cute chestnut skin wouldn't mean a thing. Instead of speaking English to Stamps, she spoke to Hector, who translated.

'She wants to know are there more of us.'

Bishop piped up, 'Hell yeah, honey. I know fourteen niggers in St. Louis alone, and two of 'em's waiting to be adopted.'

Stamps said, 'Bishop, if you don't stop banging your gums I'm gonna kick your ass right here.'

Bishop stared at him dully. Stamps, he thought, was a yellow Washington, D.C., high-breed, an educated nigger know-it-all, and now he was taking advantage of the situation to show he was boss in front of all the Italian whiteys. He made note of this for future reference and said nothing.

Stamps spoke to Hector. 'Tell her we need to sleep someplace.'

Hector translated, and Renata snapped a response at him. Hector replied, 'She says there's a house not far; just outside, beyond the wall to the right, around the corner. It has a big cross on the front door. The old man will take us there. That's Eugenio's house, the crazy man we seen up at the church.'

The four Americans looked at Renata, who shrugged and said, 'He doesn't sleep inside. He sleeps outside Sant'Anna church with his family.'

'I thought you said there was nobody there,' Hector said.

'His family is buried there. Three *bambini*. His wife. *Tedeschi. Boom-boom*.'

Renata stepped gingerly toward Train, stood on her tiptoes, and gently reached toward the boy, who still lay in his arms, limp and trembling, but the giant drew back. 'It's all right, miss, I got 'im.'

Stamps watched Renata staring at Train, her cap tipped just so, her face barely reaching his massive chest. The head of the *Primavera* was stuck under Train's arm, his shoulders were so huge that the M-1 rifle slung across his back looked like a toothpick, the boy was so tiny in his arms he looked like a balled-up chihuahua. It made quite an impression.

'Tell her it's all right, Hector,' Train stammered.

Hector's translation landed on the woman with no discernible effect. She said, 'Tell your *tenente* the boy belongs here.'

Stamps already understood. 'Cool down, *signorina*. We ain't going noplace. Train, give her the kid. They can take better care of 'im than you.'

Train, his tall frame bent inside the tiny crowded house with all the white people staring at him, felt cramped and confused. He swayed like a colossal tower, leaning over, trying to make sense of it all. This wasn't what he'd had in mind. Suppose these people were with the Germans, like the Italian mule skinners he had seen at the Cinquale? This boy had brought him luck. This boy had the power. Train had to pay him back some way. It all needed clearing up. 'I done found 'im, Lieutenant. I can takes care of him for now. Hector gave me some powder to give him.' Train pulled a packet of sulfa powder out of his breast pocket and waved it in the air.

Stamps stepped over, yanked the droopy child from Train, and handed him to Renata. He gave her the sulfa packet, too. He stared at her directly. 'This is the last of it. It'll break his fever. You gotta dilute it to make it last longer, 'cause we got no more. Hector, translate that for me.'

Hector said, 'What's "dilute" mean?'

'Forget it. Just tell 'em we'll be back for 'im.'

Train watched helplessly as the women placed the boy on Ludovico's bed in the adjacent room and began to warm water and bustle about, busily preparing. The boy awakened from his stupor and began struggling and crying softly. The women held him down against the bed. 'Maybe I oughtta stay here,' Train said glumly. He took two steps toward the bedroom. Ludovico watched in alarm as the floor creaked and groaned beneath his feet.

Stamps shot a contemptuous look at Train, stepped to the front door, and flung it open. The sound of splattering raindrops filled the room. 'Suit yourself. But tomorrow, when this weather clears, we're gonna get the fuck outta here and go back, Sam Train or no Sam Train.'

Stamps nodded at Ludovico, who followed him toward the door. The old man glanced back at Ettora as he headed out, looking for a sign on her face that would tell him something, but Ettora said nothing.

If this was the sign she was talking about, Ludovico thought glumly as he exited, followed by Stamps and the two others, it was not a good sign at all.

9

THE BLACK BUTTERFLY

In the hills of Tuscany today, you cannot find an Italian who likes to talk about World War II. The old men, the carpenters, plumbers, plasterers, and stonemasons who make their living repairing the homes of the rich foreigners who lounge in the lazy piazzas of the towns of Barga, Teglio, and Gallicano shrug when you ask them of the war. 'Too many bad things,' they say, or, 'Mussolini started the pension system,' and walk away. You can ask them all day if you want, fill them with wine, serve them pasta in olive oil draped with their mother's best sauce, and still they will not tell you. You can wait till the evening, when it is cooler and the sun has set and the children are home and the piazza is empty, and still they will not tell you. You can give them boxes of chocolate wrapped in the finest *che bella figura* style, bring them a proclamation from the mayor, feed them rare scallops from the Tyrrhenian Sea which they love, even promise college educations for their grandchildren in America, and still they will not tell you. For that war was a war of the heart, and the heart of an Italian man is strong, deep, and closed up tight, open to only a very few.

Only at night, when the grappa flows, when the women are asleep, while the rich Dutch tourists are safely tucked away in their charming Italian villas with CNN piped in and the lights are out all over town, can you learn about the war. And then it is not a discussion but rather a physical discovery, for you must stand in the middle of a village and look beyond the stone walls at the hills surrounding it. Look for a light twinkling in the distance and walk toward it. You will come to a path. The path will lead to a tiny road. The road will lead up the mountain to a tiny tavern. And if you haven't fallen on the dark trail and broken your arm or been attacked by spooks or witches or goblins, you will enter a smelly, smoky tavern to find the same old men gathered around tables telling jokes, singing songs, playing cards, and sipping grappa; and if you are lucky, two of them sitting at a card table will have a disagreement, which will degenerate into an argument, then shouting, then threatened fisticuffs. And then, just as the two old codgers stand up with balled fists to tear each other apart, someone will yell over the din of the smoke-filled room, '*How do you make a phone call in Italy during the war?*' and the two old coots will laugh and sit down and drink again, because during the war, phones and shoes were the same. Shoes were made from leftover phone wire discarded by American soldiers. You sized the thick wire around your foot to make sure it would fit, then threaded it through a piece of rubber cut from an American airplane landing tarp – the landing strip – to create a sole. You placed a rag atop the whole business, stitched it together, and, presto, a pair of shoes. Then, if the Germans came and you needed help, you quickly sat in a chair, stretched your leg across your lap, grabbed your ankle, pulled your foot as close to your mouth as possible, and yelled, 'Hello? Hello?' Because there was no one to call in Italy during the war. There were no phones, no shoes, no electricity, no food, no army, no government to speak of, no hope. Your life hung by a shoestring, dependent on the two raw goods of mankind: morality and courage, never a sure thing; food from a kind neighbor who might be a Fascist, or maybe not; a brave priest risked his life to feed you and your mother; or the partisans, whom no one dared mention, came to your aid. Phone calls? You called God because Mussolini with his fine speeches, his shiny boots, his impeccable uniform, his beautiful mistress, had been captured by the partisans and was last seen strung from a telephone pole at a gas station in Milan, his brains blown to bits, his mistress Claretta Petacci, for whom he had once built a whole train station and whose face had peeled off like onion skin when they'd shot her, strung upside down at his side. No, there were no phone calls to be made during the war. Italy was like America's wild, wild West, except it was not romantic, it was not funny, it was not even tough. Living there was like watching your mother stand in the middle of the road and get hit by a two-ton truck, watching her body fly through the air like a rag doll's, wanting with all your heart to race to the spot where she will land to catch her, knowing you cannot, so you stand there, frozen, knowing that the sound of her dead body striking the road will reverberate in your ears for the rest of your life. That's what it was like: Watching her die, every single day, over and over again.

For that reason, the old-timers in Tuscany don't discuss World War II. The teachers don't like to teach it in the schools, either. History lessons become embarrassing right after World War I, because after that it becomes personal: My father was a partisan; yours was not. What did you do? What did your father do? It's easy to claim victory now.

Everyone wants to be a winner, everyone claims to be with the partisans who fought with the Allies. But during the war, among forty-four million people and two nations, not everyone was a partisan; it was impossible for every single man, woman, and child to summon the raw courage to wander into the dark mountains, starve in the cold, sleep in holes in the earth, and take on the mighty German army with toothpicks. No. It was every man for himself, because Mother Italy was raped and cut in half: the puppet Republic of Salò lay to the north, the real Italy lay to the south, and in between the two, there you sat as the rag-tag assortment of the world's armies played footsie in the mountains, with the entrenched Germans delivering roundhouse rights and uppercuts that sent them collectively to the canvas, the Brazilians, the American Negroes, the South Africans, the New Zealanders, the British, the Gurkhas, the partisans, the Alpini, the remnants of the Italian army, all were frantically fighting to push the Germans back, stomping over you and your family and your friends, crushing and killing everything you loved and would ever love under their collective boots while the tankless Germans, who were running out of ammo and food, fought them with flamethrowers, eighty-eights, potato mashers, rusty barbed wire, and cannons manned by gray-haired Austrians and starving German boys. It was all foolishness. Better to keep quiet.

But if you stand around the old tavern long enough and pour grappa long enough; if you catch the old men in the middle of a *veglia*, a kind of story time when they sing songs and tell tales about the old days to one another; when they are weak with love, their hearts no longer closed up tight as a drum but filled with the joy of friendship, flush with the happiness of camaraderie – then, only then, will you hear the story of the war. But it is not the story you expect to hear, for the old men do not speak of war. Instead they speak of Mussolini.

He was not so bad, they say. His speeches were funny. He made you laugh. He swam ten kilometers a day. He danced like the wind. He started the pension system. Before that, old people worked fifty years for a landowner, then starved in retirement. Under Il Duce, no one starved. The trains ran on time. He built roads and bridges and libraries. He had sex with his mistresses right in his office, standing up, no small feat, but truly Italian, you know? The cities were clean. If an old woman tripped over a pipe in the road and wrote him a letter, he would always respond. He alone stood up to Hitler in 1934, sending Italian troops to the Brenner Pass when Hitler threatened Austria, while France and England fretted in uncertainty and America stuck her head in the sand. And only later, when Hitler got too strong, did the Old Man get into bed with him, and by then he knew Hitler was a madman but it was too late, for he had descended into madness himself, not for any physical reason, but because he had betrayed Mother Italy and her gallant sons, including his socialist opponent Giacomo Matteotti, whom he'd never confessed to having murdered, but whose blood was all over his black shirt and shiny boots just the same. And so the Old Man suffered and was executed, and that was fine. He deserved it. But there were others who didn't deserve to die and were executed for nothing, and still others who deserved to be executed and were not. And some . . . some who were just plain . . . And then the old men fall silent and don't touch the grappa anymore, and their eyes lose their sparkle and turn dull as they remember the scarred landscape, the desperation, their starving parents, the women selling their bodies for a piece of bread, the cruel, raping bandits posing as partisans, the red-shirt communists, and the one peasant boy from the

Serchio Valley who took the mighty Apuane Alps in his tiny hands and lifted them toward the sky, shaking evil from every crevice.

I saw him, they say. I saw him with my own eyes. He was a teenager. I was a boy myself. He came to my village on the night the sun set twice. That was the night the Germans lost the war here in Tuscany. The night he came.

The night who came?

Peppi. The Black Butterfly.

Who is he? you ask.

He was the greatest of all partisans, they will say, the kindest, the most courageous, a philosopher, a poet, a man made of truth. If he loved you, there was nothing he would not do for you. But if he did not, God help you, for there was no gun big enough, no army large enough, no force great enough to stop him.

And then the toughest old galoot in the room, the one with the two teeth, whose glass is always full and whose table is always empty, will shudder and say, My father loved Italy because of him. Because he was afraid of him. We all were afraid of him. We were afraid of his love. It was his greatest weapon. It was the greatest force you can imagine.

Why? you ask.

Because he could kill you with it.

And then you know you have gone too far, for the old coot turns away and the rest of the room returns to its business, and the innkeeper takes you by the arm and escorts you to the door. You want to know about the war? he asks. Go back to town. Tomorrow morning, stand in the piazza and ask about the night of two setting suns. Ask anyone. They will tell you all you need to know.

But why? Why will they tell me?

Because, the old codger says, as he shoves you out the door into the cold night, they know what we know. They feel what we feel. They will not be able to resist.

There is no mention of the night of the two setting suns in the histories of the Serchio Valley, nor are there any references to butterflies. The two are intertwined, and like so many things in Italy, unexplainable, unbearable in their truth, and at times unbearable in their paucity. The proud, polite guidebooks of the area cannot touch the subject. They gloss over the war and its sloppiness with the slickness of a used-car salesman. There are no structures erected in honor of the Black Butterfly anywhere in Tuscany, no national proclamation bearing his name, no scientific studies on the setting sun, no statues or murals bearing the likeness of butterflies, caterpillars, setting suns or even setting moons. In a region known for its art, its history, its glorious beacons from the past, children in school are not taught of either element, unless taught by their parents, and the elderly rarely speak of it. But if you mention the night of the two setting suns and the Black Butterfly, you will get a response. Everyone seems to know of it – and of him.

Very little seems to be known about the Butterfly's origins, for he was born in a corner of Tuscany from which few of distinction have emerged. His true name was Peppi Grotta, and he was a humble, quiet, frail poetry student from nearby Castelnuovo di Stazzema, a town of no great distinction, save for a black butterfly known to frequent its olive groves and pastures. When the war began, the young poet joined up with one of the many innocuous bands of partisans that roamed the Serchio Valley and the Apuane Alps of Garfagnana and Massa. Like most partisans, he gave himself a nickname, because the SS were ruthless in their retaliation against families. He named himself for the butterfly from his region, and distinguished himself among the partisan groups that would later form Group Valenga, a small but tough band that emerged out of the Barga region. Initially a group of twenty peasant boys, they stole arms from the *carabinieri*, derailed trains, and caused rockslides that stalled German troop movements. They were largely ineffective until the death of Gabriella Tornatti of the tiny town of Bertacchi, near Mt. Forato, a woman whose name is often mentioned in the context of the Black Butterfly, for it was after her death that the great Black Butterfly spread his wings for the very first time.

Gabriella, a lean, pretty war widow with long, curly black hair, joined a man's war in 1943 while pregnant and raising two young daughters. She hid partisans in her home, blew up bridges, shot at SS soldiers, and even launched an illegal press from her home. She was revealed to the Germans by an unknown Italian spy in her town and was arrested by a German SS commander who hog-tied her to a tree in the center of her village's piazza and demanded the names of her fellow partisans. She refused to tell. The commander tortured her to death. Her breasts were pulled off with a strange tool. Her eyes were pulled out with dental pliers. Yet despite this torture, young Gabriella Tornatti of Bertacchi never revealed the identity of her fellow partisans. She was hanged by the neck and left in the piazza.

The news of Gabriella's heroic death spread through the Apuane Alps and Tuscan valleys like lightning. It was then that the great Black Butterfly struck.

For several weeks, the Black Butterfly spread rumors in the valley around Bertacchi that on a certain date, at a certain time, he would show up with an entire army to revenge Gabriella's death. As expected, an Italian spy alerted the German authorities and the SS arrived in force on the appointed date, surrounding the village. But the Black Butterfly did not appear. He watched, hidden in the mountain forest, with his binoculars, and marked the SS commander who perpetrated the torture on poor Gabriella. The Germans departed after a few days, thinking the threat was empty. But Peppi had other plans. He secretly followed the officer's squad, which moved on to terrorize other villages in the Tuscan valleys. He waited and waited, waited a full six weeks, until the officer was relieved and rotated out. He and a small group of his men followed the officer to Viareggio, where, posing as mule skinners, they caught him along with a squad of eight German troopers who were also heading out for a relief rotation. The eight German soldiers, Peppi freed. The SS commander, though, he did not.

Patiently, and to the nth degree, the Black Butterfly exacted the same torture upon the SS commander that the commander had exacted on Gabriella of Bertacchi. He hog-tied him to a tree. He taped his mouth. He pulled off his breasts with a strange tool. He waited a day, then pulled out his eyes with dental pliers. He let him bleed. When he was done, he pulled off the commander's testicles and stuck them in his mouth, then carried the SS commander's body seventy-eight kilometers back to the same square where Gabriella of Bertacchi had been savagely killed, and waited.

Once a year, the sun sets twice a day in the Serchio Valley of Tuscany. It hits the eye of the Mountain of the Sleeping Man, and disappears behind the top oval of the encirclement of rock. It hides there for a few minutes and reappears again right through the center of the eye before disappearing down the mountain again. It was during this moment that the Black Butterfly sent a message to the people of Tuscany that would never be forgotten.

The German commanders who were running Bertacchi did not know the sun set twice, so when darkness came, they were safely settled in their headquarters near the village gates. The villagers, however, as was their custom, stood outdoors in the town square to watch the yearly phenomenon.

The sun disappeared, and darkness came. When the sun appeared again, minutes later, there, in the center of the village, was a ghastly sight. Hanged from the same tree as Gabriella was the SS commander, his decomposed body wracked and sliced, his breasts pulled off, his eyes gouged out, his testicles shoved in his mouth. A sign strung across his neck read: 'Viva Italia. Love, the Black Butterfly.' Then the sun disappeared again, and night came for good.

The sight of the German commander had the opposite effect on the villagers than what one would expect, for they had no doubt that reprisals would be swift and merciless. The SS promised to kill sixteen civilians for every SS trooper killed, and this corpse they were staring at was no trooper's. This was an officer. Many turned and fled into the woods and forests and never came back. But the few who stayed were witness to a remarkable turn of events, for the village spy who had turned in Gabriella saw the corpse of the SS man and panicked, revealing himself. He sprinted to the nearby German headquarters to tell the commander in exact detail what he had seen, but when he returned with a large squad of shaken Germans who shined their flashlights and lamps on the spot, the SS commander's body was gone. The piazza was clear. Swept clean. It was as if nothing had never happened.

The Germans knocked on doors and demanded of the villagers, 'Who has done this?' but to a man and woman, the villagers denied it, for even knowledge of a rebellious act could bring terrible reprisals against their sons and daughters. It was the cleverest of clever moves, for, as the villagers later explained, there was no body in the piazza and therefore no one would be punished, and, secretly, Gabriella's death had been revenged. No, we saw no body, they told the Germans. Nothing happened here. This piazza is as it always has been, as it was before night fell. There is a curfew, is there not? We saw nothing.

The German commander ordered the spy to be jailed for lying. He was sent to prison in Castelnuovo di Garfagnana, where news of his dastardly betrayal of Gabriella had long preceded his arrival. He was jailed with several socialists, communists, bandits, and true partisans. By the time the Germans sorted out the truth about the missing SS commander and hastily sent word to free him, he was, as they say in Sicily, calling the fishes – long dead. He did not last six hours in prison.

Meanwhile, in the town of Bertacchi, the few villagers who remained awakened in the following weeks to find at their doorsteps bread, wine, baskets of chestnuts, even jars of olive oil, which was so scarce it was almost priceless. The caretaker of Gabriella's two toddler daughters found two small sacks of pure gold bullion in a basket underneath the children's bed and two gold necklaces with the word 'Love' etched into them. The two became rich women after the war – one became a provincial governor. The Black Butterfly, however, the young poet from Castelnuovo di Stazzema also known as Peppi, was never seen by anyone in Bertacchi during or after that event. He was a rumor, a wisp, a thought, his exploits bragged about by those who admired him, loathed by those who feared he had only prolonged the agony of losing to the Germans. As the war dragged on and his feats grew, the Germans placed a price on his head, though it was senseless. How can you catch a person who does not exist? Even the Italians were not sure. He was rumored to have joined the ranks of the Buffalo Soldiers from America, who were said to be marching up from the south and fighting like the sons of black Hannibal and were so taken with him that they carried him back with them to America, where he was rumored to own a nightclub in Harlem named after him, which was filled with black butterflies that flew along the walls and ceilings as the Negroes jitterbugged to jazz music.

Unfortunately, none of those rumors was true. Peppi the Black Butterfly never went to America. He never even left Tuscany. In fact, Peppi the Black Butterfly had never met a Negro before December 1944. But it was that meeting, a confrontation in the town of Bornacchi, at the foot of the Mountain of the Sleeping Man, that would forever cement his reputation as a man who never forgets his friends, who punishes his enemies dearly, and who kills you with his love.

10

PEPPI

From high atop his perch on Mt. Caula, overlooking the town of Bornacchi, not more than five hundred feet above the tiny house where the four Negroes had spent the night, a lone twelve-year-old Italian boy sat below a shelf of rock that covered him from the driving rain and watched the four soldiers emerge from the house into the daylight. It was dawn, and the rain would not stop. It fell in endless sheets, pattering and splashing, raking across the horizon and swelling the creek that ran in front of Ludovico's house, splashing heavily against the rocky shore.

The boy leaned forward to see more clearly as the Negroes sleepily approached the swollen creek, dipped their faces in it, stood up, took a wary glance at the ridges around them without seeing him, then knocked on the door of Ludovico's house. The boy whistled softly, and the trees and bushes behind him gave way to three moving figures that emerged from the thick forest's trees and rocks like shadows. The four partisans, Italian resistance fighters, the oldest no more than twenty-six, armed with carbine rifles and bandoleers, gathered at his shoulder and observed the four Americans in silence. They watched as Ludovico opened the door, glanced hurriedly at the ridges above the house, then let the four men in, closing the door swiftly behind them.

'Old Man Ludovico's got protection now,' one of the partisans quipped.

'He's got a lot to protect, all those rabbits,' another mused.

'That tall one, that's the biggest Negro I've ever seen. Maybe he's Louis Armstrong, eh, Peppi?'

A short, thin, prematurely balding man with a small forehead and piercing black eyes, stood apart from the three and watched in silence. He knelt down on the ridge and made a small circle in the mud, drawing with a stick, ignoring the fascinating phenomenon of the Negroes below. Peppi, the Black Butterfly, looked nothing like the force he was believed to be. He was frail compared with the others, with a lightness to his frame that seemed ill-suited to the ruggedness the mountains demanded. He had turned twenty-six that morning. He'd written a poem about it the previous night. The poem was about the silences that lived inside of him, the yawning valleys where he'd left himself when the war began, before the bottomless rage inside him had grown into the silent, furious butterfly. He'd wanted to read his poem to the others when he arose but saw no use. There was no time for that anymore. He'd been promoted to lieutenant now, still a member of the infamous Valenga band, which had grown from the original twenty men to nearly two thousand, an unmanageable size, far too large for his taste. There were too many spies, too many political opinions, too many errors, and debacles abounded. To make matters worse, the Germans had offered ten thousand lire to any Italian who could kill or capture him, and as he grew more effective the offer had grown to fifty thousand lire, then to a hundred thousand lire, now a hundred thousand lire and a bag of salt, the last of which had finally closed the circle around him, buying traitors until the Black Butterfly had no one left to trust save these three – and one of them, Ettalo, was only twelve. Every morning Peppi woke up and crossed himself, thanking the Virgin Mary for letting him see another sunrise in a world where a bag of salt was worth more than a man's life. Twenty-six years God had let him live. It seemed like twenty-six lifetimes. He looked down at Ludovico's house and shoved the poem he had written deeper into his pocket.

'The Americans are not who we need to see,' he said. 'Our business is with Ludovico. We wait till they leave.'

'In this weather?'

'The Germans can't move, either. Neither can our traitor.'

'Whoever led the Germans here is gone, Peppi.'

'Maybe. Maybe not. But Ludovico has a mule, electricity, and new rabbits. At least fourteen rabbits. That's a lot of rabbits. He will show himself alone at some point, and when he does, we will ask him how he got those things.'

Rodolfo, a short, stout youth with big ears, sidled up next to Peppi, set his rifle down, and blew into his hands. He was twenty-four, just two years younger than Peppi. He'd studied English in Rome. He'd been an artist before the war. Had Colonel Driscoll seen him, he would have recognized the young man as the shabby priest who had been in camp to warn the Americans about the pending German attack.

'I say we get Ludovico before the rest of the Americans come,' Rodolfo said. 'I told them the Germans are coming. They won't be long. Once they come, we'll have to explain everything to them. They'll take over, and they'll answer to no one. Our chance will be lost.'

'No. We will wait,' Peppi said. 'Whoever has shown himself to Ludovico may come back to claim another prize. We'll see. Maybe Ludovico is not the one.'

He hoped he was right. Peppi liked Ludovico. Like all of them, he'd known the old man all his life. Before the war, Ludovico had been the town blacksmith, who gave them free horseshoes and taught them to fish for eels and play soccer. He was the first in the village to get electricity, which he'd shared with everyone. He'd walked all the way to Forte dei Marmi to get it, twenty-five miles, paying two power company men five hundred lire apiece to run poles all the way from Forte dei Marmi to Bornacchi, which, Peppi had to admit, showed great foresight. But Ludovico had changed after his wife died. He'd become bitter and aloof, retiring to his house and olive fields, obsessed with his daughter and her marriage, removing himself from village life and paying Ettora the witch enormous sums so that his daughter would get pregnant – a waste of money. Most important, he was a Fascist, and while he claimed impartiality to everyone he knew, no one could be impartial now. No decision was a decision. To not take sides was to take sides. Peppi's own brother was a Fascist who had been drafted into the Italian army and sent to Russia and hadn't been heard from for months. Peppi hoped he wouldn't come back soon, because now nothing was promised and nothing was forgiven. Rodolfo's brother Marco was a Fascist whom they'd killed in the Ruosina Pass in a firefight two months before. Marco's body fell from a ridge and was caught on a ledge of jagged rock that no one could reach. He stayed there two days before Peppi's pleas made both sides stop fighting long enough so that Rodolfo could climb up the precipice and bring his brother's body down. Fascists and partisans alike buried Marco in his beloved mountainside and stood side by side at his grave. Rodolfo wept and wondered aloud how to tell his mother. 'Marco wanted to be mayor of Bornacchi,' he said. 'Don't you remember? He taught us to mix drinks and hunt wild boar so that we would vote for him when he grew up.' The partisans and the Fascists had wept together, refusing to look at one another, but after the prayers were said and the hugs were delivered, they departed and the next day fought each other with even greater animosity.

Peppi dug his stick into the thick mud until it was buried up to his fingers. 'The Negroes change nothing,' he said firmly. The three partisans watched him in silence, expecting he would say more. But he said nothing more. Even if the Negroes had the entire American army behind them, he thought bitterly, that would not make the problem of the church go away.

Even to think of the church made his stomach hurt, and the sorrow that drowned his heart made him weak and dizzy. It was a nightmare that had begun horribly. Six weeks before, he and his little band – the sons of farmers, olive growers, and grape pickers who had taken up arms and fled into the mountains when they could no longer stand watching the humiliation and suffering of their starving families – caught two SS soldiers on patrol near an olive grove outside the nearby town of Sant'Anna di Stazzema, less than a mile up the mountain from Bornacchi, where they sat. They had caught them by accident, while one of them was pissing, and wiped them out. It was a sloppy operation, not the kind Peppi liked, full of mad screaming and terror. They had tried to capture the Germans, but one had yelled trying to alert his nearby comrades, and the other had almost escaped, then begged for his life, dying in a gurgling of blood from Rodolfo's clumsy knife wounds. Rodolfo in particular had behaved terribly and viciously, but there had been no time for admonitions. They finished the job quickly, then fled into the caves of Mt. Paladonia and split up, during which time Peppi escaped by the skin of his teeth thanks to an old farmer who routed him around a waiting German patrol while the rest were on their own. He hid in terror as two companies from the 16th Panzer SS Division rolled through the mountain with mules, dogs, artillery, and five hundred men, wiping out everyone and everything in their path as they turned over every rock, tree, and boulder trying to find him and his band. The four made a prearranged rendezvous in another village several kilometers away two days later, where a terrible fight broke out among them, which was further exacerbated by the surprise arrival of a German patrol, which forced them into the mountains again. They hid in caves and underground caverns that had been formed by nature hundreds of years before, at times forced to separate, each unsure of the location of the others, trembling as the dogs sniffed and the German soldiers chatted just feet away. They starved that way for ten days, sometimes together, sometimes apart, eating olive twigs and chestnuts, totally dependent on a woman farmer who was brave enough to supply them with a bit of bread. When they finally met up and emerged from the foothills at the woman's farm, exhausted and starving, the woman farmer had a pasty look of shock on her face. She blurted, 'They killed everyone at Sant'Anna.'

'Who?' the partisans asked.

'The SS. They put everyone in the square and shot them and burned them.'

'How many?'

'Hundreds. Maybe three hundred.' She collapsed in tears.

Peppi wandered away, stunned, as his shaken men surrounded her, pumping her for more information. Was my sister there? Did you hear any of any Encinos, or Tognarellis, or Cragnottis, were they there?

Peppi, for his part, felt inside himself a deep sickness that would remain for the rest of his life. He waited, apart from the others, sitting at the foot of a tree with his chin resting on the palms of his hands, as she told what had happened: The SS had arrived at Sant'Anna di Stazzema furious about the killing of two of their own and had posted a sign at Sant'Anna's church saying that the villagers had to leave; they were suspicious that the village was supporting the partisans. Someone – no one knew who – tore that sign down and posted another, saying 'Don't leave. Resist the SS passively. This is our town. The partisans will protect you.' In response, 150 men from the 16th Panzer SS Division gathered up 560 people from the surrounding villages, set houses ablaze, shot every living creature – chickens, animals, dogs – and took the people to the church of Sant'Anna, and shot them in the piazza. Babies were bayoneted. Young women were raped, tortured, and piled behind the church nude and then set ablaze.

Peppi knew of no partisan – or any Italian, for that matter – in his right mind who would post that sign. The partisans knew the SS rule: for every soldier killed, the Germans would kill sixteen civilians. To post a sign rousing villagers with slogans and empty promises of protection, to flaunt that kind of reckless arrogance in the face of the SS who were ruthless and increasingly desperate, was not something any partisan would do.

Peppi waited the entire night until the weeping of his men subsided, and only then did he address them.

'No partisan can guarantee the safety of any village. You know this. Maybe the Germans posted the sign themselves.'

'No,' said Rodolfo. 'The woman said the town was empty all night. There were no Germans in the village.'

'Then whoever posted that sign is a traitor, and we will find him.'

Rodolfo had volunteered to make the dangerous journey south over the mountains to Viareggio disguised as a priest, to tell the approaching

Americans of the atrocity, in the hope that the mighty American army would push north through the mountains faster. Meanwhile, Peppi and the others hatched a plan. By the time Rodolfo returned, a day later, to report that the Americans would not be coming for several days, he and the others had already checked out several of the inhabitants of the surrounding towns, men and women who could possibly be traitors. Niccolò the baker, whose son was missing in the Italian army, Fuchini the barber, who was rumored to be a communist, Marsina, the chairmaker's wife, who was said to favor the German composer Wagner, even Ettora the witch. None had checked out. The only one who was a known Fascist was Ludovico. Plus, he had new rabbits, a lot of them, and also electricity.

The partisans had arrived at Ludovico's house just before dawn and were waiting for the chance to corner and question him and decide for themselves whether the old man would pay for Sant'Anna with his life.

Peppi stood by the ridge and watched as Ludovico, followed by the Negro soldiers, emerged from his house holding one end of an electric cord. The soldiers stood outside in the rain as the old Italian waded into the shallow creek in front of his house holding his electric cord high, then suddenly plunged the cord into the water. After a few seconds, he stood up in a babble of splashing and struggling holding an eel. He held it up high, and the Negroes laughed.

Peppi stared down silently, rubbing his fingers gently against his face.

'We will not bother with the Americans,' he said. 'Maybe they are here to protect Ludovico, maybe not. But it is Ludovico we want to talk to. We'll wait for our chance.'

The four settled back into their hiding places amid the trees and bushes, and the twelve-year-old took his post again.

11

INVISIBLE CASTLE

The boy lay in Ludovico's bed and dreamed, images swirling around him like misty figurines. He dreamed of houses made of peppermint, of dancing wizards with canes; he dreamed of roosters laying chocolate eggs, and elves in woolly caps who sang loud songs and drank sweet honey-colored water; he dreamed of a giant ogre sitting in an apple orchard, his face hovering above the treetops, plucking apples with fingers so big the apples looked like peas, dropping them to the ground, where they landed in the soft earth and sprouted into beautiful flowers as tall as trees, their buds the size of soccer balls. He dreamed of trees with faces, and bats made of chestnuts, but most of all he dreamed of rabbits, hundred and hundreds of rabbits, white ones, pink ones, brown ones, orange ones, bounding through the air, cascading across his face like rainbows, stopping in midair as they leaped past, their tails erect, their ears stiff as poles, one line going this way, the other going that way. He tried to reach up and grab a rabbit as it leaped in an arc above his face, but it flew out of reach, landed on the floor, and hopped into a corner of the room while he watched, fascinated.

'You are very silly,' the boy said, laughing. He tried to get up from the bed to catch the rabbit, but realized then he was awake and too tired to move. He lay back as the door opened and an old man entered the room, spotted the creature with great alarm, and made several futile attempts to grab it before finally snatching it into his arms. The door opened again and Renata walked in, holding a bowl of soup. She regarded a sheepish Ludovico with a grimace.

'You are fooling yourself,' she said airily, 'if you don't think half the valley doesn't know about your rabbits.'

'What's one silly rabbit?' Ludovico shrugged. He pushed the floorboards aside, and a putrid, animal smell filled the room. He tossed the rabbit into the hole and pushed the floorboard back into place.

'Is it one rabbit or twenty-one? I'm starving, too.'

'Eat what you want,' the old man muttered. 'Two died. Ettora cursed the rest. Twenty-two in all.'

Renata stared at him angrily. 'You are a disgrace,' she said.

Ludovico made a motion with his hands as if to say, 'What can I do?'

Renata glared. 'If it wasn't for Ettora, you'd be dead for holding out. She's telling everyone the rabbits are bewitched and they'll get sick if they eat them.'

'I told you she cursed them!'

'She's saving your life.'

'Ahhh!' Ludovico waved his hands.

'Keep your foolish creatures,' Renata said. 'But him,' she said, walking over to the boy, 'he needs more than chestnut soup and olive oil.' She touched the boy gently. She was glad he was awake. She had watched him all night. He had lain there for ten hours – since he'd arrived with the Negroes – and had barely moved, shivering, muttering softly, not eating. He was white-hot with fever, and she was afraid he would not live through the day. She held the soup over him as he stared at her, the breath wheezing out of him in ripples.

'You will eat chocolate but no food,' she scolded. 'You will starve that way.'

The boy did not hear her. He had slipped again to that quiet place where there were no voices or sounds. Renata carefully spooned out a small bit of soup again, holding it high as she spoke to the boy. 'When your big American friend comes back and wants to eat your soup, what will you do then?' she asked. 'There's only enough for one person.'

The boy turned his face away. The woman hovering over him was confusing him, and the smell of soup made him nauseous. He closed his eyes and waited, and after a few long moments Arturo appeared. Today he was wearing a green bomber pilot's cap and a green army jacket that came down to his knees. He stood behind Renata, hopping on one foot.

'Why do you take so long to come now?' the boy asked.

Arturo shrugged.

'What does she want?' the boy asked.

'Shh!' Arturo circled around to the side of the boy's bed as Ettora the witch entered the room, feeling her way along the walls. 'She is very smart,' he said. 'Do not tell her too much.' The two women stood above the boy, talking in hushed tones to each other, while Arturo watched from the far side of the bed.

'What are they saying?' the boy asked.

Arturo leaned close and cupped his hand over the boy's ear. 'Do not pay attention,' he whispered. 'They want you to eat a slippery fish soup that is bitter and makes your tongue stick to the top of your mouth.'

The two spoke in whispers.

'Where is the chocolate giant?' the boy hissed.

'He went back to his invisible castle,' Arturo said.

'He has a castle?'

'I've seen it,' Arturo declared, stepping back to hop on his foot again.

'What's it like?'

Arturo's eyes sparkled. For the first time, the boy noticed how odd Arturo's coloring was. He was neither black nor white, but a shade of gray, and everything about him was gray as well, even the green uniform cap and jacket he wore. For a moment, the boy thought he was going blind.

Arturo danced back a moment, hopping around in a circle on one foot, then switching to the other foot. He hopped over to the boy's bed to lean in and whisper. 'It's huge. It's made of candy, and when you break off a piece to eat, it grows back. And the road to his castle is a strip of chewing gum. His pillow is a fluffy cake.'

The boy smiled. 'What else?'

'There are big statues outside made of sugar candy. The hard kind that lasts forever when you lick it. His bed is made of soft sugar dried in sweet milk. The trees outside are chocolate. The twigs are licorice sticks, and the leaves . . . the leaves are green jelly beans!'

'Green jelly beans!'

'All you can eat.'

The boy felt as if warm water were splashing over his insides. He smiled again, weakly this time, then sighed. His chest hurt and he felt sleepy again. 'Let's go there together,' he said wistfully.

Arturo held out his hand. 'Why should I go with a friend who does not share his chocolate?'

'I saved the last piece I have for you,' the boy said.

Ettora and Renata stared in disbelief as the boy, sweating and feverish, breath rattling in and out of his lungs, stopped his lethargic mumbling, turned on his side, fished a piece of chocolate from beneath the blanket, held it in the air, gulped it down, then closed his eyes.

'Go to sleep now,' Arturo said.

'Wait!' the boy cried, but Arturo disappeared as Ludovico entered the room again.

'He's bewitched,' Ettora said.

Ludovico rolled his eyes, and Ettora turned and felt her way to the kitchen. Ludovico's house was small, and the kitchen, separated from the bedroom by a doorway, was only a few feet away. Ludovico followed Ettora and watched her bang pots and pans, busying herself, preparing something at the stove. He waited for her to mention his rabbits, but she didn't. 'Did you give him the powder they left?' he asked.

'Ahh.' Ettora waved her hand. 'He won't eat. It is not as good as my medicine, anyway.' She motioned with her head to the table, on which she had placed a little cloth sack full of crushed olive leaves. 'I need some salt. It will make the devil go away. You have any?'

Ludovico laughed bitterly. It was a joke. They hadn't seen salt in months. 'Who is he?' he asked.

'He's got a lot of devil in him, whoever he is. I'll get it out of him.'

Renata entered the kitchen. 'He's beautiful,' she said. 'He's a beautiful sign.'

'He's no sign,' Ludovico said. He was tired of signs. He saw the way Renata gazed at the boy. Renata was barren. None of Ettora's pregnancy potions had worked on her. Now she would start believing the boy was a gift from God. 'He can't stay,' Ludovico said. 'Can't you hear in the distance? That's German shelling. They'll be back in another day. Then maybe we have to explain to them who he is. And,' he nodded at the window, toward Eugenio's house, where the Negroes were quartered, 'who they are.'

'Explain to who?'

'To the Germans. Maybe they'll think he is the child of a partisan. Or worse, Peppi's child. He's the one they want.'

'Peppi would not leave a child in the woods. No partisan around here would do that.'

Ludovico looked at his daughter in alarm. 'How do you know so much about Peppi and the partisans around here?'

Renata ignored that, trying to let it slide. The less said about the partisans, the better. She knew an awful lot about them, too much to say. She spoke to Ettora. 'I thought you said a sign was coming.'

Ettora looked down at some chestnut flour she had poured onto a wooden plate. 'Things happen when they happen. He is a sign for sure.'

'And the Americans?'

Ettora shrugged.

Ludovico huffed. 'I heard them trying to talk on their radio last night.'

'What did they say?' Renata asked.

'How should I know? There was a lot of scratching on it. They talked on it, but no one talked back. There are no Americans around here for miles, none between here and Vagli; none on Mt. Forato. I bet they're deserters. Sister Caprona at the convent said she scared the Jesus out of them when she rang the bell last night. Maybe they're not Americans.

138

Maybe they're impostors. Maybe they're Gurkhas posing as Americans. They're dark, too, the Gurkhas.'

There was silence. The thought was a frightening one. The Gurkhas were bloodthirsty and terrifying. They fought with the British. They wore turbans and long robes, ate raw chickens, and ran around with knives in their mouths and unsheathed swords, raping men and killing women. They seemed lawless. The rumor was the British let them out of cages during the day to fight, then put them back in at night. Even the Germans were afraid of them.

Ludovico continued, 'How many Negroes are there in America, anyway? I thought they were all slaves and died. I think these men are Gurkhas who killed this boy's parents.'

That thought seemed to press the oxygen out of the room. Anything was possible. The woods outside Bornacchi were full of bandits, redshirts, partisans, bandits posing as partisans, communists, Brazilian soldiers, even the occasional Gurkha. Nothing was safe.

Ludovico nodded at the boy, who lay mute, his eyes still closed. 'He's got to go.'

Renata's face tightened. 'Where?'

'With the American impostors. Or whatever they are.'

'The boy stays.'

'It's my house.'

'I have a house, too,' Renata said grimly. She turned to Ettora. 'What do you think?'

Ettora shrugged. 'The devil is in him. He is possessed.'

Renata said, 'There is a priest at Gallicano who will look at him. I'll take him there myself.'

'There is no priest at Gallicano, remember? He ran off.'

'Maybe he has come back.'

Ettora stared at Renata in amazement. There was a time, before the war, when the young respected their elders. They respected the old ways. Ettora would spin coins on a table and Renata would scream in delight. She took Renata's worms away by drawing a cross on her tummy and forehead with a silver coin and kissing her on the forehead. She would let Renata taste a little *vin di nugoli* made from the chestnut tree's fruit and watch her dance with joy. But now they didn't believe in the old ways. They liked the radio. And dancing. And jazz music. And priests who ran off.

'Do what you want,' Ettora said, clapping her hands in frustration as Renata, realizing her mistake, scurried about the room, busily warming the soup again. Ettora rummaged about among the items near the stove, rattling through the pots and pans till she found a spoon. She poured some chestnut flour onto the wooden plate, then grabbed the long spoon to beat the flour into finer bits. As she raised the spoon to beat the flour, her arm was frozen in midair by a loud banging on the door.

'C'mon, *signora!* Open up, baby!'

Ettora put down the spoon, and Renata opened the door. The three Italians backed into the living room to let the four Americans in. The giant one strode directly to the boy, who lay with his eyes closed. He leaned over him, his chin strap dangling down. He felt the boy's head and said something to the Spanish-speaking one. The Spanish-speaking one spoke to them.

'He's hot. You give him the medicine?'

Ettora grimaced. 'He won't take it. The powder you gave is not as good as my medicine, anyway.'

The Spanish-speaking one translated, and the giant said something to the others that Renata could not hear. The three Italians, gathered in the living room, watched as a hushed argument ensued among the Americans who stood in the bedroom over the sleeping boy. Ludovico panicked, watching the floor creak and sag beneath the four men with his twenty-two rabbits underneath it. Renata glanced at him in disgust, saying nothing.

The argument lasted several minutes, the giant shaking his head while the lieutenant spoke to him. Finally, the four emerged from the bedroom and the Spanish-speaking one said, 'We have to take him with us down the mountain to a hospital. Who knows the way?'

The three Italians were silent.

'I know the way,' Renata said.

Ludovico's face crinkled in alarm. 'You must be losing your mind. There are Germans and mines everywhere. Besides, you won't get far in that.' He pointed out the window to the pouring rain. He didn't mention that the idea of his lovely daughter walking through the woods with four foreigners, American Negro foreigners or whatever kind of impostors they were, was unthinkable.

Renata ignored him. She spoke to Hector in Italian. 'There might be a priest in Gallicano who can help him. That's not far.'

'He needs a doctor, not a priest,' Hector said.

'He's bewitched, and a priest can take the devil out of him.'

Hector laughed. Stamps, watching the exchange, demanded to know what was going on. Hector explained, and as he did, the giant Negro, who had come over to join them, peeled off and strode into the bedroom again. He hunched over the boy's bed. He shook the boy gently.

The three Italians watched in awe as the little boy awakened and opened his eyes wide in recognition. The giant held the boy's head gently and placed the sulfa powder on his tongue, then motioned with one of his huge paws for water. Renata handed him a flask. The boy drank, then vomited a little, then drank again.

'He would not eat,' Renata said helplessly.

'I wouldn't eat, either, if I lived here,' Bishop said. 'Smells like cow-butt up in here.'

The giant one ignored them. Renata watched as he spoke softly to the boy. He had a voice that sounded like crushed gravel gently scraping across a cool dirt road. He rose, and with one hand, picked up the boy and laid him across his shoulder, the tiny boy settling against his bandoleer and rifle like a rag doll. The giant knelt and with one huge hand grasped a blanket off the bed and placed it tenderly over the boy's back. He crouched through the bedroom door and approached Stamps. 'I'm ready to go, Lieutenant,' he said.

'Go where?' Stamps asked. 'They say there ain't nowhere to go.'

'Then we got to go back the way we come,' Train said. He wanted it done now. He had slept ten hours. The boy was his responsibility, till he got rid of him. 'He got to have parents someplace. Maybe they at division looking for 'im. Maybe division is looking for us.'

Bishop said, 'Shit, they ain't looking for us. What the hell makes you think Nokes is looking for us? Hector tried the radio all night. Ain't nobody on it.'

Train strode from the room back into the tiny bedroom, placed the boy carefully on the bed, and sat down on the floor next to it. The room smelled funny, reminding him of something from home, but he couldn't remember what. With one long foot, he reached over and slowly, silently, nudged the door, closing it with his huge boot. He needed to think. He heard the others talking outside the door and shut them out of his mind.

The boy had fallen asleep again. Train had never seen someone sleep so much.

Outside the door, the three soldiers and three Italians turned to Stamps, who again was undecided. He said to Hector, 'Ask the old man if there's another way outta here where there's no Germans. Even if it's the wrong way. Maybe we can reach the Tenth Division. They're over in Ferrara, I think.'

Hector didn't like it. The Italians were scared dumb, and the best thing to do would be to lay low with them. They'd survived this long, he thought, but he complied and asked Ludovico if he could help them find another way out. The old man shook his head in response.

Stamps said, 'Tell him we'll pay 'em. We got plenty of the funny money they use here.'

Ludovico continued to shake his head.

Hector sat and waited impatiently for Stamps to decide what to do next. Ettora poured the remaining chestnut flour into a bowl. Seeing the flour made Hector hungry. He decided there was no sense starving while Stamps cut his teeth on being a lieutenant. He produced a can of Spam. He had two left.

The Italians stared hungrily as Hector opened the can and the pungent smell of hash filled the room. Stamps saw Ettora watching. 'Want some?'

She motioned to a pot of boiling water, and Hector dumped the hash into it.

From the next room, they heard singing. The sound of Train's voice made all of them stop. 'That's beautiful,' Renata said.

Bishop rolled his eyes. It amazed him that someone as dense as Train could impress anyone, though he had to admit Train had a pretty singing voice. 'That nigger could put Bessie Smith out of business,' he snorted. He tried the bedroom door. It was locked. He knocked on it. 'Train,' he shouted to the door, 'when you gets signed up for a big contract, remember my fourteen hundred yards of large, that's what you owe me. Fourteen hundred bucks. Not a penny less. Won't mean nothing to a rich man like you then.'

Train ignored Bishop and continued singing softly, his deep baritone voice rising.

Sitting at the table, Stamps sighed. 'All right. We wait till tomorrow.' He spoke to Hector. 'Tell the old man we wait till tomorrow and we need to eat. We can trade.'

Ludovico shook his head. 'You should leave tonight,' he said. 'There are Germans in the mountains behind here, between us and the Americans. If you go at night through the mountains, it's safer.'

Hector saw where it was going. The old man wanted them out of his hair. He didn't give a damn. Hector didn't need to translate his response for Stamps. 'We don't know these mountains,' Hector said. 'We need somebody to show us the way.'

'I don't know the way,' Ludovico said quickly. Before Hector could translate, Renata spoke up again, in Italian. 'I know the way.'

Ludovico stared at her, shocked. She looked at him, her eyes dull and hard. 'I know the way through,' she repeated. Hector noted the tension between them. There was a game here, he decided. Something going on between father and daughter. He wanted to know nothing about it. Couldn't Stamps see that this woman was trying to make her daddy mad? And for what? To lead some coloreds through the woods? Who was she, Little Red Riding Hood? What was in it for her, anyway? Maybe she was a partisan. Or a Fascist. There were women Fascists, too. Maybe it was all a trap, a ploy to lead them to the German commanders outside the village. Hector would kill her then, if she did that, Stamps or no Stamps. He could see she liked Stamps, could see it from the moment they stepped in there the night before. Maybe it was all a ruse, her pretending to like Stamps so she could lead them all to a waiting SS squad out in the hills. A wave of shame suddenly made Hector blanch. He was glad he didn't love anybody. It was easier, safer, not to love somebody, not to have children and raise kids in this crummy world where a Puerto Rican wants to kill an innocent woman for doing nothing more than trying to help him. He was sick in his heart, sick of translating, sick of her, sick of all of them. He wanted to get out of the middle of it and go home.

He saw the room watching him and translated for Stamps. 'She says she knows the way through and will take us.' He said it twice, to make sure Stamps understood.

Stamps looked at the slim beauty dressed in men's clothing staring at him. His heart began to pound. He couldn't help himself. She was beautiful, and brave, too. By God, he'd take it around the neck for that one, swing high from an oak tree just to have one night of setting his heavy soul against the soft caress of this woman. But to take her out into the open forest, in a furious rainstorm, and possibly have her death on his hands . . . He shook his head.

'We're going to lay low back at that dotty fella's house again and try this radio twenty-four hours more. Tomorrow, before daybreak, we'll try to get out.' He stood up. 'Let's go.'

Stamps, Hector, and Bishop left, but Train stayed inside the bedroom. Ludovico closed the door behind them and watched their backs through the window until they had turned the corner. Then he turned to his daughter. She sat at the table, saying nothing. He motioned with his head to the bedroom. 'If that big monster sleeps in my bed, I am sleeping in your house,' he said angrily. She shrugged.

In the next room, the boy lay in bed, his eyes closed, resting peacefully as the giant's deep singing voice washed over him. He felt like he was floating on clouds. He opened his eyes. There was no one in the room except the two of them.

'Where is your invisible castle?' the boy asked.

Train, sitting at his bedside in a crouch, stopped singing and leaned over. 'Got no more chocolate, boy. Can't help you there.'

Train leaned forward and he and the boy stared at each other. All his life, for twenty-one years, Train realized, he'd never owned anything, and here this boy was offering him his heart. He could see it. No one had ever offered him anything in the world. The world was a confusing place. He remembered the day he was drafted. He was pulling a mule across Old Man Parson's field and his aunt Vera came out to him. She was visiting from Philadelphia. She said, 'I'm gonna kill Jing-a-ling.'

Jing-a-ling was Train's cousin, whom they also called Sticky. Jing had started a reading business for the colored of Mt. Gilead, because the last colored who could read, Reverend Willard, had run off with a fourteen-year-old named Peaches. Jing couldn't read, either. In fact, the only words he could read were 'pink' and 'noodle' and 'Cadillac,' but he told everyone it was about time the colored of Mt. Gilead started to do for theyself since the white man was always telling them what to do with his funny white dollars. Everyone agreed.

The colored of Mt. Gilead were getting their mules confiscated, going to jail for tax evasion, and getting evicted, ever since Jing started his business. It was a disaster, the letters piling onto Jing's kitchen table. But no one got suspicious, because Jing made a big score for an old man named Jumbo

146

Dawson, who had gotten hit by a white man driving from New York to Florida. The white man broke Jumbo's leg in three places and punctured a lung. His lawyer wrote Jumbo three times offering a settlement, and each time Jing, who answered everyone's mail, sent a letter back to the man with a picture of the pretty brown girl from the *Jet* magazine centerfold and a pink Cadillac, because he thought the letter was from the Department of Motor Vehicles, since Jumbo had been trying to get his license for four years, ever since his wife ran off with a light-skinned Negro named Linwood, who had a car.

The white man was irate. After Jing's fourth letter, he sent Jumbo eight hundred dollars and told him to get lost.

So no one got too suspicious of Jing-a-ling's business. The white man's ways had always been a mystery to the colored of Mt. Gilead anyway, the way he counted his money, his crops, his time. A Negro getting his land confiscated or going to jail for tax evasion or being bamboozled, these were cause-and-effect matters in a mysterious and cold world. Avoiding the white man's evil was like dodging raindrops anyway – sometimes your number just came up.

Train's draft notice was tossed in a pile of tax liens, arrest warrants, winning sweepstakes notices, free circus passes, and death notices on Jing-a-ling's kitchen table. Train would never have known he was drafted if Aunt Vera hadn't come to visit from Philadelphia and gone through the letters.

Standing in the field under the hot sun, Train's aunt Vera waved the notice in the air. 'You been drafted!' she said.

'What's "drafted"?' he had asked.

'To fight. The Japs done attacked Pearl Harbor, and the Negro's finally gonna fight.'

'Who's Pearl Harbor?'

'Git on down to High Point right now!'

His grandma gave him some bones and dust in a black bag to wear around his neck for good luck, and he was gone.

The army was a confusing place. They gave him pictures, and training manuals to read. They pointed at things for him to shoot at. They put him on a boat. They told him Hitler was a bad man. But nothing they gave him was his. All of it had to go back to them – the gun, the clothes, everything. They had been clear about that. The only person who had given him anything was Bishop. Sure, he whupped him in cards, but Bishop knew about things. He had given him knowledge. He had told him it was a white man's war. And Train had believed him, until now. Until he looked into the boy's frightened eyes and saw himself.

'I'm scared, too,' he said, patting the boy gently. 'That's why I follows the Good Book. You know what that is? See, everything's already been decided. The good Lord, He spares who He want to and He strikes who He want to. So you just have to go along. And after a while, you don't even know you're going along because you don't know that there is anything else *to* do, see. You don't even have to think about anything else.' He sang gently,

> *If I can help someone along the way,*
> *If I can help them from day to day,*
> *If I can help someone not do wrong,*
> *If I can help them through this song,*
> *Then my living would not be in vain . . .*

The boy smiled.

'You like that, don'tcha? That's an old church song, boy. My grandma teached it to me. And I'mma teach it to you. It's just words. When you say words, they don't mean much. But when you sing 'em, Lawd, they seem to get a whole lotta power. I see that now. Words, trees, rocks, everything the Good Lord touched with His hand, got power in it. You believe in miracles, boy? I got something to show you. Look'a here.' Train pulled the large head of the *Primavera* from its netting. He had polished it up all through the night, so now it was clean and shiny. 'See this here? It's magic, boy. Makes you completely invisible. Don't tell nobody 'bout it, y'hear? Tha's jus' for you 'n' me to know. You see? You rubs it like this. Like a genie in a magic bottle, 'cept no genie do come, not yet, nohow. You wanna try?'

Train picked up the boy's limp, cold hand and ran his tiny fingers across the statue head, and as the boy felt the gentle curves and slopes of the sculptor Tranqueville's great creation, the great *Primavera* of the Santa Trinità Bridge in Florence, the boy recognized that she was the woman from his first dream, the one who had waved at him in the field. She was one and the same, and he knew then that what Arturo had said was true, that his friend was a magic giant, because this woman was a piece of candy from a dream that no one could know about. This candy had to come from a magic castle. It was hard candy, too, the sucking kind, the kind he liked the most. He wanted to sit up and lick it, devour the whole thing, but he was too tired to move. He stared as the giant's huge brown eyes blinked and he gently lowered the statue head so that it was next to the boy's own, right on his pillow. The boy could have turned his head and licked it anytime he wanted to, but he decided to wait until Arturo came. They would eat it together. It would probably take them a whole year.

The boy gazed up at the giant, who appeared misty, his eyes blinking in concern. 'You are magic,' the boy said softly in Italian. With great effort, he reached up to touch Train's face. Train knelt on one knee and took his helmet off so that the boy could reach him. The boy stroked Train's face gently with one hand. 'Turn your head now,' he said. 'Please turn your head now and make it my birthday. Why won't you turn your head?'

Train crinkled his face in puzzlement. 'I don't understand what you want, chil',' he said. Suddenly, he heard the floor creak behind him, and he snapped his head around sharply to look behind him for the source of the sound. The boy felt Train's head turn, and he lay back, closing his eyes, exhausted but satisfied – when there was a boom, from the giant's magic, no doubt. When the boy opened his eyes again, through the haze of misty consciousness that clouded his vision, he saw that the chocolate giant had disappeared, and in his place he had left a most wonderful birthday present: rabbits. White ones. Brown ones. Spotted ones. Black ones. All across his bed, all over the room. Just like in his other dream. Rabbits everywhere.

12

HIGHWAY TO HEAVEN

The division on the other side of the Serchio Valley broke through on the wireless radio at three A.M. Stamps, Bishop, and Hector were sitting in a lean-to in the alley behind Ludovico's house, huddled around a small fire warming their hands, when the radio, placed in Ludovico's back window and wired to a wall outlet inside his bedroom, suddenly buzzed to life. Stamps nearly fell over as he stood to grab it and pull it down from the window. He squatted beneath the window ledge with the radio's telephone headset between his legs. The signal was scratchy and faint, but it was Captain Nokes all right, and he wanted to know their position.

'Somewhere west of Gallicano,' Stamps said breathlessly, trying to keep the relief out of his voice. 'We can see Mt. Forato.'

'Mount what?'

'Mt. Forato.'

'Where is that in relation to here?'

Stamps kept the talk button up. 'We're the ones that's lost, and he's asking directions. Dumb motherfucker.' He pressed the talk button. 'East of the Cinquale Canal someplace. Straight up toward Mt. Forato. There's a church bell tower there. That's the best I can do.'

'Have you seen any Germans in the last eight hours?'

Bishop snorted. 'No, motherfucker, just Jabbo Smith and his jug band.' Stamps waved an impatient hand to shush Bishop and pressed the talk button again: 'Negative. But there's plenty.'

'We want you to capture and hold one. It's important.'

'We're trying to get back, Captain.'

'Just hold.'

'Hold for what?'

'I'm ordering you to hold for a German prisoner, and we'll get a fix on your position. We're sending help.'

'How long?'

'Two or three days. Get a prisoner.'

Stamps kept his finger off the talk button while Bishop cursed aloud. If a German showed his face, the last thing in the world Stamps would be thinking about was holding him prisoner. He'd shoot the shit out of him and run the other way. But he kept his thoughts to himself. Nokes had said nothing about food.

'Can we arrange a drop?' Stamps asked. 'We're running out of food. We're eating nuts and berries out here. And these folks ain't the friendliest. We got wounded, too.'

'How many?'

'One. A kid. Italian kid. Needs a hospital.'

'Just sit tight till we come.'

'Kid can't wait that long, sir.'

'Hold tight, y'hear! Get a prisoner and hold him. That's straight from Colonel Driscoll. I'll radio you oh-four-hundred tomorrow. Don't move. Out.'

Stamps flung the microphone from him and stood. 'This is a joke,' he said. He glared at Bishop. 'Your fuckin' friend goes AWOL, and now this God-and-country motherfucker wants us to get a prisoner. Something's cookin' 'round here and he ain't telling. Dumb white cracker.' He paced the narrow alleyway as he spoke. The radio telephone receiver, still attached to the radio sitting on the window ledge, dangled where he'd flung it.

Bishop, still seated on the ground, grinned at Stamps. 'So he's a white cracker, now,' Bishop said. 'I thought you liked him.'

Stamps stopped pacing and stood over Bishop. 'Who said I liked him?'

Bishop smirked. 'I seen you shining up to him all the time. Been shining up to him since he joined us. And now he's a white cracker.'

'Just 'cause I ain't a tap dancer like you don't mean I like Nokes,' Stamps said. 'Besides, he ain't the worst.'

'He left us high and dry down at the canal. You told him three times to fire the eighty-millimeter and he didn't fire it. I heard that myself.'

'So what? He wasn't the only white captain sitting two miles back radioing orders to niggers two miles up front. That's how they work it all over. Plus Nokes reports to Colonel Driscoll, and Driscoll's fair. He does right by the colored.'

'Driscoll don't like you either.'

'Like I said, he's fair.'

'He's a white man, and the only reason white folks is fair 'round here is 'cause the Germans is cutting their toenails too short to walk and they're running out of white boys to die. So now the great white father sends you out here to shoot Germans so he can hang you back in America for looking at his woman wrong. You think that's fair?' Bishop pulled out a cigarette and lit it slowly. 'Now I remember why I runned up here. I got a better chance with these Germans than I got with my own. Least I know what side they on.' He took a deep drag and blew a smoke ring.

'Well, you can walk up that ridge and make friends with them anytime you want,' Stamps said.

The window above them opened and Train stuck his head out. 'What y'all fussing about, huh? We got to come up with a plan or something. This little feller's fever's coming down. Hector, you got some mo' magic powder?'

Hector waved his hand at Train to go away. Bishop said, 'The plan is to get my fourteen hundred wampums outta you and go home, that's my plan.'

As Train frowned and disappeared from the window, Stamps smirked down at Bishop. He couldn't help himself. 'Don't you feel stupid now? How you gonna get your fourteen hundred dollars up here, Bishop? There's no money 'round here.' He laughed softly.

Bishop could feel the blood rushing into his face. He glared up at Stamps, thought for a moment about knifing him, then calmed himself, ignoring the challenge. There was no money in it. He shrugged. 'I was drafted. That's my excuse. Far as I'm concerned, the Negro was better off as quartermasters and cooks. It's safer. The Army should never made the Negro into combat soldiers, right, Hector?'

Hector remained silent, watching the whole exchange nervously. He was a Puerto Rican. He had his own problems. He wanted no part in this. There was no point. 'Two or three days up here is a long time,' he said.

Stamps silently agreed.

'You damn right it's a long time,' Bishop said. 'We're on the highway to heaven up here. Sitting ducks. For what? For nothing. Over a scam. That's what this whole war is. A scam. Whites killing whites. Whites killing Jews. For what? 'Cause they dirty? I read that in a book someplace. The Germans don't like the Jews 'cause they dirty. Like all these damn Germans 'round here . . . Hell, I ain't met one German over here *yet* who didn't have nothing for soap and water to do. The Negro don't have doodleysquat to do with this . . . this devilment, this war-to-free-the-world shit.' Bishop stubbed out his cigarette. 'They better not talk that boogie-joogie to me. White folks *own* the world, goddammit. We just *rentin'*.'

Stamps was amused by Bishop's rancor. He was surprised that Bishop was so insightful. 'This is about progress for the Negro, Bishop, that's what this is about. They said the Negro couldn't fight. We're proving he can. That's progress.'

Bishop snorted. 'Progress? How 'bout that time we was on training maneuvers back in Arizona and we stopped at that restaurant for lunch, and them German POWs was being marched around out there, and they served them inside the restaurant while we had to stand outside at attention in hundred-and-ten-degree heat? And only after the so-called enemy ate inside did they serve us – from the back door, by the outhouse, on paper plates. You forgot that?'

'I remember it,' Stamps said softly. The memory was a knife in his heart, the entire company of two hundred Negro soldiers standing at attention in the sweltering heat while twenty German POWs sat inside the cool, empty restaurant, laughing and joking, happy to be safe in America, knowing they'd get home after the war, eating ice cream with the white MPs guarding them. And he, fool that he was, Mr Big Lieutenant, kept the company in line, telling them to keep quiet, hold down the chatter, cut the complaining, this is the army, dammit. Always the professional soldier, always following orders, like they taught him at officer candidate school, always playing it straight. Sometimes he felt like his conscience wanted to snap in two. He was constantly caught between the desires of his men and the demands of his superiors, who were slaves to the propaganda, too. They all were slaves. Each and every one of them. White and colored.

Bishop glared at him. 'They don't give a damn about you, and they'll forget you five minutes past breakfast when this war's all over. You'll see.'

Stamps shrugged. 'Maybe so. but I ain't fighting for them. I'm fighting for my children, if I have any. And my grandchildren, if I get some. I'm fighting for Huggs and Trueheart Fogg, remember them? And Captain Walker. You forgot him, didn't you? Yeah. That white man saved your ass. He took the point at Lucca when your squad was supposed to take it. He got stitched nine ways to Sunday 'cause of y'all. A white *cracker*. From Mississippi. Best goddamn captain we ever had. You think we'd be hung up out here if Walker was running things instead of Nokes? You think we'd be setting here?'

Bishop was silent. Walker would have hiked up that mountain and fetched them. He'd have walked it alone if he had to. He'd have cussed them out and called them niggers because he was a snake-bitten bastard, but he wouldn't have been calling them on any goddamn radio like that coward Nokes, telling them to get prisoners while their balls were in a sling. Walker had always looked out for his men. He had always kept his word. Bishop felt a pang of deep regret and looked away. Fuck it.

'Walker's dead,' he said. 'Plus, he didn't like niggers nohow.'

'Yeah, well I'm fighting for 'im anyway.'

'Remind me to tell Mr Charlie to raise your allowance when you get home.'

'Fuck you, man!'

Bishop laughed as Stamps rose and took a few steps down the alley away from them. The soft sound of Train's singing stopped him. Hector, sitting on the ground next to Bishop, his feet splayed out by the fire, listened to Train's singing, too, as it blended with the howling wind, which had returned, bringing the rain back with it. They felt the first moist drops, then the freezing downpour began. Against the background of the splattering rain, they could hear Train singing louder, some hymn. Bishop recognized it. 'Take Me to the Water.' He liked that song.

'Damn fool,' Stamps muttered. 'The best thing he done so far is to fall through the floor and find them rabbits. You can't trust none of these people here.' He turned to Bishop and Hector. 'Germans be damned, we ain't looking for nobody. We got to sit tight for two days, three days, so we sit tight. In the meantime, we better watch these ridges and hills. This ain't the best position. We're below everything. These little streets can't cover us from above, so we got to watch from the edge of town, by the walls near the gate. There's only one way in and one way out – that front gate. So we watch that. We'll split the watch up. Who wants it first?'

'What's the point?' Hector said. 'If twenty of 'em come, or even ten, we're cooked. These people here ain't gonna help us.'

Stamps felt rage boiling up inside him. He was the one with the OCS degree. He was the one with combat training. He was the lieutenant. These guys were draftees, buck privates, and now they were experts in combat strategy. 'Okay, y'all wanna be smartasses? I'll take the first watch for ten minutes, and when I get back, the next guy has it for two hours. The next guy is you, Hector.' He pointed to Bishop. 'Then *you*, Mr Mary McLeod Bethune, you go after Hector.' He stalked down the alley, and they watched his back, illuminated by the fire under the lean-to, disappear around the corner.

Bishop snorted. 'He's a smartass, ain't he, Hector?'

Hector stared at the wall of the alleyway, silent. Two days up here was just too long. He wasn't sure they'd last two hours. They'd been here fourteen hours, and he was convinced, peering at the ridges at dusk that evening, that they were being watched. He could see nothing other than blowing treetops above them, but he could feel it, the hairs on the back of his neck telling him that somebody was out there, watching, waiting. He'd had that same feeling at the Cinquale, and he was right then. He had dreams that told him the truth, and in his dreams he saw himself getting shot or captured. He just didn't want to get captured alive by the Germans. He'd heard they didn't take prisoners, and that if they did, they tortured you for information. He always had trouble with English when he was nervous. What little information he could give them, he wouldn't be able to give in English.

'In a way, it doesn't matter if division sends help or not,' Hector said. 'If they send somebody, then we have to go back with them. And do what? Fight some more. We ought to head deeper into the mountains, where nobody can find us.'

'Is you gone 'round the bend, too?'

'Train did it and look where it got him. He's in there singing songs, he got a little friend. He's stupid and happy. That's what I wanna be. Stupid and happy.'

Bishop laughed. 'I know a pretty girl in Kansas City named Doris who'll polish your knob for fifty cents. That'll make you happy. That'll bring you joy, son. You wanna play some cards?'

'Hell, no. I'm going to sleep.' The sound of Train's soft singing from within Ludovico's house meshed with the icy rain, which was falling harder now, to make a soft symphony.

'Lemme ask you something,' Bishop said. 'When we was at the church last night, what was that crazy man up there saying?'

'Don't know, but I ain't going back there again, that's for sure.'

'Something about a chicken, right?'

'I'm gonna start charging y'all for my translations.'

'Something bad happened up there,' Bishop said. 'I know it.'

'Yeah, something bad happened,' Hector said. 'Big Diesel tried to kiss you in the poker and you was gonna let him, but we stopped you.' He chuckled, suddenly feeling giddy. The memory of it made his stomach hurt – it was so funny.

Bishop smirked. 'I don't know what got into him,' he said.

Stamps reappeared at the end of the alley. Bishop glanced up at him and said, 'It ain't been ten minutes yet.'

Stamps spoke to Hector. 'Hector, get moving.'

Hector rose wordlessly. He was glad to go. Better out there than in here. He marched around to the side of the building, passed through several tight alleyways and sharp turns bordered by high stone walls, the tops of which he could not see over, enclosing God knows what. He descended a set of tiny steps and passed several dark houses until he reached the edge of the village and could see the mountains beyond it. He stood by the gate and leaned on the stone wall, the wind blowing against him. He stared at the looming mountains. Whoever was out there could see him now, he knew. He wanted to wave, to show whoever it was that he was a man of mercy, that he was Hector Negron from Harlem who had never harmed anybody in his life before he entered the army, that he never shot the man, just the uniform. He didn't hate Germans, he didn't hate anybody. He was just afraid. He hoped they would let him explain.

As he watched the ridges above him, the clouds parted momentarily, and the moon shone through the breaks and he could see the bell tower of the church where they had fled, and a taller ridge behind it. Then a cloud came and made the night total again, and the view was gone. In the dark, he heard a dog bark. Then an owl hooted and nearly made him piss in his pants. He wanted to pee badly but decided against it. Instead, he sat with his back against the wall, facing the ridges, and after a few moments he lay down and stretched himself out, resting his head on his arm. The heavy rain had ceased. Instead, several stray snowflakes blew across his face. Hector pulled off his field coat and placed his rifle on the ground; then, curling up against the wall, he covered himself with his field coat and tucked his hands into his pants for warmth as the wind howled over his head. If the Germans came down the ridge, he thought, he wanted to die dreaming of San Juan at Christmas, with the sun on his face and the ocean blowing warm sea breezes on his nose and Christmas lights and decorations everywhere. He fell asleep immediately and slept like a dead man.

13

THE TOWN

There were thirty-two official residents of the town of Bornacchi during World War II, though its history stretched back over twelve centuries. It was founded by monks from nearby La Spezia, who were lured by the area's beautiful black cypresses, natural olive groves, and thriving chestnut trees. The monks lived peacefully for nearly fifty years until the Lucchesians arrived, conquering the town in 1202 with horses and spears. They, in turn, were driven out by the Pisans, who arrived forty-five years later with bigger horses and spears, and with mules. The Pisans stuck around for forty years and built a small wall around the town to keep invaders out, but the wall failed them when they were attacked in 1347 by the Ligurians, who arrived with ladders, scaled the wall, drove the Pisans out, and lived happily ever after, thinking they'd conquered nearby Florence, until the Florentines arrived and sent them packing. The Florentines stayed for 148 years, extending the wall around the town a foot higher with mortar and embedding broken wine bottles along its top, which only served to make the Lucchesians angry when they showed up again, looking for a rematch with the Pisans. They found the Florentines instead and whipped them just for being so frivolous as to waste good wine bottles by sticking them in a wall, then cooled their heels happily for twenty-six years waiting for the Pisans to mount a comeback. They were not disappointed. The Pisans arrived in 1598 and knocked the stuffing out of them, leaving only the teeth, bones, and skulls of the survivors and sending the rest over the glass-topped wall by the dozens. The Lucchesians responded by laying low in the hills outside of town for 140 years, telling stories to their children about the wicked Pisans, who had left only the teeth, bones, and skulls of the great Lucchesian people, conveniently omitting the part about the time *they* took Pisan teeth, bones, and skulls as souvenirs. Meanwhile, the Florentines, who were feeling flush in those days from having beaten the stuffing out of the Pisans three times straight in the adjoining valley, rushed in and sent the Pisans to the dogs. A bandit warrior named Enrico the Terrible wandered by with his army, whipped the Florentines with one hand tied behind his back, then departed and forgot about the town completely. The Lucchesians returned for one last throw, only to find that everyone had grown tired of fighting and had now graduated to diplomacy, which was worse.

The four groups, Ligurians, Lucchesians, Pisans, and Florentines, settled in the valley around the town's walls and argued for eighty-seven years about who owned what and where, until Napoleon arrived in 1799 and beat the blubber out of everybody. The town sat, indifferent, for 122 years, until 1921, when a blacksmith named Bruno Bornacchi from the village of Barga, near the Serchio River, showed up and rebuilt the town from scratch. He renamed it for himself, at which point Benito Mussolini's

Fascists shot him in the foot in 1939 and sent him packing on his pony, declaring it a Fascist town. In short, the town had known pain, glory, suffering, pity, self-sacrifice, grief, jealousy, murder, mayhem, peace, war, grapes, wine, and wisdom, but it had never known the smell of good ol' stinkin' fried rabbit cooked Kansas City-style by a smooth-talking fatback lover named Bishop Cummings, who was called Walking Thunder back home at the First Baptist Saving Souls Center.

The smell wafted high over the Apennines, into every stone crevice, mule trail, street, and alleyway, and as it did, thirty-two descendants of slaves, kings, cooks, court jesters, opera impresarios, serfs, second cousins, kings, bakers, chairmakers, and blacksmiths slung their nostrils into the air as one, and emerged from their stone huts and tiny homes, noses held high. It was as if God Himself had floated down from up above.

Ludovico saw them through the window of his house. '*Dio mio*,' he murmured. 'They'll bring the Germans here.' He ran out to warn the American *tenente* but too late, as the villagers drifted out of the half-bombed homes and rubble that lay amid the shorn hills and trees surrounding the town. They walked, seemingly hypnotized, toward the three soldiers who sat around the fire cooking the single rabbit, and gathered in a circle around them.

An old man in a worn vest and weathered shirt that had once been white but now was yellowed was the first to speak. His name was Franco Bochelli. He'd fought in the great Italian victory over Ethiopia in 1936, then had had the good sense to knock his teeth out with stones to avoid serving in Mussolini's army – though at age sixty-four it was doubtful that they wanted him. He thought the three coloreds were Ethiopians.

'Viva Il Duce,' he said.

'What's he want, Hector?' Bishop asked. Three days had passed, no Germans were in sight, the weather had lifted that morning, and it was a bright, shiny, chilly day, just four days before Christmas. Stamps had forgotten all about the radio, and he was in no hurry to get up into the mountains to check for Germans now. He sat next to Bishop, his eyes watering, as the rabbit turned and its sloppy juice dripped onto the fire.

'He wants directions to Ebbetts Field,' Hector said.

'Quit fucking around. Wha'd he say?'

'Something about a duke.'

'They still got kings and dukes here?' Bishop eyed old Franco, who, seeing he was under scrutiny, pushed his toothless grin even wider, giving his mouth the look of a bottomless pit, a black O. Wrinkled skin covered his face like an old blanket draped over a pile of junk. Bishop spoke to him. 'You looks like you was a waiter at the Last Supper,' he said, smirking. Franco nodded and smiled harder. Bishop turned away and spoke to Hector. 'Tell him there ain't enough here for no dukes unless one of 'em's Duke Ellington. I done this one here for Train's little junior.'

Hector looked at the gathering of women, children, and old men. 'Shit, you tell 'em.'

Bishop rose to his feet and faced the crowd impatiently. He didn't want to take care of all these people.

He pointed to the rabbit. 'This here,' he said, speaking loudly, as if he were addressing school children, 'belongs to the boy. Inside.' He pointed to Ludovico's house. 'We' – he pointed to the three soldiers – 'we no eat rabbit. We take it to the boy. Inside.' He pointed to Ludovico's house again. He watched the Italians. No one moved.

Bishop whispered to Hector. 'Just take it and run on in the house with it.'

'Hell, no.' Hector turned on his haunches, leaving Bishop to face his audience.

A pretty young woman in a worn blue-flowered dress stepped forward. She was tall and thin, and like most of the young, she seemed sallow and slightly gaunt with malnutrition. 'Are you staying long?' she asked in Italian.

Bishop looked appreciatively at her long legs and slender hips. He did not understand a word she had said, but looking at those legs and hips, he suddenly felt the mandate of the U.S. government heavy and righteous on his shoulders. His duty was to protect these people. They were depending on him. He spoke the only Italian he knew. '*Americani,*' he said. '*Dove tedeschi?*'

The young woman, Fabiola Guidici, happened to be an art history student at the Academy of Art and Design in Florence. She was three weeks from receiving her degree when the war hit, so she fled home from her rented room, but not before discovering en route that the university's library, to which she owed several hundred lire, had been blown to bits by German shelling. She plied through the wreckage and managed to salvage several books, including *The Origin of Potatoes (Solanum tuberosum), The Life of Plautus, A Walking History of Philadelphia*, and an ancient tome by the Roman philosopher Marcus Aurelius entitled *Crates of Athens*. She'd spent the last four days eating nothing but chestnuts and reading Aurelius's *Crates*, an experience that had left her literally stuffed and starving at once. She pointed past Bishop's shoulder and said in Italian, 'The Germans are in the Mountain of the Sleeping Man. However, the sleeping man is a metaphor for the element of surprise, for the mountain does not truly sleep but merely lies in a state of unconsciousness and dormancy, until such time as he rises and shows the true meaning of nature's unequivocal greatness and love's savage fury. Who's that rabbit for? We're hungry.'

Bishop turned to Hector. 'What'd she say?' he asked.

Hector blinked in surprise. 'I think she's their lawyer.'

'That's it,' Stamps said, getting up and brushing himself off. 'Get Loody and his daughter out here.'

Hector went inside and returned with Ludovico, Renata, and Train, who was carrying the boy.

At the appearance of the giant – of whom several had heard but few had seen – carrying the small boy in massive arms that looked as if they had been sculpted from steel, the Italians stared in awe. The boy had become an appendage now, as natural a part of Train as the head of the statue of the *Primavera* that dangled from his right hip in the net sack looped around his belt. He looked ridiculous, Bishop thought, but he had to admit, Train was the only one who could get the boy to eat.

As the days had passed, Train's attention to the child had never wavered and, miraculously, the boy's condition had improved. From total collapse, his fever had lifted and his internal injuries, whatever they were – for none of them knew – gradually began to heal; slowly he began to move, a finger first, a fist, then a toe, an arm. Soon he began to sit up by himself. While the others were convinced he was still going to die, Train told Bishop, 'This boy's a miracle. He brung good luck to me. Do you believe in miracles?'

'I believes in the power of everything, especially the pictures of white men on green paper,' Bishop said.

'What about all the preaching you does back home? Don't you believes in God?'

'I believes in God at the time I'm preaching it.'

'And then?'

'Then I don't believes it no more.'

But even Bishop had to allow that the child's recovery was unlike anything he'd ever seen. He'd seen Italian children dying by the dozens. In Lucca, where he had been stationed at the medical operations tent, he'd seen them brought in as bloody messes, with mangled arms and legs, burst stomachs, chest wounds, and some like this kid, some who had no obvious wounds but something terribly wrong inside. Most died. Some died horribly, screaming for their already dead parents. Others succumbed quietly, their huge eyes fearfully following the strange mass of colored doctors and medics who scrambled to throw IVs into their bony arms and set their horribly mangled and broken legs. Then the doctors would silently close their young charges' eyes forever, sometimes within minutes after they arrived, while their parents howled. Even the most hardened of the Negro doctors bit their lips and walked away, wiping sweaty tears from their faces. Bishop had wanted nothing to do with them, the doctors, the kids, the parents, none of them; they were losers, connected to life by a single belief and subsequent string of beliefs that he'd shut out. The Old Testament. The New Testament. God. Jesus. Elijah. All bullcrap. It would have been easier if this kid had died. Now, he had to admit, he was starting to care, just a little bit. He tried to stifle a chuckle as he watched Train's kid roll around on the ground, then sit on Train's giant foot, Train lifting him into the air, giving him a ride.

'Is that allowed?' Train said.

'You can give him a ride with your foot, Diesel. It's allowed.'

'No. I mean believing in God when you preach it, then stopping after you're done.'

Bishop shrugged. 'God allows anything in this world that can happen to happen.' He realized even as he said it that this was the exact reason why he did not believe in God, and it troubled him, because it sounded not like disbelief in someone who did not exist but more like anger at the actions of someone that he, Bishop, did not agree with. He hoped Train wouldn't catch the subtle difference, and Train didn't. The giant had something else on his mind. Train was looking down at the kid, who had now untied his boots and was gleefully trying to loop the shoestrings from both boots together so Train would trip and fall.

'Like me bringing him home? Is that allowed, Bish?'

Bishop stared at him. 'Boy, you're dreaming. This child here don't belong to you. What you know 'bout raising a child?'

'My grandma knows how to do it.'

'The one who gived you that sack 'round your neck? With the dust and magic bones in it? Her?' Bishop laughed.

Train looked confused. 'This boy's an angel, Bishop. I seen his power.'

'You a fool, Train. After he poops his panties and calls his mama a few times, you'll be done with him,' Bishop said.

But the kid never pooped at all, and he never called for anyone, and as the days passed and the boy's condition improved, Train found that he could communicate with him by a series of taps. One tap meant 'yes.' Two taps mean 'no' or 'not.' Three was 'try.' Four taps meant 'I'm tired.' Five meant 'must do it.' Six taps meant 'trouble' or 'bad thing.' It took the kid a while to learn that, but once the kid burned his hand on a kerosene flare a couple of times, he figured it out.

Nights were the hardest, because the boy would not sleep. They vacated crazy Eugenio's house after a day and slept on the floor in the bedroom of

Ludovico's house so they could use his electricity to power the radio, and on the third night and each night thereafter, the boy would tap Train into consciousness, whereupon the giant would stumble to his feet and hold the boy through the night, the child tugging on him, moaning so loudly that the others would grunt fierce disapproval and force them outside. Train would pace back and forth in the alley behind Ludovico's house, carrying the boy wrapped in a blanket, rocking him to sleep, the statue's head bumping up against the wooden wall, causing further cursing and consternation from those inside. No one slept well. Stamps always posted one of them outside the house to watch for Germans, and when Train was too exhausted to walk the boy any longer, the lone sentry – Stamps, Hector, or Bishop – took over, pacing with the crying boy until he slept. The child slept fitfully, murmuring and tugging each of them, covering his ears, as if a loud noise might come crashing through his sleep at any moment. During the day, he would wander off when Train wasn't around, prompting hilarious chases around Ludovico's house and through the rabbit pen in the alley behind it, which was now mysteriously populated by two or three rabbits. Even Stamps, hard nut that he was, found himself checking for the kid each night after their short patrols, which really amounted to nothing more than walking the perimeter of Bornacchi's walls at dusk, peering at the trees in the ridges for a few moments, then hurrying to the relative safety of Ludovico's house. He had become part of their unit; his eyes were big and dark as olives, his pallor had lifted, and his complexion was smooth and beautiful as ice cream.

The soldiers fell in love with him. It was not hard. His eyes, once glazed, now took in everything around them. He hugged everyone. He sucked his thumb though he was beyond thumb-sucking years. His incoherent babblings, understood by no one, not even the Italians, came off as cooing sounds, gentle and relaxing, but no amount of coaxing could make him talk sensibly even though he appeared to be of talking age. When he rose out of bed in the mornings and began waddling like a penguin, shaking and showering each of the soldiers with hugs and cuddling, laughing with a row of straight white teeth in a dazzling smile with one front tooth missing, he melted their hearts. After months of savage fighting, with the white man at their backs whipping them and the white man at their fronts shooting at them, the boy restored their humanity, and for that they loved him. He was their hero. They called him Santa Claus, in honor of the Christmas that was coming in four days, and they fought over what kinds of gifts to get him.

Even now, Bishop watched Train approach the crackling campfire from Ludovico's house with the kid seated on his broad shoulders, riding him like an elephant, playfully poking Train in the eyes as he walked, and he had to stifle a smile. Maybe Train knew something he did not. He doubted it. Bishop watched as Ludovico and Renata stumbled out of Ludovico's house behind Train to join the crowd of villagers now circling the sizzling rabbit, its drifting aroma covering the piazza like a halo.

Stamps rose and approached the old man, whose brow was furrowed in righteous concern. 'Where's all these people from?' he asked.

Ludovico looked at Renata, who translated. 'He's related to only fourteen of them. Fifteen,' she quickly corrected herself, seeing her uncle Bruno staggering toward them from a house on the far end of town.

'How come your father got all those rabbits and they're starving?'

'They're not starving,' Renata said. 'Franco' – she pointed to the man with no teeth – 'he's the mayor. He's got more wine in his cellar than

Il Duce. Diva, over there, she has a vegetable garden bigger than the Pope's. Do any of them look to you like they're starving?'

Stamps had to admit they didn't. But they were the oddest assortment of people he'd ever seen. He was amazed at the resilience and creativity of these poor Italians who had obviously survived without the benefits of modern medicine. Many had teeth blackened by cavities, or no teeth at all. One young woman had the prettiest hair and face he'd ever seen, but a wandering left eye that roamed crazily in its socket. Others had broken noses that were not healed. Some were disfigured by broken limbs that had not been set properly, legs bent by mortar shells, still others were missing an arm or a leg, and one young girl had no arms at all. Yet they were smiling, and while they clearly did not look like they were starving, they looked mighty close to it, and all were highly interested in the sizzling rabbit that was browning nicely on the fire. Stamps looked at Bishop and Hector. 'What do I do now?'

Hector walked over to one of the four packs that lay in Ludovico's front doorway. The Americans had paid Ludovico for four rabbits, the rest of them being so diseased and skinny they didn't seem worth buying. He pulled out the rabbits and several cans of rations, their last. 'We trade. Tell 'em what we got, and see what they got. I'd give anything for fresh vegetables.'

And so the bartering began, knick for knack, tit for tat. A knife for this, a can of coffee for that. The villagers brought fish, eels, chestnuts, olives, grapes, and real wine. The soldiers produced K rations, D rations, Bishop's cookies, Bibles, letters from home, pocket knives, phone wire, bullets. The bartering went on for hours.

As the villagers traded and cajoled, mimicking the soldiers and even one another, gathering around the kid to wonder who he was, Stamps felt something was wrong. He knew better than to get close to these people. It went against his every instinct as a soldier. Yet he couldn't help himself. The kid was beautiful, plus Stamps was starting to have a good feeling. They had waited and waited for the new marching orders from Captain Nokes back at base but they never came, and as the days passed, and the orders changed from hold for four hours to hold for eight hours to hold for a day to a week to we'll get back to you, Stamps began to see his luck turning. The silent radio was his first piece of good luck within the division in two years.

The Army had been a bitter disappointment for him. He couldn't wait to join after he graduated from college. Everywhere he went, he'd read in the Negro press about the famous all-Negro 92nd Division, the Buffalo Soldiers. They were being sent to Italy to fight as men, and Stamps signed on the day after college, a decision he regretted the moment he set foot at Fort Huachuca training camp, which was rife with dissent and rancor: blacks punished severely by Southern white commanders, Negro plots to retaliate by killing white commanders, Negroes on furlough beaten to death by white civilian mobs, sometimes aided by sheriff deputies who were frightened at the thought of fifteen thousand armed Negroes in their midst. Negroes knifing other Negroes for calling themselves half Indian, Negroes trying to pass themselves off as half white. There was even an entire company of Negroes, two hundred men, the Casual Company, who refused to train or fight and were living in the stockade. The whole business disgusted him. He was alarmed by the hoops the division commanders leaped through so that poorly qualified white officers would always outrank black officers, because of the unwritten law that no colored should ever be able to tell a white man what to do. The policy had created all kinds of problems in the field – including his current predicament. Captain Nokes didn't know shit about artillery, and everybody knew it. He was from engineering. If Nokes had fired that fuckin' eighty-millimeter, the Krauts would have vacated his squad's sector at the Cinquale and they'd be at base now, getting ready to eat the turkey and mashed potato dinner they'd been promised for Christmas. Bishop was right. It was a mistake, he decided, for the Army to allow the colored to fight as combat soldiers. For what? To fight the enemy? Which enemy? The Germans? The Italians? The enemy was irony and truth and hypocrisy, that was the real enemy. That was the enemy that was killing him.

Stamps had met the real enemy the moment the colored troops arrived in Naples on the troop carrier *Mariposo*. They had climbed over the destroyed French fleet from boat to boat, their feet never touching the water, and watched the Italian civilians pouring off the harbor, paddling their small rowboats into the bay to meet the carrier. When the huge boat released its garbage, Stamps was shocked to see the Italians fish through it with their hands and nets, pulling out hot dogs, meat, bread, unopened cans of Spam and coffee. Outside the wire grate fence of the harbor's compound where the Negro troops were assembled, hundreds of Italians stood in ragged clothes – toothless old women, children begging for food. Stamps couldn't believe his eyes. The white commanders had issued strict orders not to feed the Italians. 'There are enemy Fascists disguised among them,' they said. 'You could be feeding the enemy.' But no colored soldier who laid eyes on those starving people that first day could not feel sympathy. Stamps watched every soldier he knew, even Bishop, sorry bastard that he was, fill his chow plate three or four times, then quietly back up to the fence to scrape its contents off into the pots and hands of the starving Italian refugees.

They did it every day. It was a running joke, the lines of colored men standing with their backs to the fences, the hundreds of Italians standing behind them, chowing down. And the Italians were grateful, too. They loved the soldiers back. They kissed them on the face. They touched their hands. They spread flowers on the bodies of those who died. They treated them like humans, better than the Americans did. The Italians were like the colored, Stamps thought bitterly, they know what it's like to be on the outside looking in. Feeding the enemy. He smiled at the irony of it. Who was the enemy? In America, Germans could eat first class, go where he couldn't go, live where he couldn't live, get jobs where he couldn't, and over here in Europe they were killing Jews like it was lunch. He'd read all about it in the Negro press. How the first American troops were finding giant camps full of dead Jews, burned to death, cities in Poland with human ash falling like snow from the smokestacks of the giant ovens where they were burning children, entire families. What Negro would do that? A Negro couldn't even think up enough hate to do that. A Negro was trying to make rent, save up enough to buy milk for his kids, survive this fucked-up war, and still, when the war was over, when all the fighting was done and all the people made up, a German could go to America and live well, start a factory, work in business, run a bank, while Stamps would still be . . . a nigger. He'd be lucky to get a job delivering their mail.

Sometimes Stamps felt his conscience was going to snap in two. He was constantly caught between showing his good face to the enlisted men and slogging through the bullshit that came from above him. A man like Bishop didn't understand. All he wanted was a warm place to shit and a piece of tail. Yet the larger irony of it all was that despite the war, despite the slogging in trenches, the mud, the rain, despite the sulking coloreds and the redneck captains, Stamps loved the Army. The

Army had brought him to Italy, and he felt freer in Italy than he had ever felt in his life. The Italians had a lot on their minds, that was for certain – they were in the middle of a civil war, and dying – but one thing they didn't have on their mind was keeping the colored man down. They didn't seem to care whether Stamps was colored or not. They gave the colored man something he could neither buy nor earn in America, no matter how many stripes or combat badges or hero ribbons they pinned on him: respect. Stamps quietly noted that the Americans and German POWs were alike in their disdain for the Italians. The soldiers' arrogance, their lack of respect for these dignified, humorous, spirited people who had done nothing more than to be living in the wrong place at the wrong time amazed Stamps. *And they were all white, too, all of them.* He couldn't get over that.

Italians, he concluded, didn't want their share of the cut for being white. They seemed not to care. They were looking to get to the next day. No wonder their music was so good, he thought, all that yelling and passion, all that opera. They got it, he thought. They understood it. Love. Food. Passion. Life's short. Pass me a cigarette. Gimme that grappa. Live a little. They were like coloreds without the jook joints. He decided, as he watched Renata appear out of a house wearing a dress for the first time and illuminating the piazza with her beauty, that he wanted to live in Italy someday. Right here in Bornacchi was a good start. The silent radio that had ceased barking stupid orders was a blessing. Radio be damned. He looked at the radio on the ground and actually entertained thoughts of destroying it. But he had the others to think of, and there was the small question of his dignity, of which he supposed there was a shred left. Somewhere along with his dignity, he supposed he had to throw in his training and his army discipline, too, though there actually wasn't much left of it. All the good officers he knew who followed orders, colored and white, were killed or so screwed up mentally they would never be right after the war. The hell with it. He was going to do like the rest of his men. Survive. Be stupid. Get lazy. Fall in love with a dumb kid like Train did, or maybe find out what this beautiful woman's name was. Why not? He hoped the radio never buzzed and crackled again.

A card game had started on Ludovico's steps. Two women had taken Train's boy and were trying to get him to eat an apple. A chicken had mysteriously appeared and was crackling over the fire. Wine was being passed around, and there were toasts to Christmas, which was only four days away. Out of the corner of his eye, Stamps saw Train giving a piggyback ride to a little girl. Someone had a guitar out and began to play a Christmas song. Bishop was wooing a long-legged girl by the fire. Several more chickens had miraculously appeared. It was a regular party, a real holiday party.

Hector was seated next to the fire. He broke off a piece of rabbit leg and passed it to a middle-aged *signora* and her little boy. The *signora* looked with more than mild interest at Hector's long fingers. 'Hec, something's wrong here,' Stamps said softly.

'You're right,' Hector answered him, as the *signora* grasped him by the hand and pulled him up for a quick dance around the fire. The guitarist struck up a faster song. 'But if you think on it hard enough,' he gasped, as the woman flung him in a circle, laughing wildly, 'maybe tomorrow will never come.'

14

THE GERMAN

But tomorrow did come, and with it came snow and a German.

The sun had stretched its fingers above the mountain's horizon, and snow was falling lightly on the wooded ridge facing Ludovico's house. Stamps had just emerged from the alley behind the house and was washing his face in the icy creek when the German appeared beyond the stone wall, walking down the ridge from above. Stamps saw him and flattened behind the waist-high wall, reached for his carbine, then remembered he'd left it inside. He ran inside the house to grab it and tell the others, but Train had gone behind the house to take the kid to the bathroom. Bishop and Hector were gone.

Stamps ran to the corner where his carbine stood, grabbed it, checked to see if it was still loaded, then ran back outside and took a position against the wall, his rifle aimed at the approaching German.

Across the open field and down the mountain ridge the German came, alone. He was helmetless and unarmed, his hands at his sides, staggering down the grassy ridge of the mountain as if his legs could barely carry his weight. Behind him, the bushes parted and four young men appeared, holding rifles trained on him. Stamps heard yelling in Ludovico's house and in the other houses, and Bishop and Hector appeared out of nowhere. Stamps snapped, 'Hector, go get Train and the old man.'

Hector went into the house and emerged with Ludovico and Renata.

'Oh, no,' Renata murmured, crossing herself as she ran down to the creek to join the Americans.

Stamps, Hector, and Bishop crouched, their rifles cocked, as the Italians and their prisoner slowly made their way down the ridge and across the field, and approached the creek. Renata waited until they were about thirty feet off and shouted at them. They shouted back.

'What did they say?' Stamps asked.

'They want to eat.'

'Tell them to put down their weapons and we'll feed them all they want.'

Renata shouted and the Italians responded. 'They say they'll put theirs down if you put yours down.'

Stamps looked at Hector. 'That's what they said?'

'Sounds right.'

'I ain't lowering this gun. They could be Germans disguised.'

Renata snorted. 'They're not Germans.' She motioned the partisans forward.

The Italians advanced slowly into the creek that fronted Ludovico's house and waded across.

'What you think? You think they Italian?' Stamps asked Bishop.

'If it looks like fish, smells like fish, and tastes like fish, you can bet it ain't buzzard.'

Stamps watched Renata march up to the Italians, who had emerged from the water onto the snowbank. She walked up to the one who had huge ears and grabbed an ear. Rodolfo winced as Renata shook him by his ear. 'No German has ears like this,' she declared. She said something in Italian, and the four partisans laughed.

Stamps lowered his weapon slightly as the Italians approached to within ten feet, but he kept the barrel close to his hip just in case. The leader, a short, thin, balding man with a handsome, slender face, motioned for the others to stand back. His eyes were dark and hard as pool balls, his stare as straight as a razor's edge. His face was weathered and seemed to have the wind in it, as if shifting breezes and strong gales blew about it without stirring it. He was a young man, Stamps guessed, perhaps in his mid-twenties, and while his clothing was worn, Stamps could see that beneath it the man was built for power and speed. Though he moved slowly, he was lithe and easy in his movements, like a panther or a small mountain lion. Stamps was immediately afraid of him. He glanced at the others. They were young, too. One was a boy whose rifle was nearly as long as he was.

The leader came forward to meet Stamps.

'Tell him to show me some papers,' Stamps said. Hector translated.

'This is my papers,' Peppi said in English, nodding at his rifle.

The door to Ludovico's house opened, and Train emerged, holding the boy.

Stamps glanced at him but kept the barrel of his gun up. 'Train, put that kid inside.'

Train approached excitedly. 'This boy's talking, Lieutenant. It's important.'

'Not now, Train.' Stamps kept his eyes on Peppi.

The Italian looked at Train, the giant with the head of a statue tied to his hip and the tiny child in his arms, and smiled, just for a moment. There was neither fear nor friendliness in the smile, only recognition. Stamps decided that not only did he not like this stranger with the wind in his face, he didn't trust him, either. The man was clever, too smart, and hard.

Out of the corner of his eye, Stamps could make out several villagers approaching, including Ettora, who with her poor eyesight fumbled about from side to side, banging into walls and tripping over rocks and other obstructions as she approached. Several old men and women followed her. Stamps barked at Hector, 'Tell them to stay back.'

Hector shouted orders, but the villagers ignored him. They approached, and as they did, Stamps could see they were animated. Some began shouting. Stamps couldn't believe they were the same gentle, friendly people from the previous night. Several things had gone on during the night that he didn't want to know about. For one, Bishop had disappeared with the long-legged young student from the Academy of Art and Design and Hector with the old *signora* who had spun him around for several dances. Last Stamps remembered, he'd drunk a bottle of grappa and had fallen asleep singing 'Valentino' with Ludovico and two other toothless old men. The four of them had fallen asleep together on Ludovico's floor after playing poker. Stamps couldn't remember if he'd lost the squad's three backpacks or if he'd won one of Ludovico's four sacks of chestnuts, which suddenly appeared from yet another cavern beneath the floorboards, which seemed to conceal endless treasures. He remembered only that the four of them had fallen asleep together, huddled by the fire, and that he'd awakened shivering in the middle of the night to see old man Ludovico get up and throw a fat log on the fire. He remembered thinking, in his drunken stupor, what a nice gesture that was, for the old geezer to make such an effort to warm them all. He was liking Italy more and more. He decided that if he survived the war – a big if – he wanted to stay. He'd never held an old white person's hand before in his life. He'd never slept with three old white geezers before. They'd huddled together against the cold and slept like children.

Now the bubble had burst. The Italians were arguing heatedly. He noticed that the leader of the partisans did not flinch as several villagers harangued him with pointing fingers and accusation in their voices. He seemed focused on Ludovico, who was talking with the others. Ludovico said something to the leader, who responded. Ludovico's eyes widened in what appeared to be fear at something the leader said, and then the old man stepped back and the villagers suddenly hushed. Stamps saw a flash of fear pass across Renata's face as she stared at the angry partisan.

'Tell him to come inside to eat and we'll talk this over,' Stamps said to Hector.

Hector translated, but Peppi shook his head.

'I'm in charge here. We have jurisdiction,' Stamps heard himself saying. It sounded ridiculous even as he said it. This Italian, he thought, is not like me. I'm a trained soldier. This man, he is a . . . Stamps didn't know what the hell he was, but whatever he was, he sure didn't need vexing. Renata said something to the leader that made his gaze soften slightly. The leader nodded and lowered his rifle. The four Italians, pushing their prisoner in front of them, filed into Ludovico's house, followed by the Americans.

The entire village tried to cram inside Ludovico's house to see the prisoner, except Train, who stayed in the bedroom with the boy. The partisans sat at the table, and Renata poured them bowls of soup.

Immediately, they began gorging themselves. As they ate, Stamps looked the German over closely.

He was young, maybe nineteen, ragged and filthy, with a gaunt face, hollow jaws, blond hair, and blue eyes, which stared at the food with such jagged desperation that Stamps figured he probably hadn't eaten in days. Stamps poured some soup into a cup and handed it to the prisoner. The partisans glared furiously as the German gulped the soup down.

'Where you from?' Stamps asked.

The German soldier motioned desperately with his hands, indicating he spoke no English. Hector stepped forward and spoke to him in Italian, then Spanish, to no avail.

'Now we go back,' Bishop said. 'You wanna get on the radio?'

'No. We wait till Nokes radios again. That's what he said to do.'

'What the fuck is wrong with you, man? We got what he wanted. They said to get a German prisoner. We got one. He's setting right here, eating like a butcher's dog.'

'How do we know he's a German?'

'Who the fuck is this guy? Joe Louis?'

Stamps seemed uncertain. 'Well,' he said, 'we have to wait till they radio us to tell them.'

'What for? So they can make us get six more? Hell no. I say we take him over the mountains and back where it's safe.'

'What's safe, Bishop? There's Germans over the mountains. That's what the old man said.'

'What's the matter with you, Stamps? We can't sit out here with these wops till one of these *signorinas* decides to give you some pussy. You had your chance last night.'

Stamps felt the blood rising to his face. Hector he could stand. Even

182

Train, ignorant as he was, Stamps could tolerate. But something about Bishop pushed his button every time. He saw in him every shiftless, shuffling Negro preacher he had ever known; people who acted just like whitey wanted them to act, chasing tail like they just couldn't wait to get back to the womb, smiling in front of whitey, always laughing, playing cards, shuffling, riding the railroads, playing fiddles at jook joints, drinking and shining and partying, listening to low-down jazz on Saturday and hollering the gospel to God on Sunday. They held niggers back a hundred years. He undid the Colt .45 revolver at his belt.

'I can court-martial you right here, Bishop.'

'Go 'head.'

Peppi spoke. 'This is our prisoner.'

These were the first words he had spoken to the room, and he said them in English. The tone and gravity of his words silenced everyone. It was as if a deep-freeze had suddenly descended.

'You had plenty time to talk to him before you got here,' Stamps said.

Peppi shook his head, showing he did not understand. Hector translated. Peppi nodded, then spoke in English again. 'None speak German. We hope somebody here speak German.'

'They got ten niggers speak German back at the base camp. Come with us there and we'll get it done.'

Peppi listened to Hector's translation and shook his head. 'No,' he said in English. 'He's ours.' He rose from the table, his soup unfinished, and barked an order in Italian. The other three partisans rose as one, stuffing bread into their pockets and reaching for their rifles and the German prisoner.

Bishop raised a hand toward Peppi, who drew back. 'What's going on here?'

Peppi spoke to Stamps directly in English. 'We have some questions to ask him. After he answers our questions, he can go. He is not leaving before that time.'

'Hell he ain't.'

Peppi turned and pointed his rifle at the German's head. Just then, the door opened and Train entered, holding the boy. The German, with the barrel of Peppi's gun pointed at his face, suddenly did something unexpected. He awoke from his stupor and stared at the boy, a long, glazed stare, and began to cry, babbling in German with loud, long wails. Then he bashed his head against the table. He banged it again and again with such force that the table shook, and the boy, cradled in Train's arms, began to cry in fear. Loud, terrible howls – of the soldier and the boy – filled the room.

'See what y'all done!' Train cried. 'Got him all upset.' Train cradled the child's head against his mighty chest, and with bandoleers and statue head swinging, turned and pushed through the villagers toward the doorway. The boy's wails echoed softly as Train carried him out into the snow, leaving behind the German, whose howling had modulated into bleating sobs.

Stamps was confused. He lowered his rifle.

'Christ,' Bishop said. 'Let 'em take 'im, Stamps. I don't give a damn. I ain't fighting nobody over no damn German.'

Stamps stared at Peppi for a long time before speaking to him. 'Let's talk about this outside.' He nodded at the German. 'He ain't goin' nowhere. We got a captain coming we got to wait for, anyhow.'

Peppi looked around the room, then nodded slowly.

Four of them, Stamps, Hector, Peppi, and Rodolfo, exited to talk in the snow while the other two partisans stayed, their rifles pointed at the

German. The moment the four men stepped outside, the villagers inside Ludovico's house began talking heatedly. 'I told you!' Ludovico hissed to Renata. She ignored him. She looked at the two partisans. 'Hurry up and eat,' she said.

The two boys ate.

Outside the house, Bishop paced back and forth while Stamps and Hector argued with Peppi. Finally, Bishop stalked over to Train, who was seated on a crate by the side of the house within view of Stamps and the others, the now calmer boy sucking his thumb, still cradled against Train's chest. Bishop lit a cigarette and watched Train rock the boy, then begin a series of taps against the boy's arm. The boy tapped back.

'What you doin', love tappin' him?'

'Ain't love tappin'. He talks that way.'

'Nigger, you got too much time on your hands.'

Train ignored Bishop. He was focusing on the boy, who tapped again. Train's face clouded for a moment, then he said, 'You sure?' and tapped the boy's arm twice.

The boy tapped back once.

Train turned to Bishop. 'He's scared stiff.'

'Shit. So am I.'

'He says one of them up there was on that hill yonder near the church and done a bad thing.'

'How you know he says all that?'

'I knows it, man. We got a way of talking. He says he was up there at that church.'

'So that's where he comes from. He must've seen that German up there.'

'Yeah, he seen him. He seen the Italian, too.'

'Who?'

'That one, with the big ears.' Train pointed at Rodolfó.

'That don't make no sense to me,' Bishop said.

'What around here do?' Train asked.

1 5

RUN

It took two hours to sort it out, standing outdoors in the heavy snowfall, and by the time they were done, Stamps was more confused than he had been at the beginning. The partisans had said the German was part of the 16th Panzer SS division, which had killed a large number of civilians at the church, that much he understood. Something about a sign posted. That much he also got, but the business about who posted it he did not understand. The German had indicated that there was an old man nearby who knew the whole story, and that he himself had not participated in any killings.

Given the anger in the faces of the villagers, who crowded around the German as if they wanted to kill him, Stamps understood that, too. He'd deny it to the end if he were the German, whether he'd done it or not.

But what he did not understand was the reaction of the youngster to the German, and vice versa. The crowd in Ludovico's had taken the German outside, and when Train, with the boy in his arms, had drifted closer to the angry crowd, the boy had become visibly agitated again. And the German, seeing the youngster, inexplicably dropped to his knees, repeating something in a trembling, soft voice, over and over, in Italian. The boy motioned for Train to kneel so he could move closer to the German, and he had responded to the German – in Italian, so softly that only those standing close by, including Peppi, could hear it.

That was new.

And so was Peppi's response.

The partisan had turned to his main lieutenant, the one with the big ears they called Rodolfo, and questioned him pointedly. There was a flurry of talk back and forth. Several villagers looked on anxiously.

Stamps said, 'Hector, what's going on?'

Hector had just returned from putting together the radio and signaling to division headquarters that they had a German and a problem.

'They said hold tight. Nokes is coming himself. Take him about a day. He has to go by night.'

'Great. I feel better already.' Stamps knew Nokes would watch his own tail. If Nokes got through, then it was safe to return to base.

'Something else. We're not going back. There's a possibility we might attack on Christmas.'

'What? Who said that?'

'Birdsong. He got on the radio after Nokes was out of earshot.'

'From where?'

''Round here, that's what he's saying.'

'Shit, man. There's no Germans around here, 'cept this one.'

'Well, that's what they're saying. They're saying there might be a whole bunch more.'

Stamps felt his heart faltering. 'Maybe this German does know something.'

'Hell if I know.'

Stamps looked at the German. The partisans were talking quietly among themselves, and the other villagers had gathered menacingly around the prisoner. Some began kicking him. Two old ladies threw rocks at him. Bishop placed himself in front of the German and directed them to stop, but several more had now gathered, and the small crowd suddenly surged forward, talking and cursing. Bishop tried to push them back. 'Stamps, we better move him outta here.'

Stamps agreed, though he could not understand what was happening. Clearly, the villagers wanted the German's head. Still, they didn't seem to like Peppi much either. Peppi, for his part, now seemed more interested in his own partisan soldier than in the German, talking to him in a measured but heated tone. The other partisan was shaking his head animatedly.

And the other problem, Stamps thought wryly, was that if there was one German, surely there were more Germans close by, and if division was planning an attack, well . . . That part made his stomach hurt.

He said to Hector, 'Tell these folks they're gonna have to evacuate. If they ask why, tell 'em there's an attack coming through here.'

Hector barked out the orders, which caused further consternation and questions, which Hector seemed to have trouble answering.

As if in answer to everyone's questions, they heard shelling and artillery fire in the distance. Big fire. Heavy artillery. Everyone – the villagers, the partisans, the Americans – stopped and listened.

'Shit, where's that coming from?' Stamps said.

'That's in back of us,' Bishop answered. 'Toward base.'

'Let's take him inside.'

Most of the villagers scattered toward their homes. Hector and Bishop flanked the German. Stamps faced Peppi, his jaw set firm. He stared at Peppi as he spoke. 'Hector, tell him we're taking the German inside with us. He can come if he wants, but nobody's leaving till Nokes gets here.'

Hector translated, and Peppi shrugged, then responded in Italian.

'He says he's not safe here with us. He's safer up in the mountains.'

'It ain't safe up there. Tell him he's safer with us. Let's fight together.'

The translation came, and Peppi spoke to Stamps, directly this time, with a thick accent. 'Thank you. Next time. We go see where the Germans are.' He pointed to Rodolfo. 'He will stay here to watch the German for you. And for us.' Rodolfo smiled and shrugged nervously.

Stamps didn't like it, but it was the best he could do. He looked at Peppi squarely. For the first time, he saw some bend in the Italian. 'Hector, tell him I give him my word that nothing will happen to this guy till Nokes gets here. Birdsong speaks German. Tell him I promise to let Birdsong talk to him before we take him back.' Stamps had no idea how he'd get Nokes to go along with his plan, but it was the best he could do. Either that or risk a shoot-out with these partisans, and given the granite stare of Peppi and his hardened band, Stamps got the distinct impression that would not be a pleasant undertaking.

Peppi pulled Stamps and Hector aside, out of earshot of the others. He spoke carefully to Hector, who translated. 'He says watch him close at night. Someone may try to kill him.'

'That might be him,' Stamps said wryly.

Peppi smiled bitterly and waved his little finger as he spoke. 'I am no bandit. I am not SS,' he said softly. 'I don't kill for nothing. You watch him close.' Peppi looked at the German, and Stamps had the distinct feeling that the young partisan was trying to make a decision.

With that he turned and left, his small band, minus Rodolfo, following, trudging toward the ridge from which they'd come.

Stamps didn't wait until they were out of sight. He hustled his three soldiers inside, placed Bishop inside Ludovico's living room with the partisan and the German, then posted Train and Hector at different windows. When all was set, Stamps called Hector over to the kitchen. They spoke quietly for a moment. Hector nodded and went to the bedroom, where Train was posted at the back window, facing the alley. The giant man stood at the window, his rifle propped on the floor barrel up, watching the partisans slowly make their way up the ridge and disappear. It was beginning to snow harder. The kid was jumping on Ludovico's bed, making gurgling noises and happily rolling himself in the old man's best woolen quilt.

'Diesel, Stamps wants me to talk to the kid.'

The giant said nothing. He stared glumly at the driving snow, thinking about his future. Nokes's coming meant they would have to pull back to base, and when they did, where would that leave the kid? Maybe the captain would let Train keep the boy, if he asked him the right way. Train had no clue as to what Captain Nokes was like. He'd never really heard the man's name before now. He'd had no interest in it before. It had never made sense to him to learn the names of the white captains, because they left so fast and whatever they said was law, anyway. They didn't seem to mind that he didn't know their names. All he had to do was smile and say 'Yes, sir' or 'No, sir' and that seemed to please them. They liked him. They said it all the time. They said he was a 'good Negro.' He took no offense at it. He didn't see the point of getting all riled up because a white man was running things and telling the colored what to do. That's how it had been his whole life.

But this was different. For the first time, he had a stake in something. He never really cared about Old Man Parson's mules back home, the cotton that his mother worked her fingers to the bone picking on her sharecropped land, the father he didn't know, the old rickety shack that didn't belong to them, the Army, the white man's rules. None of it had mattered to him. They put a uniform on him and made him run around, and that was fine because he got forty-one dollars a month. For fifty-two Sundays a year for twenty-one years – his entire life – he'd learned that even his own life wasn't his own. It belonged to God. Other than his mother and his grandmother, he had no stake in anyone, any place, any land, any thing, except for this little somebody. In the boy, he saw land, lots of it, a farm in Mt. Gilead, North Carolina, where he would plow mules and pick the boy up at school and bring him home, and the boy would grow to be a man, a white man, and no one would tell him what to do, because he was white. In the density of Train's own thick mind, the walls of impossibilities that loomed ahead never occurred to him, the centuries of granite, concrete, steel-strong prejudice that awaited him back in America. This boy was a miracle. He was an angel. An angel had no color. The boy was Santa Claus. Everybody said it. Everybody liked Santa Claus. The boy was like him. He was nobody. He was invisible.

Train shifted as he stared out the window. 'Nobody thinks he sees nuthin', Hector. But he sees it all. Train knows.'

'I know, champ.'

'Y'think I'm gonna have to give him back?'

'Don't know, Diesel, but I gotta talk to him.'

'G'wan.'

Hector sat on the bed and reached into his pocket for a D bar. '*Cioccolato?*' he asked.

The kid bounced up and down and ignored him.

'Diesel, I need your help, man.'

Train approached, sat on the bed, and the boy popped into his lap. Train tapped on his chest twice.

'My name is Angelo,' the boy said to Hector in Italian.

'Where are you from?'

'I don't know.'

'You remember the man in the uniform?'

'There were a lot.'

'The one just now. The one on the hill. The one who cried in the kitchen.'

The little boy's face darkened. '*Sì.*'

'What did he tell you on the hill just now?'

'He told me what he told me before.'

'Before where?'

'Before. At the church. At the fire.'

'What fire?'

'The fire at the church.'

'Where's your mama and papa?'

The boy was silent.

'*Dove mama?*'

The boy curled into a little ball. Train waved Hector back. 'Aw, Hec, leave him be.'

'One more thing,' Hector said. 'Stamps told me to ask him. Just one more thing.'

Hector leaned down, his face close to the boy. 'What did the soldier tell you on the hill just now?'

'He told me what he told me before,' Angelo repeated.

'What did he tell you before?'

'He told me to run. He told me to run as fast as I can.'

16

SENDING NOKES

Colonel Driscoll sat in his tent smoking a cigarette and staring at his reports under a candle's flickering light. The report that the Germans were amassing four regiments near the Lama di Sotto ridge, eleven thousand men – plus four tank companies with 250 Italian civilians to carry ammo – was confirmed by a second British aircraft photo and a *carabiniere* from the area, though no German prisoners had trickled in. The Germans, apparently, were holding tight and not letting anybody clear, gathering steam, which is what he would do, too, if he were they. The prisoner they had in Bornacchi was important. Driscoll turned and ordered his staff sergeant, who was standing behind him awaiting orders, to have the prisoner taken straight to division HQ as soon as he arrived.

'They can't get him here,' the sergeant said.

'Why not?'

'Patrols between us and them, and the partisans who have him won't release him.'

'Get Nokes in here.'

Driscoll had wanted to send Nokes earlier, but the old man, General Allman, had made him wait. 'We gotta be sure it's worth the risk,' Allman had said. 'Why risk more men if we're not sure the intelligence we have is clean?' But now they couldn't wait.

Nokes arrived. Driscoll, looking at Nokes's leathery neck and grizzled hair, decided he would have preferred to send Captain Rudden, because Rudden got the job done, but he didn't want to risk losing the best white captain he had. Plus, Lieutenant Birdsong was Nokes's second, and Birdsong was pretty good. He had sense. It didn't escape Driscoll, the irony of it, that he was dependent on the colored second-in-command to pull off this rescue mission. The war, he decided, was teaching him all sorts of new tricks. He briefly considered promoting Birdsong to captain, then decided against it. It would cause too many ripples, especially with General Allman, who didn't want coloreds commanding blacks, let alone whites.

'Take Lieutenant Birdsong and a squad of four in two jeeps, and bring back that squad and their prisoner,' Driscoll said.

He watched fear climb into Nokes's face. 'Can't we just get the information by radio, sir? Until the weather clears at least? Birdsong speaks German.'

'You want me to put Birdsong on the radio with the German prisoner so he can have a friendly chat and tell the enemy what we know? Is that your thinking?'

Driscoll could see Nokes didn't like the situation. Too goddamn bad, he thought. The division was short. There were not enough replacements. The Army hadn't figured on the colored getting all shot up. They'd underestimated the Germans' strength in Italy. There were no more colored troops available to replace the ones they'd lost, except the 366th Regiment, a tough, smart National Guard outfit, but they had taken heavy losses and were demoralized. Their commander, Colonel King, had quit in frustration – a disgrace as far as King was concerned – because, King said, Allman didn't want colored commanders. Well, this was war, no one had time to deal with the Negro's claims. And besides, Nokes had screwed up. He would have to make it up on his end. They needed to know where to place their strongest regiments when the Germans came. Otherwise, they could be beaten back or even overrun.

Driscoll saw Nokes eyeing the snow-filled sky outside the tent, fretting. He said calmly, 'Those four men been up there nine days, with short supply and ammo. They made it okay. You can make it with six.'

Nokes saluted, turned on his heel, and left.

Colonel Driscoll sat at his desk glaring at the candle as it burned. He had a bigger problem, a personal problem that was nearly as bad, in the form of a telegram that had arrived on his desk that morning, telling him that General Allman's only son had been killed in action in France.

Driscoll placed the telegram in front of him on the desk and tried to think clearly. Nothing in his life had prepared him for this moment. A devout Roman Catholic, he had a sudden urge to confess his sins and seek absolution, because he loved Allman, racist or not. He had to admit it to himself, even though they were polar opposites. He was a Yankee, Allman a Southerner. He was a West Point grad. Allman was a VMI grad, five feet two inches of blue-eyed, two-fisted fury. Driscoll was constantly putting out fires between Allman and the colored, whose hatred of Allman was not without cause. He was demanding. He was harsh. He did not spare their feelings. He did not care about their racial pride, and, in fact, was against it. He took risks with them. His training marches were hell. He disapproved of black officers. Any disobedience was punished severely. He made it clear that on the battlefield he would put a bullet into the head of any man who showed cowardice, colored or white.

Yet he loved and defended the coloreds, even as he despised them. How could you love a group of people and hate them at the same time? Driscoll had seen Allman at night, alone, reading over the high casualty figures, despondent, sipping brandy, roaring with rage about the Negro press, Eleanor Roosevelt, the lack of naval firepower to support the 92nd, and General Park, his superior, who commanded the Fifth Army, who was unlike Allman in every way. Park had political aspirations that reached beyond the war, aspirations that seemed more important than the lives of Allman's men, his 'boys,' Allman called them. Allman hated politicians almost as much as he hated the cowards among his troops. 'Scared niggers,' he scoffed. But the brave ones he loved. He honored. He wrote letters to their families even as he muttered that their families probably couldn't read them. He attended the bodies of the dead himself at times. He would have demoted Nokes instantly if he'd found out about that little number he'd pulled at the Cinquale Canal, hanging his men out to dry, which is why Driscoll didn't tell him and gave strict orders that anyone who did would be court-martialed, because behind Nokes there were ten other white captains just like him, and what was the point?

None of them, white or colored, understood Allman. He lived and died for battle. He'd risk the life of his white soldiers, too. He sent Driscoll, his own chief of staff, out on patrols several times. He was willing to risk Driscoll's life, and even his own, riding up to the front lines in a jeep with two red flags on it, which might as well have had a sign 'Shoot Me' plastered on the side of it. The German artillery gunners in the ridges above them, who regularly blasted to pieces any American who wasn't hidden behind a rock or tree, must have thought they were dreaming when they saw an American jeep with two red flags on it and a white man sitting in front barreling up Highway 88 outside Seravezza. The Germans weren't stupid. They knew the whites were the commanders. They blew the jeep to pieces. Allman's driver was killed, but Allman was thrown into a ditch, unhurt. Driscoll heard that several colored soldiers had cheered when they heard about it. He was furious and sought the culprits, but when he inquired, he was met with blank stares and shrugging shoulders. The coloreds did not understand Allman. He was unstoppable when it came to battle. It was in his blood. It had nothing to do with race. He was a warrior, and he expected everyone around him to be one, too.

And now Driscoll had to tell the old man that his greatest warrior, his greatest pride, was dead.

Driscoll placed the telegram on his desk and tried to think clearly. There was no easy way to handle this. The kid could have had any command post he wanted – Allman's brother-in-law was General Marshall, after all – but he'd gone with his father's wishes. They'd talked about it several times. 'To be a commander, you cannot be a humble man,' Allman always said. 'If you are a humble man, making decisions that cost the lives of your subordinates is an almost insupportable burden. You have to have ego, pride, confidence, detachment to send any man into harm's way and be able to handle the casualties that occur. That's why I want my son to serve as a lieutenant in rifle infantry first. I want him to know the full spectrum of battle before he moves to a higher level. It'll make him a better commander.'

Now that better commander was no more, Driscoll thought bitterly, and I get to deliver the news. Seated at his desk, he picked up the telegram, folded it, tucked it in his breast pocket, and marched out to

Allman's green command van, which was parked under a grove of trees just a short distance from division headquarters tent. He knocked softly, then entered.

Allman was seated at his desk, four maps before him, and the colonels of the 370th and 365th regiments peering over his shoulder. Driscoll asked if he could speak to him privately about an urgent matter.

Allman looked up from the desk, and his hard blue gaze struck Driscoll like bullets. 'We're planning an attack here,' he grunted.

'It's urgent,' Driscoll insisted.

Allman dismissed the colonels from the van. Driscoll waited until the door was closed, then handed Allman the telegram. Allman opened it and held it under the table lamp amid the maps.

The general's stern face, weathered by a thousand battles and a million disastrous combat reports, crumpled in utter disbelief and despair for just a moment as his eyes sped across the page, then righted itself. He sat at his desk, holding the paper aloft under the lamp, staring at it, motionless.

'Does my wife know?' he asked.

'Yes. Your daughter as well.'

Allman was silent, frozen, still holding the telegram.

'Do you want me to call the doctor to give you something?' Driscoll asked gently.

Allman stared ahead for several long moments, his face illuminated by the table lamp. Then he placed his hands over his forehead as if he were trying to peer into the distance.

'No. I want to sleep for a while. No disturbances till tomorrow morning.'

Driscoll swayed, the tension in his forehead tightening to a knot.

'It's December twenty-second. We have roughly fourteen hours before the Germans plan their charge. If we mount our attack, we have six hours. I can get Brigadier General Birch to handle it if you want,' Driscoll said. He knew Allman did not trust Birch. Birch was an odd man, a bachelor, and second-rate. He was a god-awful strategist. His claim to fame was that he ran a singing platoon. Driscoll knew what Allman would say.

Allman seemed far away. He sighed a moment, his head in his hands. 'Give me an hour,' he said.

Driscoll backed out of the van into the traffic and flow of the division busily clattering behind him. He stood with his face to the door for a few moments, then with a sigh turned to face the bustling tanks and men going every which way. From the top of the steps to Allman's van, he saw a figure scurrying away, carrying a typewriter.

'Captain Nokes!'

Nokes turned and walked over and saluted. His leathery face wore the expression of a puppy dog caught chewing a pair of shoes.

Driscoll nodded at the typewriter. 'What's that for?'

'Need to requisition some new socks for the men before we leave. Trench foot, sir.'

'Were you going to order out for a hamburger and malted milk, too?'

Nokes's face reddened. 'No, sir.'

'What the hell are you waiting for?'

'Just thought it'd be okay to wait an hour or so for the weather to clear, sir.'

Driscoll felt rage crawl into his face. 'Drop that goddamn typewriter right now, form that squad, take two jeeps, and get your ass out there.

Don't come back here till you have bodies or dog tags or a German or all three.'

The typewriter splattered the snowy mud as Nokes saluted, turned, and fled. Driscoll watched him go, stifling the urge to run after him and kick him in the ass.

17

HECTOR

The booming artillery fire had died down, but Stamps knew the Germans were in pause mode. Whatever was coming was coming from both sides above the Serchio Valley. Another half day and the shelling that was threatening the ridges that surrounded them would land where they stood, and they would have to move because troops would not be far behind. He stood in the dead center of the village and watched the villagers moving back and forth listlessly.

Since the firing was coming from above, crisscrossing, with them near the center, they would have to decide which leg of the X to run up. Which way to run? If only he knew the woods. He decided to take a chance and trust the partisans. Not all of them, he knew, were trustworthy. They were supposed to be approved by the Office of Strategic Services at headquarters and to carry papers stating that. Otherwise, they could be the Italian army, or spies, or Fascists, or simply bandits who went with whoever was running things, German or American, he'd seen that, too. But there was no time now. The Italian with the big ears was guarding the prisoner in front of Ludovico's house. Stamps summoned him. 'Go take a look up that ridge' – he pointed to the west – 'and tell me if you see Germans over there.'

Stamps's order took several tries because the man did not speak English, but after a few more hand signals, the Italian nodded and took off, trotting for the ridge facing the village. Stamps watched the partisan's back as he climbed the mountain. Something about the guy was not right, he felt, but he had no time to think about it now.

As he climbed the ridge, Rodolfo could feel the American's eyes aimed at his back like a sniper's scope. The American *tenente* was smart, he thought. He would have to be extra careful now. The Negro Americans had nearly ruined everything. And they had come by mistake, too! They were lost. That's what the Spanish-speaking one said. Rodolfo cursed his luck. He wanted to scream, thinking about it. He paused a few seconds and breathed deeply to calm himself. Everything could still be salvaged. Then he leaped forward, climbing the ridge until the *tenente* was out of sight.

Sporadic shelling still came from several ridges over to the west, landing on the cliffs opposite Rodolfo, but that didn't bother him. He was in no danger. Still, he was cold. He headed upward to a wide chasm, forded it by walking carefully along an icy eighteen-inch ledge that took him around it, then scaled yet another ridge that led toward an uppermost peak which he knew would afford him a view of the ridges directly across. Planting his feet into nooks and crannies, he hoisted himself up to the top of the cliff and lay on his stomach. From his position, he could see clear across the Serchio Valley, right into the eye of the Mountain of the Sleeping Man. He lay there motionless for several seconds, letting his eyes adjust to the sun, which shone directly in his face. He fully expected to see four or five advance squads of Germans making their way down Mt. Forato toward the Lama di Sotto ridge, with one or two cannon companies behind them. What he saw instead made his heart skip a beat, and he sucked in his breath.

The whitened snow trails beneath Mt. Forato were black, thick with German troops, thousands of them, marching steadily forward, clumsily stumbling and slogging down the mountain from the Sleeping Man's giant eye as they made their way toward the Lama di Sotto ridge, which led toward the Serchio Valley, Bornacchi, and the villages below. There were so many troops they blotted out the snow, pulling eighty-eights, cannons, and heavy artillery, with horses, mules, and civilians, the mass of men and machines forming a half circle nearly a mile wide, so that when they came down the ridge to blitzkrieg the valley, their flank would be several miles wide and create the pincer movement the Germans favored. There were more than he'd seen before. More than he had told the American commanders when he went to them disguised as a priest. Ten or twelve thousand maybe. And closer than he'd thought.

Still on his stomach, Rodolfo quickly slid away from the edge of the cliff, then scrambled to his feet and backtracked over the path he'd come. As he descended the ridge to Bornacchi, he saw Stamps watching him from the wall near Ludovico's. Standing next to Stamps was Renata.

Rodolfo trotted over, avoiding the *tenente*'s anxious gaze. Renata asked nervously, 'What did you see?'

Rodolfo shrugged. 'Nothing,' he said. 'They must be coming from the other direction.'

Renata translated to the *tenente*, who nodded a cautious thank you and inclined his head toward the German. 'You can go guard your friend again,' Stamps said. Rodolfo headed back toward the house, where the German sat out front, where Stamps had placed him so he could easily be seen. He felt the *tenente*'s eyes boring a hole in his back again.

Stamps and Renata watched Rodolfo take a seat on Ludovico's front steps.

'Something's wrong with him,' Renata said.

'Who?'

'Him,' she said, pointing at Rodolfo. 'He's afraid. 'I think he's afraid of you.'

'He ain't got nothing to be 'fraid of, unless he owes me some money. And even then . . . hell.' That's why they were there in the first place, Train owing Bishop money. Stamps wondered if he would have gone after Train if Bishop hadn't gone first. It all seemed so ridiculous. He turned to Renata, careful not to look her in the eye but rather staring someplace over her head. Her beauty seemed to cover everything. He noted that she was wearing another dress today, an even prettier one than last night's.

'We're going west, probably. That's where the least firing is. You all can travel with us.'

'Who?'

'Whoever wants to come. Everyone here. Evacuation. We gotta evacuate the town.'

'No one's going with you,' she said simply.

'Why not?'

'Look around you,' she said.

Stamps watched as the villagers went about their business, scurrying to and fro, even as the distant shelling began again. He was incredulous. 'They're loco,' he said.

'Loco?'

'*Pazzi*. Crazy.'

'Where can they go? The people who ran to Sant'Anna's went there because they thought it was safe. They're all dead. No place is safe.'

'There are other places,' Stamps said. 'Forte dei Marmi. Viareggio. Lucca.'

Renata shrugged. Stamps had to admit, even her shrug was beautiful. 'You can go there if you want,' she said.

Stamps snorted. 'You don't have to worry 'bout me, honey. I'm catching the next thing smokin' when they come for me.'

She didn't understand what he said. She had a hard time understanding his English, so full of slang as it was, but as she gazed at him, she understood his intentions. He was a man who could not speak in circles. He was full of points, tall, straight, so true, she felt. She looked at his chestnut-colored face, his long arms and broad shoulders, the slender, dark fingers that were now brushing the snow off his nose, his copper-colored eyes that scanned the ridges behind her. She saw that beneath his grim stare and constant frown he was essentially a shy man, and young, ten years younger than she – strong in his intentions, yet burdened with the responsibility of the others. He fascinated her, as did Bishop, though Bishop was more free-wheeling in his ways, his easy humor, his loud laugh, the cool manner with which he addressed life. Bishop laughed at the Italians, at himself, at their predicament. He was not afraid to touch, not afraid to flirt, not afraid to suggest the forbidden. Her friend Isoela said Bishop tried to kiss her and more – and that prospect, the prospect of Bishop working his warm, dark hands around her, grasping, holding her, groping, looking for some clear space, Renata found unbelievably exciting. Her husband, Renzo, had been gone a long time, and even as she hoped against hope that he was still alive, she'd found herself admitting to herself recently that Renzo had not been the most exciting of lovers. He was too attached to his stupid mother, God bless her soul. Italian men were like that, she guessed, though she'd known no other man except him, and in her life had seen few foreigners save one or two white Americans in Florence, and these Negroes, who were each so different from the image she had of their fellow Americans.

Lying in bed at night, alone, as she had for months, shivering in the cold, Renata wondered about each of them, the supple, sleepy Spanish speaker; the silent, meek giant with the odd statue head, who moved as if he carried mountains upon his huge shoulders; Bishop, with his wide grin and sparkling white teeth; and Stamps, the prettiest of them all, a dark, brooding, thoughtful flower. She decided she liked Stamps the most. As she watched him, she thought of a chestnut tree in the snow, a Donatello sculpture standing in the whiteness that surrounded them, his eyes covering her with warm, eternal cocoa-brownness, his long arms reaching out to protect her like tree limbs. She could not imagine him killing anyone. Every time she stood near him, her curiosity about him awakened the kind of excitement she hadn't felt in her heart in years, even though they'd never exchanged more than a few words. It was only a feeling she had, and she wasn't sure if it was because he was a foreigner or because he was a safer version of Bishop, about whom she also had an almost irresistible curiosity. She decided that she was just a country girl, and against her better instincts and character, she wanted to ask him question after question – where he came from, who his mother was, where he grew up.

'You Negroes seem different from other Americans,' she said. 'Why?'

She spoke just as Bishop emerged from the rear of Ludovico's house to check on the firing and ask what Stamps wanted to do next.

'Hear that?' Bishop chuckled to Stamps. 'She ain't known us a week, and already she's asking them Mary McLeod Bethune questions.' Stamps ignored him and said nothing. Bishop turned to Renata. 'We ain't so different from them,' Bishop said. 'We just different where it counts most.'

'Where's that?' she asked. She asked it of both of them, but she wanted only one of them to answer. Stamps felt himself clamming up as she stared directly at him.

It was the first personal thing she had ever asked him, and he desperately wanted to respond. This was a full woman, a real woman, not like the young girls Stamps had seen back home, the colored girls from church in their bland peach-colored hats and conservative Sunday dresses, wearing white gloves and chatting about the Jack & Jill society, which gave brown paper bag tests to see if your skin was light enough to gain admission. She wasn't like the distant white waitresses who stared across the counter at him in Washington, D.C., with a mixture of fear and loathing as they slid cold cups of coffee at him, their frumpy dresses knotted at the waist, their long hair tied into buns, their skin stretched against their faces like plastic wrapped around old beef. She looked more like the beautiful, sophisticated young women who worked in the cosmetics department at Lerner's, smelling of sweet oils and perfume, their dresses fitted just so around their slim hips, the thick leather belts tied around them carelessly, their slender, dainty white feet tucked into tiny black high heels. They would glance up from behind the shiny glass perfume counter as he, a starving college student, his long arms and legs crammed inside a fourteen-dollar green wool suit from Woolworth's, strolled past, his head held aloft, trying to maintain his dignity and composure and hiding his disappointment at being turned down for yet another sales job. He imagined what she'd look like behind the perfume counter, all oiled and lubed and smelling good, her beautiful breasts bouncing like puppies, her smiling at him as she did now, with total absorption, complete curiosity. He imagined her standing in front of the department store at closing time with the rest of the perfume department ladies he'd seen waiting for their boyfriends and husbands to pick them up, and he imagined himself pulling up in a new Packard, leaning over the passenger seat so he could flip the latch of the door and open it, her slipping inside, a grown woman, a white woman, a nigger's wet dream, the kind he'd seen in the movies, Ava Gardner, Betty Boop, that kind of woman, the two of them driving home, rushing inside, her flinging off her shoes, her dress, her underwear, them falling on the bed, and him sinking his hard stiffness into her wet bottom like there was no tomorrow.

But then he saw himself walking through his own neighborhood holding her hand as his black neighbors cackled and glared and moved away from him, knowing he was a dead man or a fool or both, imagined himself swinging from a cherry tree in nearby Richmond, Virginia, with diesel fuel poured down his throat and hot tar on his face as a white mob set his fuel-soaked body afire, and his reverie exploded in his mind like a firecracker, and he heard the shells falling and felt the cold winter air of Tuscany slapping his face again, and the white reality of it all froze his insides. You had to be a reckless know-it-all fool like Bishop to dream that way. Bishop would stick his willy in the barrel of a sawed-off shotgun if he thought there was pleasure at the other end. He knew how to talk to women. Stamps suddenly realized he was jealous of Bishop. Standing there at that moment, he hated the smiling Bishop even more.

'Ain't no difference,' he said gruffly, 'between white and colored. We're all the same back home.' He couldn't think of anything else to say.

He saw Bishop grinning and Hector circling nearby. 'Hector, you just in time,' Bishop said. 'The lieutenant here's giving out free Uncle Tom lessons.'

Stamps ignored him. The villagers were gradually returning to their homes. The distant shelling had died down again, and from out of the corner of his eye, he saw the Italian standing near the German, who was seated on the ground beside Ludovico's house. The German hadn't moved. He sat listless, motionless, probably expecting to be killed, Stamps thought. Too much was happening at once. Something about that Italian guarding him alone was wrong.

Turning to Bishop and Hector, Stamps nodded at the Italian. 'I don't trust him,' he said.

'Aw, git off your hind legs 'bout that guy,' Bishop said. 'He's on our side.'

'I still don't trust him.'

Renata said, 'He's just afraid. He's from this area. I know him.'

'I don't give a damn if he's Eleanor Roosevelt,' Stamps said. 'I still don't trust him. The Krauts are hitting us hard from the next ridge over, and he don't see nothing? He'll forget us five minutes past breakfast if them Germans come over that ridge.'

Hector silently agreed. He pulled Stamps's arm. 'Stamps, I gotta talk to you a minute.'

'Not now.'

'It's about Train's kid.'

'You got him talkin'? What did he say?'

'He says the Germans were up at that church we saw.'

211

'Oh, that's just skippy. We know that.'

'He says we got to skedaddle.'

'Who says?'

'The kid.'

'Maybe you can get a job as his personal secretary when this is all over.'

'I'm telling you, the kid knows something.'

'Forget the kid,' Stamps snapped, watching Rodolfo, who was standing near the German. 'I don't trust that guy. Get over there with him. Take him and the German to the south post, the main post at the south of the village, and keep an eye out for Krauts. And watch that Italian guy. Anything funny happens, fire two shots in the air. One-two. Like that. Got it?'

Hector took a look at Rodolfo, who seemed uneasy, and he didn't like it. 'We don't need two people to look after one prisoner,' he said.

'Nokes is coming all the way out here to get him. He must be important,' Stamps said. He felt stupid even as he said it, looking at the ragged German who sat next to the house, a kid – it was hard to believe he could be that important.

'If he's important,' Hector said slowly, 'what does that make us?' He was starting to put two and two together. Something big was coming. Headquarters needed more intelligence on it. If they'd ask me, Hector thought, I'll tell them all they need to know: We need to get the hell out. Now. Get some bomber planes or something up here, and we'll be back later.

'Why does it sound like an auction every time I tell y'all to do something?' Stamps snapped. 'This ain't twenty questions. Just do like I said.'

Hector glumly walked over to Rodolfo, and the three of them trudged off. The German marched behind Rodolfo toward the outer wall, with

Hector following them. They turned a corner and marched down a small alleyway to a tiny piazza, Hector keeping his eyes on both of them. His nerves were tingling. He was exhausted. He'd gone outside to tell Stamps about Train's kid and instead had drawn the worst assignment. He was freezing and his toes were numb.

The Italian stopped at the far wall, where Hector motioned him to one gatepost while he took the other. The entrance to the village faced a small river several yards off, and behind that the ground sloped up to ridges that ascended gradually. They could be climbed if necessary, Hector noted, if he and the others had to flee in that direction. Or, he thought with a pang of fear, they could be descended easily, too, if a company of two hundred Krauts decided to come down to kick their asses. He tried not to think about it. About four feet separated him from Rodolfo, with the German sitting on the ground between them.

They stood in silence for a moment, looking out at the ridge. Hector bet the Italian knew those mountains like the back of his hand. All the partisans did. That's why the Americans used them as guides – except for Stamps, he thought, who trusted no one. He peered at the young Italian sideways and decided he was okay, though he still agreed with Stamps on this one and watched him close. The Italian tried to smile at him, but it came off as a grimace. He was nervous, Hector could see it. The young Italian offered him a cigarette, his hand shaking, and Hector suddenly felt a burst of sympathy for him. He was scared, too. At least I have a home to go to, Hector thought. This poor bastard, this was his home, right here. He's fighting for a little shithole.

With a friendly smile, Hector reached for the cigarette, and at that moment felt something cold hit his arm. He heard the German suddenly scream and saw him kick at the Italian. Hector heard a *pflap!*, as if someone

213

had slapped him, a flesh-on-flesh sound, and instinctively turned his head to look over the wall at the hills beyond, waiting for the pain to surge through his body, thinking he'd been hit by a German sniper. In doing so, he saved his own life, as the Italian's knife, aimed at his throat for a second attempt, missed and sliced off a piece of his ear instead.

It was not till many years later that Hector admitted to himself that the German soldier had saved his life, because had he not shouted and kicked Rodolfo off balance, the Italian's aim would have been true; and in those later years, when the war which he tried so hard to bury haunted him mercilessly, presenting itself to him in his dreams, rising like a phoenix – the flesh wounds, the starving children, the cheerful Italian villagers with crippled legs and no arms who smiled at him and fed him their last crumbs – causing maniacal outbursts and trembling hands on his part, Hector often resolved to quit his life at the post office and spend his last dime to find the young German soldier so that he could fall on his knees and thank him, kiss his hands in gratitude, warm the soldier's young, freezing fingers with his own lips for saving his life. But that opportunity would never present itself, because by the time Hector fell down in the thickening snow, holding his bleeding ear, hearing the fleeing Italian's feet splashing past his face and the shouts of Ludovico and the others coming to his rescue, the German boy lay facing him, slouched against the wall with his throat slashed, blood pulsing out of his neck as he stared at Hector with neither guilt nor anger in his deep blue eyes, but rather, Hector noted, something akin to relief.

18

BETRAYAL

Peppi sat at the edge of the east ridge above Bornacchi and peered into the snowy darkness of the town below. The sound of artillery was growing closer; the heavy booms felt like they were landing atop his heart. He wanted to sob with the weight of it. Two of his partisans sat nearby in a semicircle, warming themselves at a fire. They listened to the soft song of the boy Ettalo, who sang a melody that only a child would know and tried to interest them in dominoes.

The booms of the artillery did not bother him. The approaching Germans were nothing new. He had seen them with his own eyes. They were descending from Mt. Forato, right through the eye of the Mountain of the Sleeping Man, a huge force, yes, maybe ten thousand men, but they would have to move slowly. Their size would hamper them, the snow would hamper them, the mountains would check them – there was only one trail big enough to accommodate that many men and machines as they descended through the Lama di Sotto ridge anyway.

His band could attack them easily there, hold them up for a short time by sticking a few detonated charges in a narrow pass near Mt. Procino – he knew a place there where the earth and rocks were so loose he could kick them down onto the trail with his feet – but the stall wouldn't last long. They would come, and there would be hell to pay as usual, though he was not afraid for himself. The Germans would never catch him in those mountains. He knew them like the back of his hand. Every nook, every rock and cranny he'd climbed in and out of as a boy, hunting wild boar, gathering chestnuts, crawling, hiding, playing in the dozens of caves and caverns with his brother Paolo, his cousin Gianni, and of course Marco and Marco's little brother Rodolfo.

Rodolfo.

He had heard the German clearly. He had told the boy to 'Run, run like I told you before.' The German had played dumb the whole time. He'd pretended he didn't speak Italian when they caught him. Now he knew why. Now he understood the look of accusation on the German's face when they had first captured him and he'd seen Rodolfo. The German had seen Rodolfo before. The German had seen the boy before, too, and vice versa. Something was wrong.

He mentally reviewed his band's movements in the week preceding the mess at Sant'Anna. The four of them had killed two German soldiers near Ruosina, two kilometers north of Sant'Anna, then split up. It was their common practice. He was too hot. They all knew it. It was too risky for them to be with him when the Germans came hunting for them. It was Rodolfo who had created the escape plan, and it seemed to be a good one: The three others would leave, split up, follow separate trails around the town of Sampiera, hide in the caves for two days, then meet up in Giorgina. Meanwhile he, Peppi, would travel through Mt. Ferro and head up to Sant'Anna di Stazzema to find food and supplies for them. He had a cousin there, Federico, who would help. But the plan had backfired immediately. When he had split from the others, he ran into a German patrol on the trail between Ulibi and Sant'Anna and had barely escaped. It was an unmarked partisan trail. It was impossible for the Germans to know that trail. He had gotten lucky only because an old farmer up there had warned him just before he'd approached Sant'Anna that a German patrol awaited him. Otherwise, he would have been at his cousin Federico's house stuffing his face with olives and bringing the wrath of the SS down on him and hundreds of others, which had happened anyway.

Instead, he'd doubled back, given up on Sant'Anna di Stazzema, and had met his band at Giorgini. He tried to remember whether Rodolfo was surprised or not when he'd stumbled into the village, but he had been exhausted when he'd arrived and he had encountered another problem on his hands the moment he set foot there.

Rodolfo had found some money on the dead Germans they'd killed in Ruosina. He had used it to throw a feast for the villagers in Giorgini. When Peppi arrived, the villagers and partisans were laughing and carousing in the village square, drinking grappa and roasting chickens they'd bought with the dead German's money. When Peppi found out where the money for the party had come from, he was furious. He'd chased them away from the square, emptied the remaining bottles of grappa onto the ground, and flung the roasted chickens into the dust, grinding them into small pieces with his foot. The money he found, he tossed into the fire.

The villagers had encircled him, aghast. 'What are you doing?' they cried.

'This is blood money,' Peppi said. 'If you become dependent on someone's death to feel alive and throw a party, then you are worse than the Germans, worse than even the Fascists. I am an Italian,' he cried. 'I don't kill for money and grappa and chickens. I fight for my freedom. I fight for Italy. To hell with you.'

He had stomped off, leaving the ashamed villagers to stare in his wake.

Rodolfo had not taken that well. He had followed Peppi into the forest and they had argued. It had been a snub to him, Rodolfo protested. It had made him look stupid in front of everyone in the village. What difference does it make, he said. It was our money the man had. We took back only what was ours.

But Peppi would not hear it. You can take the German's money anytime you want, he'd said. But if you kill the man and take the man's money, you are not a soldier, you are a thief. That man died poorly, he said. Don't you remember? He did not die like a soldier. He was pissing when we caught him. He was holding his dick when he died.

From that moment on, there had been a space between them, and over the ensuing days and weeks it had widened into a gap, and now it was a yawning valley, and in the middle of it sat the boy, who recognized Rodolfo, who had seen him, who had seen the German, too. But where? There were no survivors of Sant'Anna that Peppi knew of. His cousin Federico was dead. Furthermore, most of the inhabitants in the surrounding villages didn't know the people of Sant'Anna. The tiny town was a bubble, a haven for the residents of Forte dei Marmi and Lucca and Florence. They had come there for its church, for the convent where the four nuns lived since before anyone could remember. They came because it was away from the battle lines, ten kilometers from the Gothic Line, where the Americans and Germans were fighting. They came because it was safe. Peppi wanted to throw up thinking about it. He felt nausea working its way up his throat, then retreating, then working its way up again.

He sat down and dug a stick into the snow, trying as hard as he could to reason why Rodolfo would betray him. Rodolfo was a good soldier. He had seen his own brother Marco die. Peppi himself had been there. He had seen Rodolfo's resolve, had seen Rodolfo shoot at his own flesh and blood for the cause of Italy, he had seen Rodolfo's tears. They had wept together and held each other up as they stood, near to collapse, at Marco's grave. Peppi had told Rodolfo then, 'We are brothers now,' and Rodolfo had understood, for they both realized Rodolfo had crossed that most sacred line, the line of taking blood, true Italian blood, family blood, for the cause of Mother Italy. There was no greater sacrifice. It was impossible to believe Rodolfo would betray that ideal.

But then there was the money.

The price on Peppi's head had tripled. He'd learned that from Ludovico. When he'd cornered him in the town square, the old man had told him, 'I would not trade fourteen rabbits for the lives of five hundred people at Sant'Anna when I could have a ten-kilo bag of salt and two million lire for yours.' Peppi was stunned. Two million lire and ten kilos of salt were riches beyond any man's dreams, worth more than gold. The old man had said, 'I am a Fascist, Peppi, but I am not a killer of men.' He had nodded toward his daughter, Renata, who stood nearby, out of earshot. 'Her husband is dead,' the old man had said. 'He is not coming back. I want to see her married when this war is done. Maybe you will be my son-in-law someday. Or him,' he had pointed to one of the other partisans. 'Someone from around here. I want her to stay here, with me, to help me keep my rabbits when I grow old.'

Peppi had had to stifle a smile then. Ludovico was already old. 'How did you get so many rabbits?' he had asked.

The old man had smiled sheepishly and shrugged, showing the palms of his hands. 'Don't you believe in miracles?' he asked.

Only then did Peppi believe him, believe him with all his heart, because he, too, believed in miracles. Everyone did. All of Italy was a miracle. Every bit of it. Every centimeter and kilo of it. There was no reason for any of them to be alive anymore without miracles. Every hope was dashed, every dream ruined, every villa destroyed because of the war, yet there they were. Every conceivable crime and nightmare had occurred: children shot to death in front of their mothers, fathers executed in front of their daughters, men raping men, men raping children, yet there they were. Brother killing brother, mothers howling over sons, fathers killing sons, fathers losing their minds, the dogs of war unleashed in every corner. Miracles were all they had left. Miracles were what kept them alive. At that moment, Peppi knew he could not kill Ludovico even if he wanted to. Ludovico was just a frail old man. He had watched Ludovico from the ridges as the old man skinned his precious rabbits, plucked his sole chicken, and pulled out his grappa and handed it over to the Americans and the rest of the village. He'd known the old man his whole life. The old man was always cheap, Peppi thought wryly, but he's still an Italian. An Italian knows how to live. An Italian knows how to eat, an Italian likes to have fun. An Italian believes in miracles.

Traitors. Traitors don't believe in miracles. They believe in nothing.

Rodolfo had changed after his brother died. He had, Peppi thought sadly, become more like me. His silences were long and deep, his eyes were now calm, savage, and thoughtful by turns. Rodolfo's careless bantering, his bickering about the great Tuscan poet Giovanni Pascoli, his bragging about having seen the works of the great artists of Rome and Florence, whom he'd aspired to emulate, had disappeared in the weeks following Marco's death. He had become silent and moody. His once warm smile had become like ice, his laugh bittersweet, the laughter prompted not by curiosity or wonder or kindness but by cruelty. He'd chortle as he snatched bread from the baskets of old women, helping himself to the last grapes from an old farmer's vineyard, saying, 'This is for the war cause,' as the farmer's family watched helplessly. These were things that Peppi, even when the Rage came upon him, even when the Black Butterfly filled his soul with lava-hot anger, could not do. Rodolfo had killed the two Germans in Ruosina and enjoyed it, stabbing one in the chest and watching him gurgle in his own blood and choke helplessly till Peppi had shot him to put him out of his misery. Rodolfo had enjoyed the killing. He had volunteered to make the perilous journey across the mountains alone, to the American headquarters at Viareggio, disguised as a priest, to tell the Americans of the atrocity at Sant'Anna, in the hopes of the Americans sending troops there. In doing so, he had thrown off suspicion from himself. It was a clever move, Peppi thought, because Rodolfo understood how the Americans operated. The Americans didn't understand Italians. They would march their armies into Sant'Anna. They would arrest whomever they wanted to, they would find an SS or an Italian collaborator, they would conduct a summary military trial, perhaps jail or even execute someone. That would be the end of it. But an Italian would not bother with a stupid mock trail. An Italian would exact revenge, and it would not be pleasant.

Peppi pondered the possibilities. The American Negroes who blundered into Bornacchi were not what Rodolfo had expected. Nor was the German prisoner. How had Rodolfo reacted when they found the prisoner? They'd captured the German wandering in the forest outside Corglia, near Mt. Forato, clearly one of the many deserters that were increasingly leaving the German army. Rodolfo had wanted to kill the German prisoner right away. 'We need to find out what he knows,' Peppi had argued. But Rodolfo had swayed the others. 'You saw what they did at Stazzema. The woman said it was the SS. What is he? He is SS. He was there!'

It had taken every ounce of Peppi's convincing to keep them from killing the German. And even now, he was not sure he had done the right thing in leaving him with the Negroes. But he did not want the blood of an innocent man on his hands. It would not make the dead at Sant'Anna di Stazzema any more alive to kill the German if he'd had no hand in their deaths. So Peppi had left him with Rodolfo and the Negroes as a test. The German army would not arrive for at least another day, perhaps two if he detonated a few charges to slow them down. If Rodolfo wanted to test the ire of the Negroes by trying to kill the German, let him. Then the Negroes would deliver justice, not him, and that was better, for to kill Rodolfo was like killing himself. Peppi was not sure he could do it.

The war was killing him, he thought, and he realized at that moment that even if he survived it, the Black Butterfly would not, and as the Black Butterfly went, so he went. He accepted it peacefully. He would never be able to wash the blood off himself, anyway – the useless killing, the senseless betrayals of brother by brother, the rich forcing the peasants to suffer, the peasants exacting their revenge on the rich, the starvation, the death of all innocence. He felt as if he were drowning, the water surrounding him, pushing behind his eyeballs, pumping through his face and brain like a constant flu. It would overtake him and sink him. It was only a matter of time. He turned from the ridge and stared at the twelve-year-old Ettalo, singing harmlessly and dancing around the tiny fire as the other partisan, Gianni, sat with bowed head, nodding to sleep. He wondered what kind of life awaited Ettalo. The boy had no parents left. He'd learned to shoot and kill at an age when he should have been learning to hunt and fish, plant, read poetry, and study the colors of the different trees in the mountains. The boy was dead before he even had a chance to become alive. He had no hope. No life awaited him.

The rustle of the bushes below signaled Rodolfo's return from town.

'How is the German?' Peppi asked.

'The Americans made me leave. They are going to evacuate and take him, I think.'

Peppi was silent.

'We better go,' Rodolfo said. 'The Germans are coming down Mt. Forato fast. I saw them just now. Thousands of them, with lots of mules.'

Peppi rose and motioned Rodolfo over. The others followed. Peppi decided it didn't matter if they heard.

He stared out over the ridge at the towns below. He could see the glow of small fires starting in several homes. 'I think we'll head down to join the Americans,' he said.

He could hear Rodolfo's rush of breath as he sucked in. 'Why? Let's get away. We go up to Mt. Procino, set some charges to slow the Germans down, and go. The Germans are going to catch the Buffalo Soldiers in a day. They're as good as dead.'

'I don't know. Maybe we'll join the Negroes, fight with them. They asked us to.'

'What's the matter with you? We made a deal. We would revenge the church ourselves. The Americans will not deliver justice. They don't understand us. We've got to catch the traitor ourselves.'

'No. It's over,' Peppi said.

'What are you talking about?' Rodolfo snapped. 'There were five hundred and sixty people at that church, Peppi, remember?'

'What's one person?' Peppi said. 'What's ten? What do they have to live for? The war is almost over, Rodolfo. The Germans will lose. Everyone knows it. And what will become of us then? We will be peasants after the war, all of us. The Aracia mines will have our souls. The rich will be rich again, the poor will be poor. You've said this yourself many times. What's the point? I'm tired.'

'What's the matter with you?'

'It's not Ludovico, anyway,' Peppi said.

'Then we will keep looking till we find him. There are several villages we haven't checked. Let's save ourselves now, and get away from here.'

Peppi shrugged and kept his back to Rodolfo. He was afraid to look at him. Instead, he gazed over the mountain ridges into the darkness. 'I wonder if the Mountain of the Sleeping Man will ever really wake up, like they say he will,' he murmured softly. 'That's what Marco used to say. He used to wonder about it. He told me he was going to climb to the top of the eye once. He used to wonder if he was strong enough to do it. I think he could have. He was strong, you know.'

Rodolfo was silent.

'He was a good brother, wasn't he? He was like a brother to me, too.'

Rodolfo remained silent. Peppi knew him too well. Any other secret he could keep in his heart, his terrible mistake, the blood still on his sweaty hands from the fresh murder he'd committed not even ten minutes old, but this he could not. Peppi had always been smarter than all of them, even Marco.

'But Marco wasn't my true brother,' Peppi continued. 'I don't have to

224

care for his mother once the war's done. That's your job. No more art school for you. No more dreams. Because Marco, who took care of your mother, is dead and it's my fault.' He felt his heart was breaking as he talked, and he choked back a sob. The truth was unraveling to him now, and though he felt his heart peeling back in layers, he couldn't stop himself.

Rodolfo gazed into the snowy darkness covering the ridges below. 'Peppi, can you go to hell for making a mistake?' he asked softly. 'Even if you confess to God, and He forgives you?'

Peppi shrugged. 'I don't know,' he said. The confession didn't surprise him. For a moment, they were no longer two partisan soldiers fighting a war. Just two young men, two friends who had known each other since boyhood and shared every fear, every dream, every resolve, every secret. 'I'm not a priest. People think I am, but I'm not. That's why I love it up here.' He gazed at the mountaintops around them. 'I lose myself up here. Up here, I'm not the Black Butterfly, the great *partigiano*, the leader of men, the destroyer of Germans. I'm just myself. Peppi Enrico Grotta. The boy of the air. Remember when I called myself that? Scanapo, the Air Boy? When we saw that airplane for the first time?' He didn't wait for Rodolfo to respond. 'I remember it. That was something.' He turned and faced Rodolfo. 'Now look at me.' Rodolfo, whose eyes were glued to the ground, glanced up at him and was surprised to see Peppi sagged, his back bent as if a giant weight were on his shoulders. Peppi placed his hands in his pockets and sighed. 'It's like every little bit inside of me that was real, it's gone, and the rest of me . . . I don't know who I am anymore.'

The revelation soured Rodolfo. Peppi always tried to act so smart, trying to find the meaning of things. Sometimes things had no meaning. They just existed.

'I know who I am,' Rodolfo said.

'And what is that?'

'I am a freedom fighter.'

'What makes a freedom fighter?'

The rhetorical question snapped the reverie, and Rodolfo felt his anger rising. 'What's wrong with you?' he barked testily. 'Why do you ask so many stupid questions? Why are you wasting time? You can't think anymore, is that it? We would have known who betrayed Sant'Anna if we had kept the German. We could have waited and found out he spoke Italian.'

'True,' said Peppi, 'and then he could have told us about you.'

There was a long silence as the fire behind them popped and crackled. Peppi wished it were lighter so he could see Rodolfo's eyes, but even so, Rodolfo's voice told him more than he wanted to hear. He spoke in the tone of the new Rodolfo, mirthless, calm, deliberate, now clear of the subject of Marco, his weak spot distant, his resolve once again firm.

'You afraid I betrayed you?' Rodolfo said slowly. 'Is that it? You heard that stupid German talking to that boy and believe him over me? How many years do we have between us? This is war. People suffer.'

Peppi said slowly, 'Are you telling me that the people in Sant'Anna deserved to suffer?'

'I don't know what you're talking about.'

'Are you saying the people in Sant'Anna should suffer because Marco is dead? Is that what you're saying? Clue me in. There were only old people and children there, Rodolfo. Federico my cousin, you've known him your whole life, he was there. Carlina Martinelli lived there. Bruno Franchi's whole family was there, his children Guibaldo and Guido and little Maria Olimpia, who made candy floss all by herself once and gave

226

us some. They should be dead? They should be dead because of me? You think Marco would have them dead, for me? Fascist that he was, you think Marco would kill innocent children to trap me? Would he?'

Peppi's voice, though it rose in the form of a question, had a hard steel spine to it, and the other partisans, standing nearby, backed away.

'Marco has nothing to do with this,' Rodolfo said.

'Why didn't you ask me? I would have let you collect, you fuckin' swine. Now I have their deaths on my head. Forever. The devil will have me! Because you betrayed me for a lousy bag of salt!'

Peppi felt the blood rising to his face, and with it the heady feeling he experienced just before he went to battle, made a kill, stole weapons from the *carabinieri*, blew up another German convoy. The rage was coming upon him, the fury that sought to bring the silences back to him, the silences the war had taken away. Peppi was gone. In his place was the Black Butterfly, who had no conscience, no friends, no fear, just an unassailable rage and one single purpose, to bring peaceful, poetic silence back to Peppi, and to Mother Italy.

With one swift motion, he snatched Rodolfo's rifle from his hands and set it on the ground. He removed his boot from his foot, and, squatting down, stuck the rifle barrel in his mouth and placed his toe in the trigger.

'I'm going to let you collect your money, Rodolfo. You will be rich after the war. No partisan, no man, not even a traitor, can live with five hundred and sixty deaths on his hands. Just tell me one thing. Tell it to me from your own lips, and I will take my own life happily. Tell me that you betrayed me for a lousy bag of salt and that the rest of it was a mistake. That is all I ask. Please tell me. Because if I am fool enough to consort with the devil, then I belong in hell.'

Sitting in the snow with the barrel of the gun in his mouth, Peppi felt something inside him snap open, like a clogged ear that suddenly pops free and allows sound in. He heard the crackling of the fire, the snapping of twigs, and these, he understood, were the sounds of one man's soul twisting and burning in the wind. The roar of it, in Peppi's mind, was deafening and painful. Over the roar, Peppi heard a sob.

Rodolfo had turned his head away from the fire, and Peppi heard him say softly, 'God help me, it was. It was an accident,' he murmured. 'The SS only wanted you. And when they didn't find you . . . they . . .' His quiet sobs filled the trees and bushes, which swayed with the knowledge. He began backing away, toward the ridge that led to the mountain below. He stood alone, his big ears and face were pointed downward, his lean frame was silhouetted against the black sky like a ghost, his sagging clothing pressing against his body in the cold wind while Peppi and the partisans watched him, watched a man break apart before their eyes, the little pieces of his soul dropping into the snow like tiny extinguished matches, the breathlike smoke dissipating into the air, or blowing downward into the mountain night below. They felt as if they were watching a goblin being born, and they stood in awe.

As Rodolfo stood alone, crying, he silently prayed Peppi would kill him, shoot him now. Peppi had shamed him. He was relieved to accept death now.

As if hearing his silent prayer, Peppi took the rifle out of his mouth, rose, and turned the barrel toward Rodolfo. By the firelight, Peppi could see Rodolfo's eyes, and just as quickly the rage in him died, and tears filled his eyes. He threw the rifle at Rodolfo and collapsed on the ground. 'You broke my heart, Rodolfo,' he said. 'My last friend in the world, and you sold my life for a lousy bag of salt!' He began to cry aloud.

It was shame that made Rodolfo turn and run at that moment, for he had no fear left. And even as he barreled down the mountain, not even bothering to pick up his rifle, bouncing and falling over the ridge and smashing through the snow-covered bushes and brush into the darkness of the mountainside, the shame that welled up inside him crusted over into rage and a new knowledge – the knowledge that he had unknowingly made a pact with the devil, and now had to live it, and that his best friend in the world knew it, and knew the best way to punish him for it. As he tumbled down and down, he realized he'd begun his journey at the top of the mountain as an angry man who sought revenge, and now, on his journey downward, he was metamorphosing into a defeated soul, a ghost, a goblin, as haunted as the ancient, furious mountain goblins he had always feared as a child, the ones his mother had always warned him about. Except that now he was one of them. By the time he reached the bottom of the ridge and began running for the next ledge, he knew that with each step forward he was running one step closer to hell.

The other partisans dashed to the edge of the cliff and watched him run. 'Shall we get him?' Gianni, the older partisan, asked, turning to Peppi for a response.

'No,' Peppi said, wiping the tears from his face. 'Let him go.' He had an overwhelming urge to tell the other two to drop to their knees to pray for Rodolfo, but he couldn't bring himself to utter the words. Besides, the day would come when he could reward Rodolfo's years of friendship by putting him out of his misery for good. He decided to save that generosity for another time.

19

THE MASSACRE REVEALED

It was later that morning, after they had hastily placed the German's body on Ludovico's bedroom floor and laid Hector on the kitchen table to wrap the superficial wounds on his ear, that the memories began to come back to the boy. They returned slowly, in increments, and as they did, he became harder and harder to handle. He became irascible, throwing temper tantrums and fits. He had one unstoppable, roaring crying spell. Renata's soothing and Ettora's sweet chestnut soup he ignored. The playful tugs and tossing of Hector and Stamps did not amuse him. Chocolate, even chewing gum, did not move him. He had retired to that silent, safe place, where there was no front, no back, no middle. He waited for Arturo to come, but he would not come. Only the giant could soothe him, and it took all of Train's caresses and hugs, his deep chest, his huge arms, to bring comfort to the boy. The giant never talked. He simply stayed there, like an immovable object, and held the boy close. The boy wouldn't leave his huge arms.

It was from within the giant's arms that he told them all he could, as the Italians and Americans listened and Hector translated. He told them his name: Angelo Tornacelli. Yes, he had been at Sant'Anna di Stazzema. One morning many Germans came. They marched his mother and his grandfather to the square. There was a big fire there. People were burning. A little baby was burning in the fire with his arms out like this – he demonstrated – and had a long stick stuck through him. Some Germans were eating lunch and listening to accordion music as the fire burned. A soldier – that one, he said, pointing to the dead German who lay in Ludovico's bedroom – he took my mother and several others to the side of the church. He told us to turn around. He fired his gun in the air and said, 'Run! Run as fast as you can.' My mother ran, but I was afraid to run because of the fire. My mother came back to get me. A second German came around the side of the church and saw the people running. The second German shot the running people. He shot my mother. The other German, that one – he pointed to the dead German again – he shot the German who shot my mother. Then he picked me up and ran into the mountains. Then he was gone and there was the old man. That is all I remember.

'Then how do you know the Italian partisan with the big ears was there?' Hector had asked.

Because he was the one in front of the house when the Germans knocked at the door and told us to come out, the boy said. He told my mother not to be afraid, that he would try to protect us, that the Germans just needed to speak to us in the square. The one with the big ears, he started it all, the boy cried bitterly. I wish he had never come.

The room listened to the boy's words with rapt attention. Even the old man, Ludovico, wiped tears from his face. Then Ettora the witch explained the rest of the story to the others in the room, weeping bitterly as she spoke. She had talked to Peppi. She knew several people in Sant'Anna. She had not known the full story of what had transpired there, but now she knew after having talked to Peppi. Rodolfo, his righthand man, was a traitor. Rodolfo had posted the sign at Sant'Anna telling the residents that the partisans would protect them. He did that to cover himself, so that any one of the bands of bandits who roamed the woods posing as partisans would be blamed when the Germans marched into the village. In actuality, he had led the Germans to Sant'Anna to catch Peppi, whom he had lured there. But Peppi had been saved by an old farmer from Bornacchi, Salvo Romiti, who'd warned him that a German squad was waiting for him on the trail to Sant'Anna. Ettora had heard this from Salvo himself.

Peppi detoured, and the SS came to Sant'Anna anyway, and look what they did, the devils! Rodolfo lured Peppi there and when the SS couldn't find him, they had a killing party. Would that I meet them at the gates of hell, she cried. I would string them up by their thumbnails myself! And Rodolfo! I have a special potion for him! If his father were alive he would kill him! Poison him! She followed this with a string of expletives, the likes of which Ludovico, in more than sixty years of knowing her, had never heard her utter. He had never seen her so angry before, and after years of watching Ettora's calm, deliberate, silent leadership, to see her lose control that way was like lifting the lid off the tin can of reason that held them all together. Ludovico realized, as tears streaked down Ettora's face and she yelled and cursed, that she was what he'd always known her to be: his ideal woman, his ideal human being. Strong, vulnerable, beautiful, her colorful beads and bracelets disheveled, her red dress tattered and worn, she wiped her lovely, cutting eyes with a rag as she sobbed and yelled, standing next to the tall Negro Americans, who, after only eleven days of being with them, patted her on the back and placed their long arms around her shoulders to comfort her, though had they understood the vile oaths she was muttering they might have sprinted from the room. He admired them then, and was grateful for their presence, because it was all he could do to keep from rushing across the room and wrapping himself around Ettora to tell her that it was okay, that he loved her and always had, that she needn't cry, that they were just poor people, poor people caught in a trap, and God would open the door soon.

And now he must take her and Renata to hide someplace because the Germans were coming again, and if they didn't want to end up like the poor wretches of Sant'Anna, then they must do as the Negroes said. But where does a person run when the world is destroyed? To a refugee camp in Viareggio, to shit in trenches behind wire grate fences and die of disease next to German POWs, the same German soldiers who tried to kill your family, while the British and American soldiers feed you scraps and laugh at you? The whole notion made Ludovico cry again, and he had to cover his face.

Ettora's rant died down slowly, like a hurricane, and a cone of silence covered the room. Fat Margherita spoke out. 'I don't care about Sant'Anna,' she said. 'They're gone now, in heaven's embrace.' She crossed herself. 'What about us? What about now? The Germans are coming again.'

'Who cares?' said Franco Bochelli, the old man who had knocked out his teeth to get out of serving in the war. 'I need a drink. It's almost Christmas. Come to my house and finish the rest of my wine before the Germans get it.' With that he rose and left the house, followed by the two cock-eyed teens, Ultima and Ultimissima, and nearly half the village, for what else was there to do? Christmas, after all, was coming, and Franco had some of the best wine in the valley, and they would drink it all, God willing, and perhaps there might be some left over for the night of Befana, twelve days later, and if they weren't all worm food by then, they would drink what was left.

Stamps watched these exchanges with puzzlement. He looked at Hector for translation, but Hector simply shrugged. 'They're gonna get drunk,' he said, motioning with his hands as if he agreed. What the hell else was there to do? He wanted to join them, but Stamps pulled him and Train aside. He told Train, 'Get the boy from this room and as far from that German's body as possible. Hector, post outside the back door in the alley. Train, you sleep for three hours, then you relieve Hector. I'm going outdoors a minute.' He needed to reconnoiter. Hector and Train watched him leave.

Stamps stood outside Ludovico's front door, watching Ettora staggering away with Ludovico following. He knew he had a situation on his hands, but he had no clue as to what to do about it. His orders had been to hold. And he had held tight. He had the German, too, until Hector fucked it up. The hell with it. Nokes would handle it when he got here. If ever there was a crime, he thought, this was it. OSS handled this kind of stuff. All he'd wanted was the turkey and mashed potato dinner they'd been promised for Christmas. Instead he had what they called back at headquarters a 'snafu': situation normal, all fucked up.

Stamps re-entered the house, which was now quiet. He lay down on the floor and slept fitfully for an hour, dreaming of burning pews and a bayoneted baby and accordion music. He'd learned from the other Italians that the crazy man, Eugenio, whom they'd run into at the church their first day, was a decorated lieutenant in the Italian army. He'd moved his family to Bornacchi because his home, outside Lucca, had been shelled to bits. There was no food in Lucca, no economy to speak of, no bread, not even fresh water. There was a river near Bornacchi for fishing and washing clothing, there were chestnuts to pick there, and clean well water to drink, and his children could see the sunrise. They could even muster up a few lire working in the nearby Aracia mines. Eugenio was happily on his way home from the service when he learned that his wife and eight children had been visiting a cousin in Sant'Anna when the Germans came to town. They all were dead and being buried in a mass grave outside the church when he arrived. He'd tried to fling himself into their graves, wanting to follow them. No wonder he'd lost his mind. Stamps felt nausea working up in his throat and his hemorrhoids burning. He rose after an hour, his mind in a fog, barely able to think.

That wasn't the only problem. The shelling had resumed again and was getting closer. The villagers refused to leave. Train was still in love with the kid. Bishop was off someplace as usual. The electric power had disappeared from Ludovico's house, and the radio was useless without it because the dead batteries would not hold a charge. They had to wait for Nokes. He'd better hurry the fuck up or we're gonna take our chances and walk home, Stamps thought. He hoped Nokes was bringing a lot of men. He'd have to. The whooshing noises he heard overhead – the *woo, woo, woo* with the big smash at the end – meant there was a lot of eighty-eight traffic out there. He could see smoke on the horizon and smell phosphorus in the air, which meant the Germans were using flamethrowers to clear forests, homes, and even people. They weren't bullshitting. This was not defensive fighting, which the Germans had been doing in his fifteen months there. This was offensive. They were coming, from all sides.

He could not determine exactly where the heaviest shelling was coming from, because as it grew louder, it echoed along both sides of the mountain, though it appeared to be from the east. He decided the Germans were heading west toward the coast. Well, we're going that way too, he thought bitterly. Regimental headquarters in Viareggio was southwest, and he figured if he and his men had to make a break, it would be in that direction – southwest, though there seemed to be a lot of traffic that way, too.

Hector, his ear wrapped in gauze and pieces of old sheets that the villagers had ripped up, was standing by the window watching the ridges. Stamps walked over to him.

'Hector, how long you think it takes to get from regimental head-quarters in Viareggio to here?'

'Colored man'll make that run over those mountains in two hours. White man it'll take a day. Puerto Rican do it in five minutes.'

'Very funny.'

'Cool down. Nokes will bring a squad, then *adiós*, we're gone. The Germans are not close enough yet.'

'Well, who they dropping artillery on?'

'Who cares? It ain't us. Maybe it's the Brazilians. Or the Gurkhas. They're around here, too.'

'Great. That's just skippy.' Stamps couldn't stand the Brazilians. He'd visited their camp once. It was filthy. No latrines. They didn't even bother to bury their shit. The Gurkhas were even worse. They were psychotic, with their long robes and swords and screaming death cries. He heard they died by the dozens from tuberculosis because their bodies weren't used to the cold. If the Germans wanted to shell them, more power to them.

'Where's Bishop?' Stamps asked.

'He disappeared with one of those *signorinas* last night. I 'spect he's finishin' up.'

'Go get him.'

'If it's all the same to you, I'd rather not walk 'round here no more.'

'Shit, would you like me to call a cab?'

'Man, I was stabbed today! I don't know every nook of this place. I'll keep watch here.'

Stamps exited the house and marched through the piazza. A few villagers had gathered their meager belongings and were heading west down the road toward the coast, maybe to stay with relatives and friends or in American refugee camps. He noticed, however, that most villagers were going about their business as if nothing were happening. These people are crazy, he thought grimly. He supposed if he had to make a choice between his home and a crowded, dirty refugee camp, he'd stay home, too.

Home. What the fuck is that?

He turned a corner and was marching up a flight of stairs when the door to a pink house with only one shuttered window opened. A young child, carrying a bucket, emerged from the front door, followed by Bishop, buttoning his shirt. Bishop saw Stamps and frowned. Stamps approached.

'What?'

'We got a situation.'

'I ain't goin' no place.'

'The Italian partisan stabbed that German.'

'No shit. Is Nokes still coming?'

'He don't know, so he's still coming.'

'It don't matter then.'

It bothered Stamps that Bishop was so casual about the stabbing.

'While you was stokin' your little johnny, the kid was telling us the SS is 'round here; they killed a bunch of civilians up at the church we were at.'

Bishop shrugged and tucked in his shirt, taking deep breaths of the fresh mountain air. He looked liked he had just finished taking a morning constitutional. 'Imagine that. At a house of God, too.'

Stamps had an overwhelming urge to yank his Colt .45 out of its holster and part Bishop's face with it. He imagined Bishop's face being blasted into oblivion, looking like burnt oatmeal and metal. That's how Huggs had looked at Cinquale, his brain splattered over the hot tank. Stamps suddenly felt slightly nauseous, thinking of the charred pews, the outstretched arms of a baby, bayoneted. He wished he hadn't heard any of it.

He glared at Bishop and said, 'Man, what is your problem?'

'None of this is my problem. I ain't gettin' all tongue-tied over white folks killin' each other. When's Nokes coming?'

'I want you to get all our gear, the Italians' mules, radio, everything, and get it over to old man Loody's house on the double. If you hadn't sent that doofus over that ridge, we wouldn't be here.'

'I didn't send that dense nigger noplace.'

'Hell you did. Beat the guy out fourteen hundred bucks, then sent him over there. Stupid motherfucker. What were you thinking about?'

Stamps watched Bishop's breathing slow and a deep, burning anger descend upon his face. Bishop's eyelids drooped heavily. Stamps realized, for the first time, how dangerous Bishop was. He could feel it. The man had power. He'd always thought of Bishop as a sheep in wolf's clothing, a two-bit hustler. But now he could see it – could see what Train saw. The man had power. The power of the devil.

'You like it here, don't you?' Bishop said softly. 'Out here, the law is what you say it is. You just like the white man. Keep changing the law so it fits you. You said before we're gonna get Train. Then you say we gotta get a German. Then we get the German, and you fucked around playin' "America the Beautiful" for these honey drips here, and now the German's dead and we're stuck here with them, waiting for the real white man to show up while the Krauts is fittin' to throw us in the chicken fryer. So you changed up, you got to live with it. Not me.'

Bishop was standing on the top steps leading to the front door of the house as he spoke. The door behind Bishop opened and Renata emerged, wearing a red dress and holding a pack of American cigarettes, no doubt a gift from Bishop. She took a quick look at Stamps and departed swiftly.

Bishop watched her go, then smiled slightly at Stamps.

'And I grilled that ass, too. She sucked my roscoe and everything.'

Stamps leaped on Bishop and grabbed his throat. The two crashed through the doorway of the house and fell inside the darkened quarters, smashing tables, chairs, and rolling toward the open brick hearth. Spoons, ladles, and wooden bowls flew about. Bishop was pummeling him, but Stamps could feel nothing. He choked Bishop until Bishop's eyes bulged and he began to strike desperately with more force. He struck Stamps's head again and again, granite-hard blows that did nothing to weaken Stamps's grip. Then Stamps felt a blow on the other side of his head. His arms were ripped from Bishop's throat, and he was pulled back, gasping and sweating.

Hector stood between them, his chest heaving.

'Jesus!' Hector said, his head swiveling as he looked back and forth at Bishop and Stamps. 'Settle up on your own fuckin' time. C'mon, get your shit together, man! Nokes is here.'

NOKES ARRIVES

The boy felt himself slipping off the edge of the world, floating in a sea of black and white with the strange sound of the accordion guiding him, so he shut his mind and looked for Arturo. It wasn't as hard to do as it once had been, but now Arturo didn't come as often. The boy squeezed his eyes tight, until the outside sounds were gone. Everything disappeared inside him, and there was only blank space and no beginning, end, or middle, and after a few moments Arturo appeared.

'You don't come easy like you used to,' Angelo said.

Arturo shrugged.

'I saw the one from the church,' Angelo said.

'We agreed not to talk about it,' Arturo said.

'I'm afraid of him,' Angelo said.

'That's why the chocolate man came to you.'

'He's run out of chocolate, though. I even checked the pocket where he keeps it. There's no more.'

'There's plenty more. You'll see.'

Arturo disappeared, and Angelo opened his eyes and saw two jeeps in the distance, rumbling and bouncing up the mountain road. A Negro and a white man rode in the first jeep, followed by four colored men in the second jeep, one manning a fifty-caliber machine gun mounted atop the rear. Train placed the boy on the ground and stood at attention. Stamps, followed by Bishop and Hector, stepped in front of him as the jeeps approached.

The vehicles slammed to a halt, and Captain Nokes leaped out.

'How the fuck did you get all the way up here?' he asked, charging up to Stamps, who stood with his legs spread, hands on his hips, his clothing disheveled, still sweating. Stamps didn't bother to answer. He gave a half salute, then turned away and picked up his helmet, gear, rifle, and other belongings and walked toward the second jeep. He wasn't going to ride back with Nokes in the lead jeep. The hell with it.

Nokes watched him, furious. 'Where's the German?' he said.

Stamps pointed in the direction of Ludovico's house. 'In there.'

Nokes glared at him. He didn't like the attitude. He was exhausted. It had taken fourteen hours to get around Ruosina, mostly with Italian alpine mules pulling the jeeps through mud and snow, with the shelling getting heavier every minute. How these four Negroes had ended up twenty-three kilometers from base, deep on the wrong side of the Serchio Valley, was something he simply could not fathom.

Nokes barked at Birdsong, who was behind the wheel of the lead jeep. 'Find out what his problem is while I get the prisoner.' He glared at Stamps. 'You got two minutes to button your men up.' Bishop and Hector glumly gathered their helmets and moved slowly toward the second jeep, too. They had no plans on riding back with Nokes either. Nokes started toward Ludovico's house, then noticed Train standing with the statue head dangling from his waist, holding the boy in one arm. 'And get rid of that kid,' he said.

'Been trying to, suh,' Train said, 'but I guess he won't let me go. He's a nice little fella.' He held Angelo, wrapped him in a blanket. 'Take a look.'

'Get rid of him.'

'I don't know what to do with him, suh. I can't leave him here, so I figured to bring him along. He don't talk much, but he do tap. See? Watch this here. One tap mean –'

Nokes took a step toward Train. 'What is the matter with you?'

Train straightened and saluted again. 'Nothing, boss. I'm just saying that, see, this young'un here, he don't . . .'

He stopped in fear as Nokes took two long strides at him, closing the distance between them, facing him with such rage that the big man leaned backward. Nokes's eyes blazed like fireballs. His jaw reached Train's chest, and he stood so close to him with his face thrust forward that his spit flew into Train's face. 'What the fuck is wrong with you, soldier?'

Train tried to stammer a reply but could not. 'I . . .'

'We spent two days risking our asses getting here for you! Good men are dying for you! Good white men, your commanders, are holding back the attack for you! And you're telling me about some kid?'

'I . . . I feels sorry for him, suh.'

'*You* feel sorry for *him*. *You* feel sorry for *him*?'

Nokes realized his error as soon as he said it. Talking to a nigger that way with four armed niggers in the jeep, four more in front of him. The kid began to cry.

Nokes lowered his voice to an even pitch, trying to keep a tone of command in it. 'Button up and get in the jeep and let's get outta here, soldier.'

Train didn't move. A slow rage began to creep into his face.

'Ain't no cause for that kind of talk in front of no child. You ain't got to make him cry now, suh.'

Stamps stepped forward. 'Cool it, Diesel.'

'Naw. Ain't no way to talk to no child, making him cry 'n'all, cussin' and carryin' on.'

Stamps faced Nokes. 'He don't understand, sir. He's slow in his mind. It was my idea to bring the kid. We got 'im down at the Cinquale. We was trying to find out where he belonged. He won't leave us, is all. I told Train here to take 'im. It was my idea.'

The four black soldiers in the second jeep stared silently as Captain Nokes hesitated. He'd always dreaded a moment like this: alone, out in the open, within easy reach of German artillery and rifle fire, with eight Negroes and ten Italian peasants looking on and no white American in sight. He wanted to beat the crap out of Colonel Driscoll, that Mr Hoo-ray Yankee bastard, acting like this was just another white outfit fighting the Germans. These Negroes were screwing white women – he'd seen that himself back in Naples. They'd have to be re-educated once they got home. Nobody considered that, he thought bitterly. Every fiber of his being felt violated. He wasn't even supposed to be here. He was supposed to be with the 10th Mountain Division, good white men who were on the other side of the Apennines, but he had no pull at division. Now he was stuck here on Christmas Eve with a bunch of chicken guzzlers on a hill in who-knows-where-goddamn-Italy. He couldn't believe it.

'Birdsong!' he snapped.

Lieutenant Birdsong stepped out of the lead jeep.

'Deal with this while I get the prisoner. If it's not together when I get back,' he pointed to Stamps and his men, 'I'm court-martialing all four of you. Now where's the damn prisoner?' Stamps pointed at Ludovico's house, and Nokes stomped away, muttering, sweat oozing off the back of his neck despite the cold.

Stamps watched him go, knowing the explosion that would follow. He stifled an urge to follow Nokes. He wanted to see Nokes's face the moment he walked into Ludovico's house and saw the German dead on the bedroom floor. He was curious. Why not? He was already in a shitpile, anyway. He hoped to drag Nokes down into it with him. Served him right for screwing up at the canal.

Birdsong stepped forward, awakening him from his reverie. The two had known each other since officer candidate school. Birdsong wore a frown of resignation on his face. He waited till Nokes was out of earshot, then said, 'Stamps, tell you big man to loosen up.'

'Bird, I can't do nothing with him. He won't let anybody near the kid. We got a situation here. Got a bunch of civilians killed by the SS up at the church about a kilometer up that ridge. What we gonna do about that?'

'We're gonna get the fuck outta here like the captain said, that's what we're gonna do about that.'

'Why you so strong for him? Ain't nobody done a thing to him.'

'He's a captain, that's why.'

'Why you so uppity, then? I ain't seen you down at the Cinquale when we was getting our asses kicked.'

'I was there.'

'I see you got some new stripes out of it, too. 'Fore you know it, you gonna be a big white captain like him.'

A couple of soldiers in the jeeps laughed, but not all of them, Birdsong noted. He shot a glare at the culprits and saw that all the men, even those who hadn't laughed, were looking on in sympathy at their muddy, filthy comrades. Stamps glanced at Bishop and saw his eyes in dangerous, half-droop mode. He didn't know if that was for him or for Birdsong. He didn't care. This thing was winging way out of control. A crowd of Italians had now gathered behind Stamps and his men, Ludovico, Ettora, and Renata among them. Stamps wished they hadn't come to witness this faceoff. It didn't seem decent. These people had enough problems. He glanced over his shoulder at Renata and felt affection and shame. She owed him nothing. She was a free person. She'd belonged to him only in his dreams. And now she had to stay here, had to keep living this nightmare, while he would go home to his own.

Birdsong said evenly, 'I got to follow orders out here like everyone else, Aubrey. You know that. I'm asking you – not telling you – to please get your men together, lessn' we all face a court-martial when we get back.' He glanced at the ridges behind him. 'If we can get back.'

'All right then. Bishop, Hector, git your rags together. Train, give the boy to Miss Loody here.' He nodded at Renata without looking at her. He couldn't look at her again. She had broken his heart. He deserved it. Served him right for dreaming so high and wrong.

'She ain't his mama,' Train said.

'I know, Diesel, but you got to give him up.'

Train's heart was pounding, his head swimming. 'She don't know him like I know him, Lieutenant. He ain't got no mama. He got to go where somebody can tend to him. I got a grandma can do it.'

Stamps saw Birdsong roll his eyes as Hector touched Renata's arm and leaned in close and whispered in her ear. She stepped forward and gently removed Angelo from Train's arms. The boy began to wail and kick. Bishop and Hector converged on Train and tried to push him toward the jeep, but the boy broke free from Renata and leaped back onto Train's legs. Train swept him into his arms.

'See, he don't want to go,' Train said glumly. The men in the jeep laughed.

Stamps turned away and picked up his helmet, gear, rifle. Fuck it. Let Nokes handle it. He turned around just in time to see Nokes charge from Ludovico's house, on his face an odd mixture of disbelief and outrage. A thunderous round of artillery struck behind Ludovico's house, forcing Nokes to bend over for a moment; then he straightened again and stalked forward. Hector winced as he approached. Now the shit was really coming.

'Is this a joke?' Nokes said to Stamps.

'No,' Stamps said.

'The fucker's dead in there.'

'I know.'

'He's dead. How did he get dead?'

'Somebody killed him.'

'No fuckin' kiddin'! No *fuckin' kiddin'!*' Nokes was furious. 'Didn't you put a man on him?'

'I had a man on him. The Italian partis –'

'You had him and you fucked up, y'understand! You fucked up, *Sergeant* Stamps!'

Stamps silently fought the anger rising in his throat. It had taken him three years to earn those lieutenant's stripes. Three years of work. Gone in a blink. He could hear artillery and small-arms fire drawing closer. Big booms that shook the ground. He saw a grove of trees shorn off beyond Nokes's shoulder. Long-range eighty-eights at work. In a moment,

German helmets would be peeking over the ridge. They were coming from the east, from above, after all – at least he had been right about that.

Birdsong said, 'Sir, we gotta pull out.'

Nokes didn't hear. He didn't care. He backed off, hands on his hips. 'Shit . . . Goddamn, sap-sucking, yellow-bellied, son of a bitch . . .' He was kicking at the snow. He seemed to have lost touch.

'Please, sir,' Birdsong said, 'we gotta roll.'

'Okay, goddammit.' Nokes was panting now, staring at Ludovico's house, where the dead German lay. Finally, he climbed into the front of the lead jeep. To Stamps he said, 'You're in trouble.'

Train stepped forward.

'Please, suh. I jus' . . . I just wanna explain something 'bout this child heah . . .'

Nokes undid the holster holding his service revolver. He said, 'I'm gonna court-martial you, soldier. I gave you an order to load up.'

Train stood silently, still holding the boy, then slowly set the Italian youngster on the ground behind him and carefully placed his helmet on the boy's head. The child, with Train's helmet covering nearly half his face, peeked out at Nokes and the others from between the giant's knees.

Behind him, Birdsong heard the four soldiers in the rear jeep stirring. 'Ain't no need to shoot the man over no child, sir. We can take him back to headquarters. We got room.'

'Yeah, ain't no problem to take the child, suh. Let's go, suh . . .'

Nokes glanced at them out of the corner of his eye. To Birdsong he said, 'Lieutenant, take the kid.'

Birdsong jumped out of the lead jeep and approached Train slowly. 'Don't make it tough on me, big fella.'

Train didn't move. 'You bet' not come no closer.'

Birdsong lunged to grab the kid, and with one hand Train grabbed him by the neck and squeezed, lifting Birdsong into the air. Nokes yanked his carbine out of its holster, and as he did so, Bishop, standing behind him in front of the second jeep, flipped the catch off his M-1 and stuck it in Nokes's ribs.

The four soldiers in the second jeep watched in shock as Train held Birdsong high in the air by the neck. Stamps leaped on him, but Train's strength was too great. 'For God's sake, put him down, Diesel,' Stamps begged. The four men in the rear jeep leaped out to help Stamps free Birdsong from Train's grip, but the giant's power was too mighty. He held Birdsong high, and for the first time, Ludovico, standing behind them, saw the truth, saw what he had spent a lifetime trying to imagine: He saw Train silhouetted against the Mountain of the Sleeping Man behind him, the smaller men uselessly grappling with him, dangling like flies as he shrugged them off with mountainous strength, and Ludovico knew then that he'd seen a miracle, that Ettora's spell had worked, that the Mountain of the Sleeping Man had awakened to wreak vengeance and to claim his true love, except his true love wasn't a fair damsel after all; it was this child of innocence, a child who had survived a massacre, a miracle boy who represented everything that every Italian held dear, the power to love, unconditionally, forever, to forgive, to live after the worst of atrocities, and, most of all, the power to believe in God's miracles. That this child of innocence had brought this American to them was an even greater miracle, for behind this giant would come many more Americans, all because the Negroes and the child had come to Bornacchi by mistake. But this was no mistake. The war was going to end, and they all would be free soon. Ludovico watched, awestruck and terrified, as Birdsong's feet dangled high above the ground, his face turning blue. Birdsong was pummeling Train with his fists, then his palms, then with slaps, until his strikes became weaker and weaker and his body began to sag. Only after several long moments did the five men manage to force Train to release his mighty grip – just as the artillery around them began to thunder louder and machine-gun fire began to reach the town's outer walls.

The four men scrambled back into the rear jeep. Birdsong lay in the snow where he'd been dropped, grasping his neck and sucking air. 'Christ!' he said. 'What's wrong with you, man! The hell with you!'

Artillery was banging all around them now. The villagers who had returned to watch the event, frozen in terror, were backing away, fleeing. But Renata, Ludovico, and Ettora remained, transfixed, watching.

Bishop withdrew his rifle from Nokes's ribs, and the captain quickly holstered his revolver and leaped into the driver's seat of the lead jeep, starting the motor. Two men from the rear jeep leaped out and tossed Birdsong into the back of Nokes's jeep, then remounted their jeep. Nokes swung his jeep around. He pointed his finger at Bishop as if to say 'You' but said nothing more, and roared off. The second jeep, holding the other four men, roared to life as well and swung around in a tight circle for Stamps and his men.

The shelling was hammering all around now, striking several houses. The Americans and the villagers could see the Germans' helmets mounting the top of the ridge above them to the east and then descending. The second jeep hesitated a moment, waiting for Stamps, Hector, Bishop, and Train to jump in. The soldiers yelled, 'For Chrissake! C'mon!'

Stamps nodded to Bishop and Hector. 'Y'all g'wan.' They didn't move.

Shelling had reached the other side of the village. It struck a house and then walked in their direction.

The second jeep roared off.

The four soldiers watched as the two jeeps, in single file, flew through the gate, forded the tiny creek in front of it, then hit the other side of the ridge, bouncing upward and churning up snow and mud as they headed across the western curve of the mountain. They saw the eighty-eight shells whizzing toward Nokes's jeep, which was in the lead, explode in front of it, pop behind it, then strike it dead on. The jeep exploded into a ball of flames as the second jeep veered around it, flipped on its side, and fell over the ridge, tumbling over, then exploding into a fireball.

It was as if they had never been there.

From the direction that Nokes had come, they could see the helmets of the Germans bobbing down the ridge. The artillery fire was hitting the houses and flying into the air like tiny flocks of birds, striking the stone houses and sending chunks of debris airborne into the piazza, the rocks and shrapnel striking the stone walls with loud pops. They could see the backs of the villagers who had fled over the rear wall of the village, the skirts of the women disappearing over the southern ridge, blowing in the winter wind like stray flowers.

Stamps tried to think. If they were surrounded, their best bet would be to get to a high point to fight the Germans off. The ridge above Sant'Anna's church was the highest point.

'Follow me,' he said.

The soldiers and the remaining Italians followed, save one. Ludovico turned to see Ettora standing alone in the piazza as shrapnel pinged around her and artillery shells whizzed by. He peeled off, leaving the others as they fled toward the rear wall, his old frame shuffling through the snow back to Ettora. 'Come,' he cried.

Ettora shook her head. She was pasty-faced. She sat down in the snow.

'Please, come. Ettora, get up.'

She looked at him as she squatted on the ground in the snow, Indian fashion. 'My eyes are not so good,' she said, 'and I'm tired.'

She had cracked, Ludovico knew it. The Sant'Anna thing had done it. He decided to humor her. She could be stubborn. He knelt. 'Your eyes are fine,' he said. 'They look fine.' He wanted to say they looked beautiful but could not bring himself to say the words. He cursed himself. If he could not say it now, could he ever?

She smiled at him. She had always known what he felt. She knew him like a book. 'My spell worked, didn't it?'

'Yes, it did. It worked.'

She laid her head against his arm as he crouched next to her. Only then, as she turned on her side slightly, did Ludovico see the blood oozing from her stomach, from around a large piece of shrapnel, its hot metal end still poking out.

From behind him, Hector, who was last, behind Stamps and the others, heard a howl, like a dog yelping. He turned to see Ludovico leaning over the old woman, the line of red from her stomach making a small trail in the snow. Renata saw it, too, and tried to run back. Stamps grabbed her, and she kicked and screamed at him. 'Get him, Hector!' Stamps yelled.

Hector didn't want to go back. There were several Germans not a hundred yards off now. The village was in chaos, people running back and forth, smoke pouring out of houses, Germans kicking in windows on the other side of the village. He decided he wouldn't go. He'd had enough pain. He wanted to die with San Juan on his breath, dreaming of the beach at Christmas, the lights, his mother nearby, the smell of rice and beans in his nose. Hector Negron from Harlem was not going any fucking place. Hector Negron from Harlem was no hero. Fuck Stamps. Hector Negron was no soldier. Hector Negron was a boy who could barely read but could speak three languages by the time he was seventeen. How about that? Everything he did had error in it. He was a mistake, as his father used to say, a mistake that made more mistakes that were followed by still more mistakes. No mistake is going to be made unless my son Hector is involved, his papa used to say. At times he'd wanted to kill his father, the old bastard, and now, at the moment of his imminent death, Hector saw him, saw him bright as day, standing in front of him. It made him furious that his father, drunk as always – drunk from San Juan to Harlem – would stand there screaming at him, telling him he was nothing but a shit, a dirtbag, scum, even at the moment of his death. Yet Hector did what he always did when he was a boy back home in San Juan. He ignored the drunken screaming, hoisted his father onto his back, and carried him home, as his mother had always instructed him to do. Only when he was clear of Bornacchi's wall did Hector realize that the screaming man he was carrying over his shoulder was Ludovico, and that his father, thank God, was nowhere to be found. He was already dead, long ago, back in America.

THE STAND

The shelling was all around them now, and they fled through the deep, slippery snow up the road, following the Italians toward the square and the church. They'd left the mules they bought from Ludovico in the alley behind Ludovico's house – they were useless now, Bishop said. Renata knew of a cavern near the church where everyone could hide.

Train saw no hiding anywhere. It had all seemed too confusing to him, a big mystery, the shouting captain, grabbing the man by the neck, the boy. All he wanted was a bath and some sleep and to get home. He had the vague notion that his grandma would take the boy, but he had no idea how to get him home. He'd thought he would hide him – he was small enough – in his pack and get him on the boat and maybe nobody would tell; or maybe he would pay Bishop back his money and Bishop would help him; and then when they got home he'd show him Old Man Parson's field where his dog was buried and you could hear him still barking at night. There were all sorts of things that fathers did with their sons. That's how it was done, wasn't it? He wasn't sure.

Train was sorry the captain was dead. The man had tried to wrong him, but he wasn't worse than anyone else, people who took his money, ordered him around. He had wanted a simple thing. Now it was all gone bad.

The few Italians in front of them splintered off into the woods and disappeared, but the soldiers, Ludovico, and Renata pressed on, led by Stamps. They followed the twisting road around the ridges and up to the church again. The screaming man, crazy Eugenio, was gone. In his place was the angry swishing of shells, which sounded like a windstorm. The shells whipped past them, hitting rocks and sending boulders careening down the mountainside. Every so often, one of them leaped to the side to let a boulder pass, and tree branches landed in the snow around them with loud cracking noises. Train was amazed at how beautiful everything was. Every time he felt invisibility coming, it made things beautiful. He felt it coming now. He wanted the boy to become invisible with him today, that was his goal. If he could've closed his eyes, he would've closed them and wished it for the boy, but he had to follow the rest, so instead he wished it with his eyes opened, and he squeezed his hands like he was squeezing his eyes tight, and in doing so, he squeezed Angelo so hard the boy cried out and then looked at him and said, 'You're squeezing me too hard.'

'I'm sorry, feller.'

'You tired? Is that why you're squeezing?'

'Awful tired.'

It didn't occur to Train until he had climbed over the next boulder and set of ridges that he'd understood every word the boy had said.

'Good Lord, is you . . . ?'

'Where's your invisible castle?'

'I . . . What you say, boy?'

'Is heaven a place where the houses are made of candy and you can break off a piece and eat all you want?'

'Why, I guess so, boy.'

'And if you want it to rain in heaven, it'll rain, but not on other people, just on you. Is that right?'

Bishop was four feet off. Train caught up with him. 'He's talking to me, Bishop! He knows everything. He can talk good now! Can it rain on two people in heaven, Bishop? At the same time? Can it?'

Bishop turned to him angrily and said, 'I just 'bout had enough of you, man. G'wan. Git out away from me. Fuckin' idiot.'

'I jus' wanna know. Can it rain on two people at once in heaven? What do the Bible say on it?'

'Ask me on the boat going home, nigger. I just wanna tell you, you don't owe me no more money. Don't do nuthin' for me. Just keep off me, y'hear?'

'What'd I do, Bishop? I'm jus' telling you, the kid spoke to me. He speaks English. Look!'

He looked down at the little boy just as he felt a pop. The boy gave a shudder, and suddenly was pasty-faced and still. Train shook him.

'Good God, Bishop! Bishop!'

Bishop walked on, following the others to a small ridge adjacent to the church. As the giant placed the boy down, a German machine-gun emplacement began chewing up the piazza from a nearby ridge. Train set the boy on the ground in the open piazza in front of the church, fully exposed to the machine-gun fire that raked the square.

From across the piazza, the three retreating soldiers looked back and saw the giant kneeling over the boy as artillery shells and shrapnel flew about him and machine-gun rounds ricocheted off the church bell, making a ghastly *ping-pong* sound. Chips of the church façade whooshed past him, rocks and debris were falling on him, but the giant colored man appeared oblivious, unfazed, as if he were in a Sunday park reaching down to touch a flower. He gingerly reached a large hand down and gently shook the child, then removed his helmet and leaned in closer to talk to him. Finally, he placed the boy over his shoulder, the child's lifeless arm slung across the giant's forearm like a white stripe. The giant continued to stroke the child's head and talk to him gently, as if the tender words and gestures would awaken the boy and make the whole nightmare disappear.

Bishop, standing on a ridge above the piazza, leaped down and ran back toward Train. Stamps yelled, 'Let 'im go! He's made up his mind already.' Bishop ignored Stamps and dashed toward the piazza, ducking behind trees and rocks as he ran.

Bishop was five feet from Train, debris and fire ringing off every rock and tree, when he saw Train get hit. The giant looked up in surprise, then leaned over on one knee. He placed one hand on the ground and gently lowered the boy, placing his body between the machine-gun fire and the boy. He yanked the statue's head out of its netting and cradled it in his arm as rounds hit him again, this time square in the chest, and knocked him five feet from the kid and onto his back in the center of the piazza. 'You can't touch me,' he screamed. 'I'm invisible!' Bishop saw Train's face then, and in that moment, the moment between Train's dying and his own imminent sweet release from life, he realized everything he had missed in his own scurrilous life, the opportunities lost, the friendships destroyed, the blown chances, his opportunism, all couched behind the granite wall of distrust and hate that he'd built between himself and others, because of the white man's ignorance, because of his own lies, and most of all because he'd given up on God so long ago. As Train raised his head in agony, Bishop heard the words, 'You made my mother die!' and he wondered how Train knew it, knew the true reason for his lack of godliness, and it was several moments before he realized that it was he who had uttered those words and not Train, who lay on his side ten yards away from Bishop and five feet from the boy. The machine-gun fire ripping up the piazza walked back over to Train and hit him again. The giant, incredibly, turned on his back and breathed in gasps, still alive.

Bishop saw Stamps cross the far side of the piazza and open up on the machine-gun emplacement, which was inside the ground-floor window of a nearby stone house. He saw Hector run around to the side of the house, fall behind some debris, then get up and rip a hand grenade from his belt and toss it inside the window. He heard a boom, then the machine gun spit again. Hector had missed. Stamps ran up and fired dead into the machine-gun emplacement even as slugs hit him and cut him practically in half. Bishop saw Stamps fall nearly inside the window, his hand ripping a live grenade from his belt and dropping it over the sill of the window as he almost fell inside it. The force of the explosion lifted Stamps into the air and slammed him against a tree. His face, Bishop saw, was a mangled mass of flesh. The fire from the second machine gun, also in the house, ripped across the piazza past Train's back a third time as Hector crawled around the side of the window and from beneath it tossed a grenade inside before rolling away. The explosion blew, and the machine gun quit. Bishop ducked behind a large tree that shielded him from the fire and headed toward Train in the center of the piazza in a crouch. He was just three feet away from Train now, shielded behind a large piece of concrete debris. He could hear him coughing.

'Stay there a minute,' Bishop said.

Train lay on his side, staring at Bishop, his eyes wide. 'I's all right. I's all right. I'mma pay you back. Every cent.'

'Be quiet.'

'Lord. I can't breathe. I can't turn my head. Is the boy livin'?'

Bishop glanced over Train's shoulder. 'He's living,' Bishop lied. 'Hector got him.' He suddenly felt ashamed, ashamed that lying had always come so easy to him.

'Tha's good. Tell Hector he's got to take him home. You can't take him with you, Bishop, all that gambling and stuff you does.'

'Why, Train, did I ever tell you the story about Shine and the signifying monkey?'

'Forget that. You gonna do like I said? My grandma'll pay you ever cent you is owed. You makes Hector promise to take him home.'

'I'll do it. Now shut the fuck up.'

'Lord, Bishop! I see the dog at Old Man Parson's place! He's buried in the field out back. I knew he was there! I hear him barking! And there's Uncle Charlie, fiddlin' . . .'

Bishop reached out and grabbed Train, trying to pull him behind the piece of concrete. He finally managed it after the third try.

The giant's gaze was blank.

Bishop didn't know why he did it, but he had to. He sprinted across the open piazza and swept the lifeless child into his arms. The machine-gun rounds pinged all around him, heavy shells were falling now from the American bombers, which had finally arrived. He sprinted across the piazza again to the cover of the church doorway. He ducked under the doorway, right under the bust of Sant'Anna, and in the shadow of the charred, blasted-out doorway, quickly examined the child.

Bishop couldn't see where the boy was hit, but he was clearly dead. Probably shrapnel of some kind. Dime-sized shrapnel would take anybody out. He turned to run inside the darkened, burned-out church, and it was at that moment, as he turned to run, that he felt himself get hit in the back. The bullet didn't feel hot, as they said it would. Rather, it felt cool. But the force of it was strong and made him kneel. *The love*. He got up to run again and felt himself get hit in the back again, and he knelt again. *The Love*. He felt cool air blowing in his throat, then felt himself, rising, flying high into the church rafters, high, across the pulpit, over the broken and charred pews, then around, still holding the boy, until he was face to face with the statue of Sant'Anna. And as he stared at her, he understood what Train had understood. She was breathing, she was crying, she was real, she was the most beautiful thing he had ever seen in his life. He understood it all then, who God was, why the mountains were formed, why rivers ran from north to south, why water was blue and not green, the secrets of plants, and his own purpose in running up the ridge after Train. He had found his lost innocence, found it in the giant's belief in love, the giant's belief in miracles, the giant's love of a boy who was one of God's miracles. Bishop felt himself floating down, and he placed the boy on the ground, grasped his tiny head, took a deep breath, and as two more bullets passed through his chest and into his liver and lungs, snapping the veins like twigs and he felt his life draining from his feet, he pressed his lips to the boy's lips and softly breathed two big puffs of air into the boy's mouth and felt him twitch. He gently laid the boy's head down. He saw the bust of Sant'Anna above him smile, then he rolled onto his back and closed his eyes forever. Deep and comforting silence descended on everything he had known and would ever know.

*　　*　　*

The boy, lying beneath the bust of Sant'Anna, opened his eyes. The giant was gone. It seemed silent. He looked up and saw Arturo standing over him. 'We have to go,' Arturo said.

'Am I going to heaven?' he asked.

'No. You're going to Forte dei Marmi.'

'Where's that?'

'I'll show you.'

'Who's there?'

'Your father.'

'Is my father the giant?'

'No, your father's Ettore. Remember him?'

And suddenly, the boy did. He remembered it all. He remembered everything. And it suddenly came to him that he was not going to be allowed to remember any of this, that all of the life forces in the world made it so that some things needed forgetting in order for life to continue; he understood that there are some things that demand forgetting; he realized that the innocence that God reserves for children had been conferred upon him and would soon leave him, and that the intolerable tragedy of war would be forever etched in the memory of others but not in his. He understood at that moment that Sant'Anna di Stazzema would become merely a memory, a dry fig in the wind tunnel of history, the place forgotten, a museum perhaps, the 560 victims never truly revealed to the world, lost even to the Italians who would take up residence in the village just months after the war. He realized that the Negroes were merely vessels to lift him from his past memory of pain to his present of future happiness, that Sant'Anna would not let him remember such pain, their pain, his pain, any pain. He would forget it all. He knew it instantly the moment he touched Arturo's hand, whom he also realized he would forget, for God would not allow him, the sole survivor of that singular church massacre in a war filled with massacres, to linger in such pain. It would be gone, they would all be gone, and he was glad.

But it was going to be hard, he thought as he grabbed Arturo's hand and began to run down the road, past the Germans who were now fleeing, past the lone American survivor, Hector, who lay hiding at the window of an adjacent house, past Renata, who lay riddled with bullets, and the sobbing old man Ludovico, who stood over the body of his only, beloved daughter, to forget the man who was chocolate, the chocolate giant who wept tears of soda pop and made it his birthday just by turning his head, who taught him how to be invisible.

EPILOGUE

THE LAST MIRACLE

It was a warehouse fire in Canarsie, Brooklyn, the fourteenth in as many months, set by the mistress of the four-term congressman from that very same district, that kept young Tim Boyle of the Daily News from following up on the story he broke about Hector Negron, the Harlem postal worker who snapped that December morning of 1983. But Boyle's story about Hector's murder of an innocent customer and his possession of the missing head of the Primavera from Florence's Santa Trinità bridge shot around the world, as these things sometimes do, and then was almost instantly forgotten, replaced by fresher and newer atrocities. Boyle, for his part in breaking the Canarsie story wide open, was promoted from the coal mines of the newspaper's city desk to the political affairs desk in Washington, D.C., where he flourished, bringing down several congressmen in sex scandals and later landing a cushy talking-head job at an NBC affiliate, where he bombed.

Meanwhile, Hector had not spoken a word to the cops since his arrest and was transferred to Manhattan's Bellevue Psychiatric Hospital, where he spent

265

several weeks in isolation while psychiatrists tried to figure out why and how, during his WW II service, he'd managed to gain access to a priceless artifact, and even more important, how he'd shipped it home – oh, and by the way, why he'd kill somebody, too. Hector wasn't telling, and after the Italians arrived to claim the head, it seemed a moot point. The city of Florence, knowing how swiftly the winds of democracy in America could change with the tide of public opinion, hastily dispatched two representatives to retrieve their lost artifact. We want no problems, they said. We just want the head. After some initial wrangling with a couple of museums and the state department, the statue's head was packed in a wooden box the size of a milk crate and whisked back to Italy, where the furor over what to do with the remnants of the four statues on the Santa Trinità bridge continued, and the head sat in a vault – or so everyone thought.

In all the hubbub and fuss, the poor sap who'd walked into the post office wearing a big diamond on his wedding ring and whose face was lifted from his skull by Hector's thirty-eight was practically forgotten. He turned out to be a mechanic from Kingston, New York, named Randy Mitchell, and had Tim Boyle of the Daily News not been dispatched to snoop around the Brooklyn congressman's literally smoking underpants he might have discovered that Randy Mitchell was born Rodolfo Berelli of the tiny town of Valasco, just two miles from Sant'Anna di Stazzema. He might have discovered that Rodolfo Berelli had come by boat to America with the wave of immigrants that had pushed their way in just after the Second World War, with half a million lire in his suitcase and tiny bags of salt stuffed into his pockets and his socks, salt that turned out to be worthless in America.

Rodolfo, like Hector, had buried the war, and even in the moments before he died, he did not understand why Hector pointed the gun at him. He thought that he'd stumbled into a bungled robbery at the post office. It was only at the very last instant, when Hector turned his head slightly, revealing the lopped-off ear, surgically repaired but still mangled beyond anything resembling normalcy, that Rodolfo realized the moment he had always dreaded had finally come to pass, that as Peppi, the great partisan of the Serchio Valley, had promised him, even as Rodolfo and his paid Gurkha accomplice had choked him to death and strung his body from a bathroom shower fixture to make his death appear a suicide just weeks before the war ended, the Black Butterfly had exacted his revenge, even from death, as he had promised.

In those last moments, Rodolfo did not resist, for he had come to realize during that war that it was not his destiny to become like the great painters and poets of Tuscany whom he'd admired, like Paolo Uccello and Giovanni Pascoli, but to be like Iago, the sly fox who engineers the death of Othello for personal gain, only to meet his own awful fate. The money he had gained for arranging Peppi's death had bought him his passage to America, but not much more – half a million lire was nearly worthless in America. The 560 dead at Sant'Anna di Stazzema he saw in his dreams each night. They visited him individually, not dead and burned, but alive, quite whole, and smiling. The children sat in his lap and toyed with his ears, the mothers chatted easily with him about the impossibility of doing laundry by hand, the fathers told him jokes and laughed with him, slapping him on the back. And each dawn, just before he woke up, they would burn before his eyes, drying up like toast, their skin roasting and crackling like fried bacon as the flames ate them alive, and he would burst awake in a cold sweat, his nostrils still smelling the burned flesh, the taste of blood on his tongue.

He lived a depressed man in hiding, a man in subterfuge, his past as well camouflaged as the priest whom he had once been disguised as in his clever attempt to bring the Americans to Sant'Anna di Stazzema, before Peppi and the others discovered the truth about his treachery. He was a mystery to his simple American wife, a small-town girl from upstate New York who lived for bingo and the Jack Benny Show. His two kids were strangers to him, his son a draft dodger who joined the protests against the Vietnam War, his daughter a college dropout who moved to Ohio and picked up spare change posing in nudie magazines for a while before marrying a dairy farmer. He was disconnected from them, and oddly enough, it was his tragic death that brought them together, for they came to realize after he died that they had never truly known him, and in not knowing him, realized that they had never known each other. The three became a true family then, talking to one another in ways they hadn't done ever before. That was all the good they got out of him, which, when you consider his history, was a lot.

But Hector got very little. He sat in Bellevue for weeks as prosecutors and psychiatrists pressed him, trying to make him talk. He saw no sense in it. He'd buried the war. He saw no sense in going back. He had no children, no wife, no living relatives; he was bereft of dreams. Even his late wife, before she died, knew little of his war service. Hector had spent most of his life after the war coming home from work, flopping on the couch, drinking beer, and watching years of television movies that lionized white GIs, who became part of WW II American lore and myth, so much so that in his daily drunken stupors Hector began to believe that perhaps what had happened to him during the Second World War had not happened at all; that perhaps the coloreds and Puerto Ricans were only quartermasters and cooks as the history books said they were, that the fifteen thousand colored men of the 92nd Division whose lives were ended or changed forever by what historians nicknamed 'The Little Battle of the Bulge,' the Christmas Day attack on the Serchio Valley that decimated Sommocolonia, Barga, Castelvecchio di Pascoli, Fornaci di Barga, Tiglio, and several other Tuscan towns, were actually something that he'd created in his mind, that perhaps he'd dreamed it all.

He drank heavily over the years, staying dark in his mind. His only contact with the reality of what he once saw was the statue head, which lay buried in a shoebox in his closet, which he'd picked up off a sweet and gentle dead man whom he had been afraid to love, a reminder of a miracle of a tender and sweet little boy he had once seen, or thought he'd seen, rise up like an angel and float away from death – or did he see it at all? He was afraid to remember. He didn't want to talk about it. The prosecutors finally gave up, and the murder case limped to trial without much notice, shuffled to the back pages of the New York papers, confined to one paragraph, lost in the constant flow of fresh-breaking child murders, psycho bombers, arsonists, and madness that are the meat and bone of New York journalistic life.

So it was with little fanfare that a tall businessman with an Italian passport and papers listing business addresses in Rome, Versailles, and the Seychelles islands, off the coast of South Africa, arrived in New York City and headed directly to the offices of the powerful legal firm of Carrissimi, Brophy, and Biegelman, who promptly dispatched a young attorney to attend Hector's bail hearing – the young attorney carefully chosen to give the impression that this was one of the firm's pro bono charity cases, though in actuality, the Italian businessman was among the firm's most powerful and richest clients, and the attorney handpicked and carefully briefed – on the pain of death if she screwed it up – to give carefully worded instructions to the judge, himself a former member of the same law firm, who curiously chose not to recuse himself from the case, that Hector's bail of two hundred thousand dollars would be guaranteed by the firm through a trust fund they had established for their pro bono cases. The judge bought it, and in doing so earned the unenviable task of explaining to the press two weeks later how Hector had managed to drum up two hundred thousand dollars' bail, obtain his passport, and flee the country. He essentially vanished, was rumored to be in Italy of all places, or perhaps South Africa, but it was never known, for the day Hector Negron shuffled out of Superior Court in lower Manhattan accompanied by his young attorney, he was never seen again in New York City or on the shores of America. (The judge, by the way, later recovered, running for the office of senator and later for Congress, where he served four consecutive terms as the representative from New York's second district.)

Hector, for his part, never remembered the bail hearing, or the hasty night flight to South Africa by private jet, stopping only once, to refuel in Tel Aviv. By then, the sleep apnea that had plagued him during the war was full blown and he had been cut loose, freed from reality by the sight of the Italian partisan who'd killed the German during the war and was, by Hector's account, responsible for the death of so many people as well as his own sweet release from normalcy. He had been trapped at Sant'Anna for two days after his comrades died, hiding in a house, eating rations off the dead German soldiers around him felled by American bombers, until the 92nd Division troops, led by Colonel Jack Driscoll himself, arrived, the colonel later personally pinning the Silver Star for bravery on Hector's chest. But that was gone from him. He wanted to forget it all. He was in a fog, brought on by Bellevue Hospital's drugs and the terror of his own memories. Only days after his arrival in the lovely, peaceful surroundings of the Seychelles, where attendants in floppy skirts and sandals brought him lemonade and rare fried fish, pasta draped in melted cheese and olive oil, did he come to his senses and realize that he had not died.

For the first few days, he said nothing. He sat on a beach chair staring out into the ocean not far from a young man clad in a robe and bathing suit who also sat nearby on a beach chair, reading Shakespeare in Italian, sometimes napping, snapping awake with a start and a shudder that told Hector that he too had been a soldier someplace. The stranger sat beside him every day for several hours, and after several days of waiting for the stranger to speak, Hector finally broke the silence. He spoke not to the man, but to himself, for something about the stranger stirred something deep inside him, and he felt himself forced to utter a revelation that he'd never revealed to anyone, including himself.

'I am the last one,' he said. 'I was the only one left. Me and the old man who had all the rabbits. His daughter died, and when he saw her dead, he died of sorrow.'

The young man rose. He had become tall now. The years after the war had not been kind to him, years of starvation, watching his peasant father struggle and eventually commit suicide, unable to process the lingering bitterness of the war. He had become a race car driver for a while, daring death, defying it, tempting it, and it was his lack of fear that had made him rich. He attacked safety problems like a kamikaze pilot, developing his own line of safety products, products that turned things on and off, moved them up and down, buttons that turned on safety bags, knobs that loosed straps and belts, hoses that blew air, held you tight, loosed life-giving oxygen, strapped you in, kept you safe, freed your hands, turned you over from one side to another so that you'd breathe again. He flipped businesses as if they were pancakes, piling them up like steaks on a plate as they multiplied, one, two, three, ten times, because there was no risk in business, no risk in life, no risk in losing money, no risk in anything. People paid him gobs of money to control their risk, because they did not understand that there was no such thing as safety, no such thing as control. Sant'Anna di Stazzema had been safety, Sant'Anna had been control, and control, he had learned, was death. Safety, he had learned, was the greatest risk of all, because safety leaves no room for miracles. And miracles, he had learned, were the only sure thing in life.

But whom to explain that to? They would not understand. They did not want to understand. Hector, the young man knew, was one person in the world who did understand.

'You are not the last,' he said. 'There was one other.'

A small cloth satchel sat beside the young man's lounge chair. He picked it up, and his fingers undid the string wrapping it. Even before he finished, Hector knew what it was, and the old Puerto Rican, his body aged and torn by arthritis, rose out of his chair and fell into the arms of the young man, who dropped the head of the Primavera onto the sand and hugged him tight, holding the fragile elderly man as the chocolate giant had once held him, and as Hector's bitter tears of release fell on his shoulders, they both realized they had finally found what each was looking for. They had found yet another miracle, and they were finally free of the last one.

ACKNOWLEDGMENTS

This book began many years ago, when I was a boy of about nine, sitting in the crowded living room of my stepfather's brownstone in Fort Greene, Brooklyn. My stepfather and his brothers, Walter, Garland, Henry, and their friend Missouri would sit around a table under a bare lightbulb drinking Rheingold beer and Johnny Walker Red on Saturday nights, flinging tall tales across the room like bullets. My uncle Henry, a World War II veteran, was my favorite. He'd sit at the table, clad in porkpie hat and suspenders, cigarette in his teeth, his glass full of whiskey, telling jokes that made the men guffaw, while me and my sister Kathy sat under the table bleary-eyed and sleepy, waiting for our mother to show up from work. Invariably, Uncle Henry would fill up on joy juice, grab me affectionately by the ear, and holler, 'Boy . . . back in the war, the Italians, they loved us! And the French . . . oh, la, la! We was kings over there!' My sister and I would roll our eyes as he rattled off another old war story. The stories had no meaning to me then, and I barely remember them. He spoke of fires that lit black forests, and frozen dark bodies stiff with cold, and jeeps that flipped on their sides and burned while he ran for his life. What I remember most about the stories were not the stories themselves but rather Uncle Henry's pride. He spoke with such pride. He was so proud of what he'd done.

It took the better part of thirty years before that pride shook me awake one night and began to spin itself into the web and labyrinths of characters who now inhabit this book. They came alive on their own, without prodding, through the stories of the many men and women, from both America and Italy, who shook the demons of their memories off long enough to sit down and reveal to me that same pride that my uncle Henry had. These men and women have a moral character and fiber that, sadly, is missing in our world today, where the level of social progress is measured not in leaps and bounds of moral justice and thirst for knowledge but in the feet and inches of television ratings, survival shows, and video games that teach our children war in a world where 125 million children go to bed hungry every night and real wars are waged on innocent civilians by hidden terrorists who call these murders righteous acts of God.

Nonetheless, I am thankful to these survivors of the so-called Good War, the veterans of the 92nd Infantry Division who fought in Italy, the Italians who fought with them, and the Germans who fought against them – they were victims all. Many of these men and women sat with me, unlocked their hearts, and told stories that sometimes caused their hands to shake and tears to roll from their aged eyes. Most I have interviewed personally. A few I have met only through their written accounts. Sadly, many of them, both in Italy and in America, have died during the writing of this book, and those that are still alive are in their twilight years. If you see one, shake their hand.

Thanks to Florentino Lopez, the miracle survivor of the Sommocolonia tragedy at Castelvecchio di Pascoli; Captain William E. Cooke, Captain

Lloyd Parham, Ed Price, Captain Harold Montgomery, Joseph L. 'Steve' Stephenson, Denette Harrod; my late uncle Henry Jordan of Brooklyn, whose stories about the war, heard when I was a child, inspired this book; the Honorable James 'Skiz' Watson, George Cherry, the Reverend Edward Belton, A. William Perry of the Huachucan Veterans Association; Albert O. Burke, president, 92nd Infantry Division Association; John Fox of Cincinnati, a Medal of Honor recipient; Wendell Imes of St James Presbyterian Church in Harlem; Edgar S. Piggott, Rufus Johnson, Jesse Brewer, Deacon 'Wooley' Gant, Thomas 'Buddy' Phox, David Caisson, General Edward Almond, Captain John Runyon, Otis Zachary, my cousin Herbert Hinson, E. G. McDonnell, George 'Bro Wimp' Wimberley, Robert Brown Sr, David Perkins, James Usery (former mayor of Atlantic City, NJ), and Spencer Moore, the walking historian of the 92nd. Thanks to Richard Hogg, Terry Brookens, Perry 'Mack' Barnes, William Little, Arthur B. Cummings, and Sinclair Smalls.

Others to thank include Arlene Fox, Ruth Hodge (Museum Curator for the State of Pennsylvania, Harrisburg) Solace Wales, Barbara Posner, and Robert A. Brown, Ph.D., University of the District of Columbia. Special thanks to Hondon Hargrove and Mary Penick Motley, whose historical works on the 92nd were written with clarity, accuracy, and honesty. Also thanks to Jehu C. Hunter and Lieutenant Colonel Major Clark for their work on that subject as well. Deepest appreciation to the wonderful staff at the U.S. Army College in Carlisle, Pennsylvania. Thanks to Jodi Reynolds of Los Angeles for her wonderful transcription work.

And a special, heartfelt thanks to Lieutenant General William J. McCaffrey of Arlington, Virginia, the former chief of staff of the 92nd Division, a pioneer of racial integration in the U.S. Army and a man of profound insight, wisdom, and truth, whose guidance proved to be a beacon.

I am equally grateful to the many Italians of the Serchio Valley, who gave their time, their stories, their hearts, their wine, and their wisdom to this project: Alfredo Lenzi, Roberto Dianda, Roberto Tonacchi. The late Manrico Duchessi (the great Pippo); his legendary lieutenant Tutsiana; the late partisan Leandro Puccetti; Bernardini; Franco and Giovanni 'Gioni' Tognarelli; Mrakic Antonio and Frugoli Antonio. Also thanks to Lodovico Gierut, author of *Stage nel Tempo*, the Museum of Sant'Anna di Stazzema and its curator, Enio Mancini. Thanks to Enrico Tognarelli, Maria Olimpia Tognarelli, Malcolm Tognarelli, Dononi Diva, Del Frate Vaina, Fabiola del Frate, Bruno Bonaccorsi, Manule del Frate, Poli Gloria, and Gualtiero Pia. Special thanks to the Ricci family of the Seychelles and Castelvecchio, the Ricci Foundation of Barga, Italy, and the late entrepreneur Giovanni Mario Ricci of Seychelles, South Africa, whose bravery and generosity during World War II changed the lives of several American soldiers forever. Special thanks to Romiti Alderano and Salvo and all the brave farmers and survivors of Barga, Italy, who survived the war by the skin of their teeth. Thanks to Professor Umberto Sereni – the mayor of Barga – and to Anna and Paolo Zaninoni, for their wonderful insight and guidance as they read this book in its earliest form. Thanks to the Museo Storico della Liberazione of Lucca – its directors and curators, including Samuel Bennardini, General C.A.T.O. Gualtiero Alberghini, and its founder, Holocaust survivor Nusia Hoffman. A special nod to Professor Bruno Wanrooj of Georgetown University at Florence, whose insights and knowledge proved to be invaluable; thanks to the Italian Studies Institute of Floral Park, New York, and Good and Plenty at West Forty-third Street in New York City. Also thanks to Bafico of the Institute of the Resistance in Genoa.

Special thanks to my gifted Italian researcher, Patrizia Rampone. I

MIRACLE AT SANT'ANNA

extend my deepest gratitude to the Bogliasco Foundation in Genoa, founded by Jim and Marina Harrison. Without the help of the Bogliasco Foundation and its wonderful staff, including Anna Maria Quaiat, Alan Rowlin, and Ivana Folle, this book might not have been written. Thanks to the American International School of Genoa, Gary Crippen, and Dr Marco Lagazzi for his insights into Italy today and yesterday.

My deepest gratitude to my wonderful agent, Flip Brophy, attorneys Mark Biegelman and Vinny 'Skywalker' Carissimi, and my gifted editor and friend, Cindy Spiegel at Riverhead Books, whose brilliant insight led to whatever magic may lie in this work. And finally, thanks to my wife, Stephanie, my ultimate force, who pushes me to dream big and who teaches our children, Azure and Jordan, that God's love is the greatest miracle of all.